LIAR'S BALL

Liar's Ball

BEHIND CLOSED DOORS
2

K.F. Johnson

One Ironwoman Publishing

One Ironwoman Publishing
Grayson, GA 30017

Cover Design by Christine N. Davis
ISBN : 978-1-954469-01-3

Contents

1

Brenda

How do you tell your best friend that you saw her fiancé having sex with another man? I wasn't sure what words I was going to use, but I knew the majority of them would probably be four-letter ones. I'd gone to my boyfriend Lane's auto shop, Hamilton Auto Repair, because I needed a shoulder to cry on; not to bear witness to consensual sodomy between my estranged half-brother, Julian, and my best friend's fiancé, Paul.

Ironically, Julian didn't say a word to me at all. He just straightened his clothes and avoided eye contact with me.

"Brenda, wait!" Paul begged in his Jamaican accent as he chased me down the hall into Lane's office, where I'd gone to get my purse and keys.

"Paul, get the hell outta my way! You can save your sob story for Rhonda with your cheating ass!" I yelled.

"But let me explain for a second before you go and ruin my life!"

"Ruin your life? Are you serious? I caught you having sex with a man when you're engaged to my female best friend, you bastard! You're the one ruining lives! Get the fuck out of my face, Paul! And move out of my way!" I screamed, feeling my light-skinned complexion turning fire-red.

"I know, I know, but just let me talk to you. I didn't even realize what I was doing until it was too late," he pleaded, grabbing my wrist as I shoved past him.

I stopped in my tracks and shot him a disbelieving glare.

"What? When the hell was it too late? When you bent him over, or when your balls were knocking his?" I hollered, pushing his hand from my wrist and continuing my quick stride.

I expected him to continue his pleas, but he stopped where he stood, watching me as I exited the EMPLOYEES ONLY door out into the auto shop's waiting area.

"Is everything okay?" Donna, the slender brown receptionist asked with wide eyes as I rumbled past her.

"No. Tell Lane I'll call him later when he comes back please," I said, exiting and getting into my black BMW that was parked in front of the shop.

I sped towards Rhonda's job with fire in my heart and tears in my eyes. I couldn't believe I'd actually just seen what I saw. Paul? Mr. Macho Jamaican who constantly criticized other men for looking like "batty boys"? The day had barely started, and it was already the worst!

Pulling onto the highway, GA 400. I kicked myself for never bothering to buy a car charger. I hated being easily accessible by cell phone, so I rarely kept it on me or worried when it went dead. This time I was sorry I'd let it run out of juice because there were so many people I needed to call, but I couldn't call anyone. I thought about what I was going to say to Rhonda, over and over in my head the entire 20-minute drive to the Coca-Cola plant in Alpharetta. Rhonda was on staff as a chemist there. I hated to have to tell her at work, but I knew if I waited, Paul would get his story to her first, if he hadn't already.

When I pulled into the plant parking lot, I took a lot of deep breaths, and grabbed my purse from the passenger's seat before getting out. I gave the woman at the front desk my name and told her that I was there to see Rhonda Pierce.

"Okay, I'll buzz her extension," the older, white-haired woman said with a pleasant smile. "Ms. Pierce, Ms. Brenda Andrews is here to see you...okay. She'll be right up, Ms. Andrews."

"Thank you," I replied, taking a seat in the red cushioned waiting room chair and dropping my sunglasses down to my eyes from the top of my head. Squirming a bit in my seat, I straightened my beige off-the-shoulder shirt, brushed lint off of my Capri pants, and crossed my legs.

Suddenly I had the urge to bolt. I knew this was totally going to break her in two, and I was going to have to be prepared to help her pick up the pieces.

"Girl, what are you doing here? I hope you weren't trying to surprise me for lunch, because my break was over 30 minutes ago," she said, approaching me in gray dress pants and shirt with black flats. Her shoulder-length, jet-black hair was pulled back into a neat bun, accentuating her chocolate-brown skin complexion.

I stood and hugged her prematurely, causing her to tentatively return the embrace. "What's wrong?"

"Can we talk somewhere private?" I asked, hoping my voice wasn't quivering.

"Umm, yeah. They've got some stone tables and benches out back where people go for lunch sometimes."

"Okay."

"Whoa. Whatever it is must be really crazy for you to come to my job. What did your mom tell you?" she asked, as I followed her out of the building. "You look like you've seen a ghost."

That would have been better than what I actually saw.

* * *

Rhonda led the way with a jovial pep in her step that made me feel guilty to be delivering such bleak news. We sat down across from each other as she placed both palms on the table, leaned forward and said, "Okay, spill it! What did your mother say?"

I took a deep breath and nervously rubbed the back of my neck. I'd gone to my mother's home earlier in the day to discuss something she wanted to tell me, but that wasn't the topic of my current mission.

"She said a lot of stuff. It's not important though, Rho. That's actually not what I came to talk to you about," I said, adjusting the sunglasses on my face again.

"Oh...okay," she said, turning her head like someone had blown a dog whistle and she'd actually heard it. "Can you take those damned sunglasses off? I feel like I'm having a conversation with some obnoxious celebrity."

I removed them but directed my eyes away from hers. "I went over to Lane's shop when I left her house to talk, but he wasn't there. I went to the employee bathroom while I was waiting for him, and I heard some sexual-moans and groans through the vent."

"Whoa! Oh my God, please tell me you didn't catch Lane with another woman? Not Lane!" she began to whine.

"Well, that was what I thought at first. I followed the sounds to the supply room, and I saw...I saw..."

"Who was it? Donna? Girl, I am not surprised. I knew her little innocent receptionist act was bogus. Every time I go in there, she's super sweet, but I know, I know she's a phony."

"No. It wasn't Donna," was all I could manage to squeak out.

"Brenda, spill it already! I don't have a lot of time to talk since my lunch break is over," she said anxiously.

I took a long pause and answered, "When I opened the door, I saw Paul, having sex, doggy-style."

Her eyes seemed to glaze over, and the color washed from her face. "What?" she asked. "With who?"

I dropped my eyes to look at my hands. I couldn't bear to look into her face while I shot her with the next bullet. "With a man."

"What the fuck!? No, you didn't! You couldn't have seen my Paul having sex with a man! Maybe the bitch looked like a man, but it couldn't have been a man!"

Her reaction startled me. "I saw it with my own eyes."

"You couldn't have!" she cried. "He wouldn't do that to me. We're engaged, for Christ's sake, and he's not gay! It couldn't have been a man!"

"It was a man, Rhonda. It was Julian."

"Julian who? Who the fuck is Julian?"

"My half-brother," I mumbled.

"This is not happening," she whimpered, with tears staining her gray silk shirt.

"I'm so sorry, girl. I really didn't know what else to do. I couldn't hide it from you once I found out, but I didn't want to hurt you," I pleaded.

She cried hard and loud. Even I was beginning to worry that someone from her job would hear her. She was totally deconstructing.

"Rhonda…"

"Just…don't!" she yelled at me. "How the hell am I supposed to go back to work right now? Why would you do this to me?"

Huh? Why would I do this to her? Maybe I was the crazy one but, last I checked, I wasn't the one that proposed to her, then proceeded to dick down the nearest man. What the hell?

She turned her head toward the sky and attempted to wipe away tears quicker than they could fall, without success.

"I gotta go," Rhonda said, storming off the way we'd come.

Had she just shot the messenger? She wasn't actually mad at me, was she? I slowly picked up my purse from the table and walked back to my car. I just wanted to lie down, go to sleep and wake up to another day, because this one was already a wash.

The entire drive home was spent holding back tears, but they'd already begun to drop by the time I finally arrived. I typed in the code to the front gates and drove up the short path to the house, parking in one of the spaces inside the 4-car garage. When I opened the door, my Mini Pin Zeus was anxiously awaiting, wagging his nub furiously, barking and leaping in the air with excitement. I put my purse and keys down on the counter in the foyer, bent down, and picked him up.

"Hi, baby," I said to him while dodging the ninja-like quickness of his tongue. I was really in need of some love and a hug.

Kicking my shoes off at the doorway of the living room, I walked over to the huge black sectional and sat.

First my mom dropped not one, but two bombs on me earlier in the day, and then I witnessed everything I never wanted to see in life; just before getting chewed out by my best friend for trying to help her.

Can I get a do-over?

* * *

To say my mother and I had a rocky relationship would be to say Michael Jackson was somewhat of a celebrity. Our relationship was more like a quarry. My brother, Brian, and I rarely wanted for much materialistically in our youth, but we also got an abusive, adulterating, alcoholic father, and a phony, glutton for punishment, drama queen of a mother as a bonus.

If not for my father's suspicious drowning a few weeks after Easter forcing us all to interact, my brother and I would still only be speaking to my mother on holidays and birthdays. Oh, yeah, and my father's bastard son Julian, who we discovered existed during the funeral proceedings. That was simply the icing on the cake in our latest family drama.

Julian looked like my brother Brian's more manicured, long-haired, gay doppelganger. It was a very unpleasant first meeting, and consequently led to blows while everyone was preparing to head to the burial site. Luckily, we still only had one body to bury at the end of the day.

I hadn't seen that mystery slut Julian, or even thought of him, until his surprise appearance at the shop.

My head was hurting, and my eyes felt heavy. I hadn't eaten all day, but I had no plans to do anything more than sleep now. Zeus snuggled with me as I sat back and closed my eyes.

The next thing I knew, Lane was kneeling down behind the couch with his arms over the back of it, staring at me.

"Oh my God!" I yelped.

"Sorry, sleeping beauty, I didn't mean to scare you," Lane replied sweetly. "I'm surprised you didn't wake yourself up anyway, as loud as you were snoring."

"Really? You think it's funny to sneak up on a woman whose been held hostage before?" I scolded.

"I wasn't trying to sneak up on you. I came into my own home, jingling keys and all. I wouldn't—"

"Okay, okay, I'm sorry. Forget it," I interrupted.

The way he said 'I came into my own home' sounded like a subtle hint that I was wearing out my welcome. I wasn't in the mood to fight.

"What time is it?"

"Quarter after seven," he answered, walking off and ascending the spiral staircase.

I pulled the scrunchie from my bushy ponytail and followed suit behind him.

When I entered his bedroom, I sat on the black chaise in front of the huge picture window and waited for him to emerge from his walk-in closet. I knew he'd gone to take off most of his jewelry, clothes and wallet in there, as always. Soon, my 6' 4", dark-brown and chiseled boyfriend emerged wearing nothing but gray boxer briefs and diamond studs in his ears. Yummy!

"So, Donna said you came by the shop today and something went down with you and Paul, but she didn't know what it was. I tried to call you, but you know how that goes," he said, meaning that I couldn't be reached. "What happened?"

I refocused from his abs to his face, bringing my feet up onto the chaise and leaning my chin onto my knees.

"Paul didn't say anything?"

He looked dumbfounded. "No. That's why I'm asking."

I took a deep breath and hoped his reaction would be better than Rhonda's. "I heard sex noises coming from the supply room while I was waiting for you, so I opened the door and caught him and—"

"Oh, damn, don't tell me he was back there banging Donna?" he interjected.

Wow! If Donna knew how shady people thought she was for no damned reason, I bet she wouldn't like it.

"No. He was having sex with my brother."

"Your brother?" he exclaimed.

"Not Brian. Julian," I corrected.

"Get the fuck outta here!" he said disbelievingly. "Are you kidding?"

"I swear. Right there in your supply closet. There's no mistaking they were screwing."

Lane's mouth was agape.

"Can you believe he had the nerve to ask me not to tell Rhonda, too?"

"I bet he did. Crazy thing is, he's the most homophobic brother I know and... Wow... Paul was on the DL. I guess the 'down low' population in Atlanta gets bigger every day," he lamented. "This is crazy. So, what did your brother say?"

"Not a damned thing. He didn't even seem fazed. You think he targeted Paul or something? You know, to get at me and Brian?"

"Targeted him? I don't know how fucking your best friend's fiancé would be getting back at you, but hey, I guess if anybody would know your family, it would be you."

Lane had no idea how far from the truth that was.

"Can you believe Rhonda was actually pissed at me for telling her? And she kept tripping about finding out while she was at work," I complained.

"You went up to her job and told her?" he asked disapprovingly.

"Yes," I began, already on the defensive. "That's my best friend. I would want to know as soon as she found out if roles were reversed. I thought she would, too."

He continued to shake his head and walked into the master bathroom. "I should have known too much time had passed without there being some drama. Trouble follows you like a stray puppy, woman."

I frowned. Is that how he thought of me? I would have disputed his statement if I'd had a leg to stand on, but I didn't.

In fact, I hadn't even scratched the surface of the drama unearthed at my mother's house that morning yet.

She... was a murderer.

2

Brian

I couldn't wait for my boy Ike to come and pick me up so I could get away from the one woman in this world I wanted to choke on sight. The meeting with Trent to solidify our partnership as owners of Eat Your Art Out restaurant had gone as planned; until his wife showed up to retrieve her iPad. I had no idea that he was married to Gabrielle Riken, my dating anti-Christ. I caught her deep-throating a guy from my Spanish class my senior year of college, and later spent a couple of nights in jail for assaulting her.

Although it was more than eight years ago, all of the hate I felt for her was reborn when she walked into Trent's office. Neither one of us acknowledged that we already knew each other, and Trent was none the wiser to our façade.

She was just as beautiful now as she was then, except her hair was cut into a curly style that came just below her ears now, and she was dressed like a stylish businesswoman. We kept the small talk very small, and she left as quickly as she came. Now as I waited for my ride, I couldn't shake the burning anger that sweltered in every muscle in my body.

Ike's silver Audi pulled up in front of the restaurant and I quickly got in, smoothing the wrinkles out of my brown linen pants and beige shirt.

"How'd it go?" Ike asked, turning down the jazz music on the radio as he backed out and drove towards my place.

"Everything went as planned with me and Trent. We were able to agree on pretty much everything except the specifics of my office," I said, leaning my elbow against the door and peering out at the moving cars. "That, and his wife."

"His wife? What's his wife got to do with anything? She didn't like your ideas?"

"It was Gabby."

"Who was? His wife?" he exclaimed as I nodded. "Gabby is his wife? Aww, damn!"

"Of all the fucking people in the world, I'm about to be partners with that she-devil's husband," I scowled.

"Unbelievable. So, the deal isn't off though, right?"

I didn't answer. This was exactly the type of restaurant and partnership I wanted until I could get enough experience and gain a customer base to own my own; but I didn't want anything to do with Gabby. At all!

"Well...how often are you really gonna see her though? I mean, unless she's part of your partnership, why even sweat it? All that shit with her was years ago. You've moved on with Nadia, and she's married. Case closed. Water under the bridge."

I cut my eyes at him and inhaled deeply. Water under the bridge? What kinda pansy-ass forgiveness talk was that? No dirt done to me is ever water under the bridge. I don't forgive, and I don't forget. That's the difference between Ike and me. He was my best friend, but we were polar opposites. He's the 5' 10", brown-skinned, receding hairline, average nice guy, and I'm the 6' 1", hazel-eyed, curly haired, brown-skinned lady killer. My standards for acceptable treatment were understandably higher than his would be.

"We didn't discuss how often she'd be around, but I don't want to have to hear about her, either. Trent seems like the type of dude that talks a lot, and I could see how pussy-whipped he was when she came in," I hissed, remembering when she'd made me feel that way.

"So, he's cool working with his wife's ex?"

"Hell, if I know. She didn't say anything about it and neither did I. He introduced, we said hello, and that was it."

"See now," he said, shaking his head. "You're about to set the tone like y'all have something to hide."

"Y'all? I'm not the one that's married to him," I retorted. "She could've said something to him. I just met the man. I don't owe him anything."

"I still say you're playing with fire. I know if I was about to go into business with a dude that my wife dated for two years, pressed charges on, and nobody told me..." Ike shook his head again. "I'd be mad as hell."

"Well, for all I know, she's planning on telling him later. I really don't give a fuck to be honest," I decided at that moment. "I'm gonna let that be between them."

"You're about to be partners with this cat, you better think, or rather re-think, how you go about dealing with his wife. I'm telling you, you don't want to start off a business relationship like that."

"As long as that bitch keeps her distance, everything should be golden. My business is with him, not her."

"Brian, you can't be serious. With as many of our college boys that we still hang with, how long do you think that secret is gonna remain a secret? Your sister isn't gonna be able to keep a poker face once she finds out, and you know Tara still talks to Gabby sometimes."

Tara, Ike's bitch-ass wife. That's all I needed. That spiteful, grudge-holding, loudmouth, to get a whiff of this news, and it would-be all-over Atlanta before I got out of the car. I hated that he married that barracuda.

"Well, don't go running home to tell your big-mouth wife then. This is between me and you for now, capeesh?"

"Yeah, yeah of course," Ike said, scratching his head as he turned into my apartment complex. His nervous tell. He might as well have just said, "You know I'm lying like hell, right?"

"Look, man, I'm serious. Don't get to gossiping when you get home. What I tell you is between us, and not for your motor-mouth wife to weigh in on."

"Dude, stop calling my wife names. I said I'm not gonna tell her. But I still think you need to 'fess up to ol' boy so it won't come back to bite you in the ass later."

I wasn't listening. It was Gabby's responsibility to fill her man in on her past, not mine. My mind was made up. As long as she understood her boundaries and stayed out of my way, nobody would get hurt…or at least I wouldn't.

* * *

"B, how can you stay here after all of the death and bad memories associated with it? I don't blame Brenda for moving out," Ike inquired, parking in front of the walkway near the stairs.

"Believe me; I'm already looking for another place. I can't even front like it's not strange being here now that she's moved, and Kelly is gone," I answered. "In fact, I might be moving out in the next few weeks if I can decide between a condo on Cheshire Bridge Road or a house on Pharr Road. I was also looking at a crib off of Wieuca Road. You know I can't go too far outside of Buckhead."

Ike nodded and reached to turn the radio volume back up.

"Well, I guess that's my cue to get the hell outta your car then, huh?" I said jokingly as I opened the door.

"Nah, it's not like that, but I love this song. The band was playing it when I took Tara on our first date to—"

"On that note, I'm outta here," I interrupted, as I slid out of the car and closed the door behind me.

Ike used his controls to roll the passenger's side window down. "You ain't funny," he said with a half-smirk. "I can't wait for you to start talking all mushy about Nadia so I can throw shade at you, too."

I shrugged and headed towards my apartment.

"Don't hate! Congratulate!" Ike yelled out the window, backing his car out and driving off.

I reached my apartment door, inspected it to make sure it was in the same condition it was in when I left, then put my keys in to unlock it. I felt uneasy coming home ever since I'd survived being ambushed and shot by a crazy stalker in my apartment.

I secured all of the locks back in place once inside and went into my bedroom to settle in. Glancing out of my patio door and laying my wallet on my dresser, I sat on the bed to take my shoes off and thought of my cousin, Kelly. My aunt and uncle owned the apartment building and they'd let her manage it. She constantly barged in on me unexpectedly and got all in my business, but she was my favorite cousin. Unfortunately, the twisted fuck that held me captive was also in cahoots with my sister Brenda's dysfunctional stalker Edwin, and Kelly became a casualty of their rage before it was all said and done.

The police shot and killed that bitch Gwen who'd shot me, but not before her accomplice killed my cousin and attempted to do God knows what to my sister. Edwin pled guilty and got 25 years without parole, but it wasn't enough to soothe the grief my Aunt Tonya and Uncle Donovan felt. They sold the apartment complex to my sister and me and moved back to Columbia, South Carolina, where most of my mother's side of the family are from.

My little cousin was truly missed.

I heard keys jingling in the front door and knew it had to be Nadia letting herself in.

She was talking to someone on her cell phone when she entered and locked the door behind her.

"I doubt that she's that stupid," she was saying into the phone. "But anyway, I'm over at Brian's now so I'll call you back...well, you worry enough for both of us then, 'cause I'm not about to waste another minute of stress thinking about it. I'll talk to you later...okay...bye."

I watched her kickoff her black wedges, lay her pocketbook down on the coffee table in the living room, then do the "I gotta pee really bad" shuffle into the half-bathroom just outside of my bedroom. I shook my head, thinking how easily I could have predicted her every move, sans the phone conversation. For some reason she had an aversion to taking a bathroom break while she was working unless it became impossible for her to hold. Of course, that meant she'd be scurrying into pee after work. My sister seemed to do that a lot, also. I shook my head and chalked it up to women's logic.

I lay back on the bed with my hands behind my head and stared up at the ceiling. For a moment, I wondered who Nadia was talking to on the phone, and what she was talking about. Then I caught myself. What the hell? Seeing Gabby after all of these years must've pinched my trust nerve. I wouldn't have given two shits about Nadia's girl chat conversation yesterday.

"Hey, baby," Nadia said, flopping down beside me on the bed and kissing my cheek minutes later. "How did your meeting go?"

"Good," I answered.

"Good? That's it?"

"That's it. I liked the place, we agreed on the deal, and he liked my menu additions. We're probably gonna start revamping the menu, re-marketing, and remodeling next week after the lawyers seal the deal and the ink is dry," I replied, looking into her beautiful brown face.

"Nice. So, did you like him? What kind of personality type is he? 'Cause, you know you can be a handful, and you don't always play well with others, Mr. Andrews," she teased, with a bright smile gleaming through her light-pink lip gloss.

"A handful? See, now if you were giving me head more often, you'd see that I'm way more than a handful," I taunted.

She rolled her pretty brown eyes and widened her smile. One of the things that originally attracted me to her was her resemblance to the actress Halle Berry. I'd wanted to crush Halle ever since she was in that movie Swordfish with John Travolta. Now, as I looked at Nadia, the words to Joe and Big Pun's song played in my head, 'I'm not a playa, I just crush a lot.'

"You are so nasty!" Nadia exclaimed, with a big grin and a love tap. "Maybe if you spent more time using your mouth, rather than running it, I would."

"Your wish is my command," I answered, flipping over on top of her and kissing her deeply. "As long as you used the baby wipes."

She giggled and playfully punched me in the stomach. "Of course!"

* * *

My tongue traced the nape of Nadia's neck and I inhaled the sweet smell of her favorite perfume, GLOW by Jennifer Lopez.

"You smell good," I said to her between kisses.

"Umm..." she moaned. "You feel good."

Mini-me stood at attention, as he always did whenever I was close to her. I hadn't been in love, or even wanted to be in love, since my relationship ended with Gabby; but I felt like I was falling in love with Nadia.

Nadia pulled her shirt up over her head and grabbed me by my ears, kissing me passionately and snaking her body into mine.

"I love you," she said, before another deep kiss was planted.

I unhooked her bra clasps and used my tongue to lick one beautiful breast after the other while my hands removed them from their lace harness. I loved her, too, but I didn't want to say it out loud. Something about saying it felt...weak; and seeing Gabby again served as a reminder that being weak left me vulnerable to being hurt.

I continued tasting, and descended her sleek body, skillfully sliding her pants and panties off at the same time. I could almost feel the heat coming from her wet box in anticipation of the expert oral I was about to perform.

I'd always been an excellent lover, but with Nadia, I actually felt invested in her pleasurable outcome. For the first time in years, I cared whether a woman came first, or at all, for that matter. She thrust her lower lips into my tongue stroke with a rhythmic dance that only a woman in ecstasy could manage. I grinned, pleased with myself as I worked my own pants and underwear off.

"Oh my God, baby, please...please don't stop," she pleaded.

Within minutes she was shivering and crying out, just before I plunged my stiffness into her convulsing cave. She began to say something again, but I stifled it with a fiery kiss while our bodies did the sexual samba. She felt so good, and after 20 minutes of our synchronized movements, I was having a hard time controlling the urge to release my orgasm.

"Oh, Brian! Oh, baby! Oh, my God, I love you!" she cried out, emphasizing the last words.

I buried myself deeper inside her, grasped the back of her head with one hand and her ass cheek with the other, just as I poured my soldiers into her womb. We collapsed shortly afterwards onto the bed. I was naked from the waist down, and her nude body was glistening with sweat.

We were both panting lightly when she said, "Why can't you say it anymore?"

"Say what?" I asked, knowing exactly what she meant.

"That you love me? You've said it before; once. But now it's like you won't. Don't you still feel it?" she asked, with a distressed expression.

"I still feel it. Don't I show you that?" I asked, touching her cheek.

"But you don't say it. Why not?"

I sighed and grimaced uncomfortably. "Nad, you know how I feel about you. I said it once. Why do you need me to keep saying it?"

"Well, how else would I know if you've changed your mind then? You might have loved me then, but not now. If you still love me, then why can't you say it back when I say it to you?"

The sassiness in her voice signaled her growing attitude, which in turn, triggered mine.

"Why do you need me to keep saying it when I've already said it? Ain't nothin' changed between us since the last time I said it, so why are you so insecure that you need me to keep stroking your ego with it?"

"Stroking my ego? Are you saying I'm insecure just because I want my man to reciprocate when I say I love you? Are you that self-centered and warped that you think returning a simple I love you is a sign of insecurity?" she replied, sitting up abruptly with blazing eyes.

Clearly, my honest answer was going to escalate this little tiff into an argument, so I lied.

"No I'm not saying that," I answered robotically. "I'm just saying that if I've already said it, I don't see why you need me to reiterate it every other day or while I'm knocking it out the frame. We're not supposed to be thinking during sex, we're supposed to be fucking."

She glared at me, and if she were a bull, I'm sure I would have seen her steamy breath coming from her nostrils.

"While you're knocking it out the frame?" Nadia said with a neck roll. "I never realized what a raving romantic you were before," she spat sarcastically, scooting to the bottom of the bed and gathering her clothes.

"Oh, so now you're mad? For what? I just confirmed that I love you and you're still trippin'."

"You are such an arrogant asshole."

"And you already knew that before you fell in love with me, so why are you acting all brand-new now? I can't believe you're having a hissy fit over this petty shit. What's your fuckin' problem? You lookin' for a fight?"

She didn't respond at first as she fastened the clasp on her bra and slipped her panties back on.

"You're about to talk yourself into a real problem if you keep talking to me like that," she threatened.

I chuckled at her foolishness and got up to go to the bathroom. If I'd have bothered to look back at her, I was sure she would have been shooting daggers at me, but I didn't give her the satisfaction. Whatever lames she'd dealt with before me must've caved to her tantrums, but I wasn't about to let her control me. This was the part about being in a relationship that I was never going to concede to; letting a woman have her way because she could pout like a 3-year-old.

Fuck that! I got played once by a female, and that was already one time too many.

I whistled as I let my anaconda loose in the bathroom, but she must've had cheetah in her blood because I heard my apartment door slam before I'd even had time to flush the toilet.

Whatever. She'd live.

3

Julian

I let the top down on my lavender Mercedes Benz CLK 63 convertible and put my purple-trimmed Versace sunglasses on as I drove off from Hamilton Auto Repair's parking lot and my hair blew in the wind. That was an unexpected score to the turmoil I had originally intended to reap on my siblings' world. Even I hadn't expected Brenda to show up at her boyfriend's shop and catch me and Paul in all our glory. If that wasn't the cherry on the cake, I didn't know what was, but damned if it didn't spoil my plans to keep Paul as a possible blackmail card in my pocket.

It was too bad; I hadn't been able to snag Lane's fine ass, but word on the street had been a pretty firm 'No' when one of the children (what some of my gay brethren and I referred to ourselves as) reported back on their attempts. Besides, it was rare to catch him out of his office, if he was even in the shop at all, the times I came in. There would have been no better "How you like me now?!" than to get him...but that ship had sunk way before it sailed.

Paul, on the other hand, was an obvious mark. I wasn't fooled by his over-the-top Jamaican machismo whenever I came in to get my baby, my Benz, serviced. Sure, he put up a good front for those who didn't know any better, but he put out all of the right signals and winks to let me know he was down for the get down, and more than willing to service me. I never gave his raggedy ass a second thought until I found out he was dating my snooty half-sister's best friend.

I used to dream of a relationship with her and my half-brother because I didn't have any other siblings, and my mother was now in a mental institution. Information I didn't care to share with my long-lost siblings at our first meeting. My Aunt Linda was the only family I had left that would give me the time of day, and that was probably because she didn't have any kids of her own. Since I was the product of an affair, I was my father's dirty little secret until I showed up at his funeral.

I would have preferred to be introduced to them sooner, and in a better setting, but my father wasn't a fan of that idea when he was alive, and my Aunt Linda insisted I attend his funeral with her when he passed. It was interesting seeing them up close and personal, since I'd only seen pictures of them or out casually at a few events around town from afar.

Brian and I both had hazel eyes and looked like GQ magazine's next black cover models, but he was maybe an inch or two shorter than me and wore his hair and clothes in a predictably boring way. Brenda was pretty, but she didn't have our hazel eyes, and her hair looked like she needed some professional attention, along with a good perm.

I was nervous and excited to see them; and I hoped the somber circumstances would open them to making our first meeting a cordial one. Aunt Linda was convinced they wouldn't be surprised I existed, but simply surprised to meet me. Clearly, she'd been mistaken.

Brian started questioning me like a detective on an episode of The First 48, and then had the gall to call me a faggot when he didn't like my answers. Well, this faggot commenced to whooping his ass as a reminder that I was still a man! It was ugly, and certainly not the introduction I'd been looking forward to. As it turned out, they had more secrets than Victoria in their little family circle anyway, because Aunt Linda ended up in her own cat fight with the Wonder Twin's mother, and later told me why.

Miss Snooty Toot herself, Brenda, was her mother's lovechild with some guy that had not been identified to the family. My aunt was ready to reveal it during the melee, but their mom put a bit of a beating on my poor aunt before she could get the whole story out. That was the day I decided that I'd make them regret how they treated me...and my aunt.

Aunt Linda was also convinced there was some foul play regarding their mother's accounting of how my father died, but honestly, I didn't care. He'd only bothered to see me maybe twice a year, if that much. It was my aunt that showed me love from the first time I met her until the present day. I could've led off the massacre with exposing Brenda's suspicious parenthood to her, but I was saving that little doozy in the event that I couldn't come up with anything more salacious.

Apparently, Brenda wasn't a big fan of Aunt Linda, and even refused to call her "Aunt" when addressing her. My aunt wasn't sure why she felt that way, but suspected it was just a casualty of their mother Olivia's disdain rubbing off. Quite frankly, I was underwhelmed by the supposed beauty of Mrs. Olivia Andrews. I admit she did look good for a woman her age, but my mother had her beat by a mile in the looks department. Even in her current state of psychosis she was a beauty. I could spot a phony bitch from a mile away, and Olivia didn't even need to be that far for me to see her character.

They were all so full of themselves, but only God knew why. With the exception of Brian, they were only slightly above average-looking, and none of them seemed to be living in the lap of luxury. Here I was, the owner of my own hair salon, sporting a top-of-the-line Mercedes Benz, wearing designer everything, and living in a plush home in Glenayre where celebrities like Usher Raymond live, yet no one acknowledged me.

Neither my father, his wife, nor his bougie kids could live up to my successes, from what I knew. I sort of wished they'd been more open when we'd first met, so I could flaunt it in their faces, but it didn't work out that way. Oh well, I didn't fret over their foolishness and insistence that I wasn't part of their family. I would simply show them, better than I could tell them, what a mistake crossing me had been.

Sooner, rather than later.

* * *

When I arrived at Hair to The Throne, my salon in Roswell, I was greeted with the "Hi's" and "Hey's" from my staff and clientele. My first appointment of the day wasn't until 3:00 p.m. so I had a lot of time left to BS around and chit-chat until then. The six stylists I employed all had a client in their seats and there was one waiting in the lounge area at the front.

"Good afternoon, Mr. Julian," Raul, my receptionist greeted me as I strutted past him.

"Good afternoon, Raul. I hope this lovely client hasn't been, and won't be waiting long," I replied with a clenched-teeth smile. I absolutely hated to have clients who were not seen at the time they were scheduled. Being a stickler for time was a quality I was proud of, and anybody who didn't appreciate, or wasted mine, would only get one chance to do it.

"Yes," he answered, batting his fake eye lashes and craning his neck at me with pursed lips. "She's early."

"Umm...okay," I said continuing to my office in the back of the salon.

I had barely sat down in my paisley lounge chair before Nick came into my office with his fo-hawk at attention, his mouth twisted and his expected bitchy attitude, closing the door behind him.

"Where have you been?" he questioned with folded arms across his baby-blue buttoned-down dress shirt.

I rolled my eyes and put my hand to my head. Oh boy...here he goes. "Don't start, Nick."

"What do you mean, don't start? You leave the house early this morning without a word, you don't answer your phone, and now you come waltzing in here after lunch like it's all roses and tulips," he scolded, shifting his skinny-jeaned legs and furrowing his perfectly lined eyebrows. There was a time when I actually cared how Nick felt, was moved by his reddening face when he was angry, and worried that he would leave me if I didn't prove my love...but that was then. These days, all I cared about was me, and what I wanted. I'd grown tired of Nick's constant nagging, incessant snooping, and more importantly, boring sex. Boring was right next to being dead in my book, and I wanted no part of either.

"I told you I had to get my car fixed in the morning before we went to bed last night," I answered exasperatedly, as I scrolled my phone to see how many times this fool had actually blown up my phone since I'd turned the ringer off earlier.

He sucked his teeth and swiveled his head like it was on wheels. "Don't they usually give you a loaner? And what about ignoring my phone calls?"

"Nick!" I yelled. "Bring it down a notch. You're all questions and no listening. They didn't have any loaners available at the time, and I had to leave my phone in the car on the charger because I forgot to charge it last night." The lies rolled off my tongue as easy as cake. I didn't really care if he believed me or not, but I had to give him some explanation.

"Oh my God, Julian! Stop lying to me! I know your ass did not sit up in no grimy car repair shop for all this time, especially without a phone. You've been using that repair shop excuse way too many times anyway. You got this luxury car but it's always in the shop. What's that about? You think I'm stupid? Who you going to see, Julian? Do they work at that place or are you going somewhere different altogether?"

I pushed the ringer volume up on my phone just as my best girl-friend Tia was calling and her ringtone blared Beyoncé's song "Single Ladies."

"Who is that this time? Let me see it! Let me see how many other phone calls you answered in between my calls," Nick demanded, attempting to grab the phone from my hands as I withdrew it to my chest.

"I will slap the taste out of your mouth if you try to grab my phone again," I threatened, shoving him backwards.

As usual, he was overly dramatic about it and threw himself further than my slight push could have actually propelled him, into the door. Anyone watching would have thought I'd whacked him with a two-by-four if they didn't know better.

"I can't believe you just put your hands on me!" he yelled, clutching his chest.

What a sissy I'd gotten myself mixed up with. Personally, I felt like I was born gay. I knew I liked boys from as early as I could remember, but I could turn it down, or turn it up at my leisure. Nick, on the other hand, was molested as a child and God only knows what he was actually intended to be, but he sometimes acted so prissy that even some women have scoffed at him.

I can't say for sure if being born verses being "made" was the difference in how gay a person acted or not, but in my opinion, us "natural-borns" had more authentic and tolerable attributes for general living. It was the stereotypical traits that typically didn't attract me, but Nick had weaseled his way into my life a few months after my mother was committed and my judgment was off balance then.

Now, I'd been feeling like our relationship was stale. I was consistently underwhelmed with his Viagra-popping sexual performances, and his clingy tendencies annoyed me more than gnats on a corpse.

There was a knock on the door, and Raul let himself in without waiting for a reply.

"What is going on in here? Is everyone okay?"

I exhaled in annoyance at both of them. Drama Queen 1 and 2, in the flesh.

"No everyone is not okay. Julian has been cheating on me and he's too much of a coward to admit it, so instead he's resorted to domestic violence," Nick whined, leaning his body against the wall like a wounded elk.

"Why don't you leave me then if you're so sure I'm cheating? Every time I breathe outside of your presence, you say I'm cheating. I can't talk to anybody unless I'm cheating. I can't go anywhere unless I'm cheating...can I take a shit without cheating, Nick? Huh?" I ranted. "You know what? You got me. I'm cheating. I'm fucking a mechanic at the shop, my suit tailor, the salon supply guy and Raul, too. I'm just a slut. I'm sleeping with everybody. You wanna add anybody else to the list?

Let me go out into the salon and see how many clients I can bag. Happy now?"

Nick's Puerto Rican face turned beet red as he brought his hand to his mouth.

Raul gasped at the absurdity of the thought. "Okay, I didn't realize this was just a lover's spat. Y'all keep my name out of this mess," he said, sashaying back out and closing the door behind him.

"I'm sorry, Julian. I know my jealousy can get carried away sometimes. But you know I get crazy when you ignore me. Especially when you're being so mean."

I knew the scroll of cheat partners would turn the tides; especially once I added Raul in for good measure. Raul was strictly a one-dick man and everybody who knew him knew it. Largely because he never shut up about his precious Jason. First rule of getting away with cheating; confuse them with the truth, then play the victim.

"I'm sorry," he repeated, approaching me with teary doe eyes.

Yes, you are, Nick. Yes-you-are, I thought.

* * *

Eventually, after I listened to Nick beg my forgiveness and explain how afraid he was of losing me for nearly five minutes, I got him out of my office so I could be alone. Sometimes being me is exhausting. I'm in such high demand and have so many priorities to juggle that nobody but me could ever handle being me.

I looked at my watch and saw I still had nearly two hours before my client was due in, so I returned Tia's phone call as I grabbed the stereo remote control from my desk and hit the POWER button. By the time Anita Baker had begun singing "Rapture," Tia'd answered the phone.

"Hey, baby," she answered.

"Hey, chica-lica. You rang?" I asked, happy to hear her voice.

"You booked up for the day? I have a restaurant review in Cumming at four o'clock, and I was gonna invite you."

"I wish I was cuming right now," I joked. "But I've got a client at three."

"You are so nasty," Tia chuckled. "What trouble has your ass been out there getting into? You missed my calls, and your man has been blowing up my phone looking for you. I didn't pick up, of course, because I wasn't sure if you told him you were with me or not."

"Girl, please. I backed that nag down as soon as I made it back to the salon. I was a bit preoccupied getting a tune up," I said, tooting my butt up and looking back at it as I sat in my chair.

"Oh, brother. With the mechanic guy again? I'm telling you, be careful with him. A lot of Jamaican men on the DL have anger issues about their sexuality. Whatever you do, don't do that choke-out sex, or any freaky violent stuff with him," Tia advised in her cute British accent.

She was an Atlanta transplant from Canterbury, UK, and had been my bestie since our first day of cosmetology school together. She later decided it wasn't for her and quit. As things turned out, she was friends with a food critic who appreciated her palate for food and ended up hooking her up with a job at an online magazine as a food critic.

"You are way too paranoid. Don't be a racist. All Jamaicans aren't like that," I playfully scolded.

"No, seriously. You know my friend, Devin; he used to date this Jamaican guy who wasn't out to his family yet. He was really troubled about it. It was like a love-hate relationship, where he hated and loved Devin at the same time for being gay. After what happened to your brother and sister, I'm surprised you're not staying away from their crazy-ass circle anyway. You're not still plotting on them, are you?"

I sighed and got up to pace my office. Brenda and Brian's kidnapping by their stalkers had been all over the television a few months back, and Tia and I followed the coverage pretty closely while Brian was recovering. I had mixed feelings about my estranged siblings, but I didn't wish death on either of them. In fact, I was happy to hear, via Aunt Linda, that Brian had survived his bullet wounds, and Brenda had escaped unscathed. Admittedly, I had been extra careful about whom I'd dated on the side after their situation, but I'd since regressed to my easy, casual interactions. My plans to make them regret how they treated me also included making them want to build a relationship with me in the end, although I hadn't quite worked that angle out yet.

"It's sort of...on hold," I answered.

"Julian. You have much more important things to do with your life than trying to screw up theirs. If they don't recognize you, so what? For 28 years they haven't made a difference; why bother now? Plus, I know you believe in karma. That mess that happened to them was too crazy to be anything other than karma coming back to get them. Don't let that type of shit happen to you; or bring it around me either," Tia declared.

"You weren't thinking about karma when you enlisted me to help you cut the cords off of all the appliances in David's house though, now were you?" I countered, as I looked at my reflection on the mirrored salon product shelf.

She giggled. "No, but that was different. He owed me fifteen hundred dollars. I was simply being karma coming back to him."

We both paused dramatically, and then laughed together at the foolishness of the statement. That was my bestie, all right. She always knew how to spin a story to her advantage.

"You think I've earned some bad karma for getting Paul caught while he was fucking me doggy style at the shop by Brenda?" I asked dramatically, knowing Tia would react to my news.

"What? You've got to be lying! Your sister caught her best friend's fiancé with you, bent over?" she shrieked.

"I'd already got mine, but she saw us before he got his. You should have seen her face. Hell, you should have seen his face! Kodak moment!"

"Get the fuck outta here! But I thought you hadn't seen her since the funeral."

"I haven't. I guess she was there to see her man, but she saw a hell of a lot more than that!" I laughed aloud again.

"What did he say to her?"

"Girl, I don't even know. I was so shocked to see her that I tuned both of their asses out, got my clothes, and got the fuck outta there before somebody might have started shootin' or something. My momma didn't raise no fool!"

"Bonkers! I can't, with you right now," Tia said, chuckling. "Did he get fired?"

I shrugged and started dancing to Stevie Wonder's "Do I Do" playing in the background.

"I don't know. I told you I didn't stick around to check on the damages."

"Well, you keep me posted when you find out, bitch," she said. We called each other bitch almost as regularly as we used our given names.

There was a knock on my office door and Raul entered again, without waiting for a reply.

"Excuse me, but there's trouble in paradise. Melanie over-processed some lady's hair and tried to send her out into the world lookin' a hot mess, chile'. Of course, she didn't wanna pay to look like 'Side Show Bob,' so now the lady wants to talk to the owner," Raul explained.

"Side Show Bob?" Tia chuckled on the other end. "All I can picture is that stupid clown from the Simpson's standing in your salon with an attitude."

I sucked my teeth and told Tia I'd call her back as I headed out the door. As always, I was in demand.

<h1 style="text-align:center">4</h1>

Brenda

I ordered Chinese food for dinner and we ate while watching the movie The Best Man on cable in the living room.

"You're real quiet. Still thinking about Rhonda?" he asked, putting a fork full of shrimp fried rice in his mouth.

I tried to choose my words very carefully. "I am but, I don't want to wear out my welcome any more than I already have by talking too much, either."

He stopped chewing momentarily and then continued, leaning back into the pillows on the couch before swallowing.

"Meaning that you think you've worn out your welcome?"

"Haven't I?" I asked with a raised eyebrow.

He eyed the flat screen on the wall, twisted his mouth, then back at me. I sat opposite him on the huge circular black sectional, eating my food from the large coffee table we shared between us.

"Why would you think that?"

"Because you just seem annoyed lately when you see me, and some of the things you've said give me the impression that I've stayed too long. I understand that. You didn't expect me to be here this long, and neither did I. I'm working on getting my own place already, though. Hopefully it will be soon," I replied expressionlessly.

It was a truthful enough answer. I did understand how he might be feeling, but I wasn't as okay with it as I would have him believe. I looked forward to seeing him every day and being in his arms at night. I hadn't been making any effort to look for another place since I'd started crashing at Lane's house, but I was about to.

He sighed and took a swig of his beer.

"Brenda, I've never said you've overstayed your welcome, and I haven't been pressing you to leave, either. Where's all this coming from?"

"It's coming from you being irritable, Lane. It's obvious when you're saying things like, 'Trouble follows you like a stray puppy' and emphasizing 'in my own home.' Sometimes the looks you give me—"

"Hold on, hold on, hold on...what? Just saying 'in my own home' means I want you out? And the comment about trouble; damn, Brenda, that's just the truth!" he protested. "Because as far as I'm concerned, me acting like I'm tired of you is all in your head, like a lot of the other assumptions you make about me. I haven't been doing or saying anything that warrants your feeling."

I diverted my eyes from his gaze disbelievingly, and disinterestedly watched the movie. Yeah, right. I can't tell, I thought.

"What's that look? You don't believe me?"

"So, you're sitting here telling me that I'm not getting on your nerves and you're not ready for me to go?"

"I'm not saying you never get on my nerves, like right now," he said, cracking a smile, which I did not reciprocate. "But that's normal with anybody. And the stuff I take issue with, we can probably work out," he answered, resting one arm across the back of the chair and the other across his torso.

"Since we're talking, let's really talk then," he continued. "I opened my home to you of my own volition. I knew you weren't going to stay with your mom or Rhonda for too long, and you made it clear you weren't going to live in your old apartment again. I could have offered you a place in one of my brother's apartment buildings if I didn't want you here with me, Brenda. But I didn't, and I haven't."

"Yeah, I know you haven't, but sometimes I feel like I'm walking on eggshells talking to you. You wear your feelings on your sleeve, Lane. When you don't like something, it's obvious," I insisted.

"Listen, baby, our relationship moved from 0 to 60 in a matter of days, and it's only natural that we're gonna start seeing sides of each other that aren't so rosy. I'm laid back most of the time, but as you've found out, I'm a neat freak. You..." he shook his head back and forth with a smirk, "are clearly not. You don't put things back where they belong, or at least not the way they belong, and it drives me crazy. I've been living by myself for a long time, and it's gonna take some adjusting for me."

"I know that, but I'm still learning you and I feel like I'm living with my grandmother sometimes. 'Don't touch that, clean that up, put that back, what are you doing with that?' all the time. I'm a little uncomfortable. And the way you look at Zeus when he jumps on stuff, or even lays on the rugs sometimes, is—"

"All right now, I admit I had to warm up to the dog being in my zone and lying on stuff. But, I like the little dude. And I do not act like a grandma about my stuff," he interjected. "Most of the time," he said, smiling. This time I returned his grin slightly.

"Come sit next to me," he ordered, patting a cushion beside him.

I sighed, pretending to protest, but I was happy he wanted me closer.

"Baby, I have been trying to conform. I promise I have. But I don't always know what the problem even is," I said, sitting beside him as he brought me closer with one arm. "I know I've been a little flighty at times, but I'm still trying to get my bearings back and stop being so paranoid about everything."

"You're right, and I might not always be as sensitive to that as I should be. It's not because I want you to leave, though. Sometimes I bring stress from work home, or I'm just moody. I'm still learning you, honey, and I honestly don't know what the woman I want, wants."

I guess that was fair. Shit, I didn't know what I wanted either, if I was keeping it 100 percent.

One thing Lane could be counted on to be is a straight shooter; and that was the thing I had the hardest time with, since I'd been trained from infancy that appearances trumped reality.

I was uncomfortable being transparent.

* * *

I let my hand rest on Lane's bare thigh and tried not to focus on the bulge in his boxer briefs that seemed to be beckoning me. I twiddled my fingers together on my lap and left my nervous eyes to rest there.

"More drama followed me this morning," I advised meekly.

His breathing was so slight; I looked up at him to ensure he hadn't completely stopped. Lane's dark eyes seemed uneasy, and his expression was tight.

"Okay," he prodded.

"My mother wanted me to come over because she was trying to be the catalyst for my father to develop a relationship with me."

His eyes widened. "She's been talking to his ghost?"

I smiled and realized how bizarre I must've sounded phrasing it that way.

"No. She told me that she'd had an affair, too, on the man I thought was my father, after she found out about Julian. The man she had an affair with, is my father. He was the married PI she hired to follow my dad...I mean, her husband."

Lane's jaw was yet again open. "Wow. Wow, Brenda," was all he could manage.

"I know, right? That's how I felt. As a matter of fact, I actually threw up."

He hugged me closer. "So now, he decides he wants to know you?"

I positioned myself so that we were eye to eye and straightened my posture to adequately deliver the next little tidbit of news.

"How about he, is the new man she's been seeing all this time since my other father died. Avis is his name," I spat, pursing my lips. "Umm hmm, but wait," I advised, holding my index finger up dramatically. "Even that isn't everything."

On that note, Lane gulped down the rest of his beer like a defendant waiting for a verdict and leaned back on the couch.

"She admitted...to putting a drug in my father's drink that night. The night he died. GBC, GHB...something like that. So that he would be incapacitated in the pool and drown. But she said he just stayed on the float; so they tipped him off into the water."

"Holy shit," he replied gutturally. "Your mother told you she murdered your father? Just like that?"

"Well not just like that, because I had to pry it out of her; but yes, she ran the whole thing down to me. My dad...her husband, was gonna leave her for another woman, and even though she wanted to be back with Avis, she didn't want to lose everything she had with my dad. If you knew my father, you would know he wasn't gonna let her have anything. So... Avis and Jenny helped her commit it, and cover it up. Supposedly the drug is untraceable unless they have some reason to be looking for it specifically."

"Brenda, you gotta turn her in. She can't just kill a man and then live happily ever after," he declared.

"I can't. She's my mother, Lane. And besides, you didn't know him like my family knew him. He was ruthless, violent, and—"

"I don't give a damn if he was the Grand Poobah of the Ku Klux Klan; she murdered him. They mur-der-ed him," he stressed, pronouncing every syllable.

Not only was I baffled by his sudden allegiance to justice for a man he didn't know from a can of paint, but I was also becoming increasingly more annoyed by the fact that he habitually cut me off in conversation.

Now I was shaking my head. "No. I'm not gonna tell. I promised her I wouldn't, and besides, if the cops didn't see a need to investigate, I'm not gonna give them a reason to. Her life's probably better now without him, anyway. Mine and my brother's, too."

"So, are you giving out murder passes now? Gwen was saying a lot of the same type of shit about your brother, but I bet you wouldn't have been so understanding if she'd have succeeded in killing him. Wake up, woman! Shit, I think just knowing about it and not saying anything is a crime, too. It might be under concealing evidence or something like that," he droned.

Damn! Now I wished I could erase his memory or reverse the time back to before I told him about it. Who knew Lane was such a goody two-shoes? It wasn't like she'd killed his dad. And it was a virtually painless death...I think. The horror stories I relayed to him from my past alone should have been enough for him to feel where I was coming from, though. Besides, what was diming my mom out really gonna do? Not that I was particularly a fan of hers either, but she was still my mother, no matter what. Moreover, Robert Andrews deserved exactly what he got.

"We're talking about a man who broke my shoulder slamming me into a wall as a teenager. The man who tried to choke the life out of me when I caught him cheating on my mother in our home. The same bastard who knocked my mother so hard on the side of her head that she lost five percent of her hearing. The guy whose illegitimate son was just introduced to his kids at his funeral! Need I go on? Nobody is mourning his loss except probably his girlfriend."

"You cried at his funeral, didn't you? Wasn't his sister the one flipping out on your mom in the church? People attended it, didn't they? Whether he was loved by 1 person or 100 people, you can't just decide he should die and kill him! I can't believe you're sitting here defending your mother's motives for killing someone, and actually expect me to help keep it secret! I'm not about to go to jail for—"

I cut him off this time. "Nobody's going to jail if you don't say anything! Damn! I'm sorry I even told you."

"I'm sorry you told me, too! Now your drama is my fucking drama!" he yelled, standing up.

Oh boy! Here we go with the drama thing again.

"No, it isn't! Just...just hear me out for a min—"

"Hear you? I already heard wha—"

"Stop cutting me off, goddammit!" I shrieked, looking up at him hovering next to me. "Just listen to me! Nobody but the three of them knew what they did until she told me. Now I've fucked up and told you, because I thought you would keep it to yourself. I know it's a crime, Lane. I know what she did wasn't right; but it's already done. He's already buried, and the police aren't even thinking about it," I pleaded, grabbing his hand gently. "Why turn everyone's lives upside down for nothing? Including yours."

His eyes glazed over, and his breathing was loud and quick.

I leaned my head against his arm with his hand in mine and waited for an answer.

* * *

The seconds he stood in front of me felt like hours, waiting to hear his decision. I even surprised myself a bit with the fervor I had expressed in getting him not to call the police. It wasn't until he was adamant about telling that I realized how strongly I felt that we shouldn't. My motivation wasn't entirely in saving my mother; it was partially due to my curiosity about my real father. I didn't want him to get locked up before I could get to know him.

"Fine," Lane conceded, pulling his hand from my grasp and walking towards the stairs.

"Lane!" I called after him.

He stopped on the first step and glanced back at me. "What?"

Clearly, I was going to need to give a more sentimental reason for my stance, else both I and my mother would look like cold-hearted bitches. "Please don't be mad at me. I... I don't want my real father to get locked up before I can even meet him. I have a sister who's three years older than me, too. I just want to get to know them and... obviously, if he's in jail, I won't be able to do that," I appealed.

He turned fully around and faced me. "You've had time to process this long before you told me. I need time to digest it and wrap my mind around everything you just put on me today. Between Paul and your half-brother, your new bio-daddy, and murder she wrote, I need an aspirin."

"I do have some good news if you want to hear any of it," I said apprehensively.

"What?" he answered, as though he could barely spare the energy to ask.

"Well, you know how I was saying I wanted to start writing again instead of going back to work as a financial broker?"

He just stared at me.

"Umm...well, there's a woman named Payton Christianson who co-wrote books with the lady who escaped that serial rapist in Texas last year, and a couple of other women who escaped stalkers and attackers. Payton contacted me yesterday about maybe writing a book on escaping Edwin and helping the police get to Brian in time. We're supposed to meet in a couple of days about it," I told him with a forced smile.

"Yeah, that is good news," he replied with an even sorrier smile than the one I wore. He then turned and continued up the steps.

I spun back around and looked at our open Chinese food cartons, forks, cups and other things left on the table. He had to be very upset to have gone upstairs without putting his food away. He really did like organization, and disorganization drove him nuts.

I didn't know what to do. I'd planned to call Brian and tell him the details of my meeting with my mother, but given Lane's reaction, I was now wary of how my brother would take it. He was unpredictable; especially when he didn't like the subject. He and my mom were on better terms than they were before he was shot and got the kidney transplant, but that didn't mean he wouldn't get her locked up and still sleep well at night.

Lane was right; this was a crime, and here I was acting like Katie Couric, about to report the news to everyone. I reminded myself of Rhonda for a moment; she, too, was typically the mouth of the south, which I usually complained about. The thought of her brought my mood down. I couldn't believe she'd actually turned on me for bringing her the truth about Paul.

In hindsight, maybe I should have waited until she'd gotten off of work. But I didn't want him to get to her first and twist the whole story around to make it look like I had my story wrong. Furthermore, what were the odds that Julian would be the bottom to Paul's top, at Lane's shop? Yeah, it was common to mix and mingle in the same friend groups out in the Atlanta dating scene, but my brother and I hadn't seen a single hair on Julian's head before the reveal at Saviors Sanctuary Christian Church for our father's home-going. Now all of a sudden, he's in my life, ripping everything I think I know apart.

I wanted to get in contact with him and see what he was really all about. I'd planned on doing it before, but now, I was more anxious than ever. Whether it made me a gossip or not, I was most definitely going to call Athena and let her know what I'd witnessed. She, Rhonda and I have been down like four flat tires since our first day of Pre-K.

If I had a pass to blab to anyone about Rhonda, it was Athena.

I put the food away, cleaned up the table in the living room where we sat, turned off the television and grabbed my cell phone from the charger in the kitchen as I steadied on the stool. The phone rang twice, and then she answered.

"B-rocka! What's going on, girl?"

"Hey, chubby. What you doing? Stuffing your little face?" I teased. Athena was nearly six months pregnant, and 9 times out of 10 when I spoke to her, she was eating.

"Actually, I am," she chuckled. "A corn dog dipped in vanilla ice cream. Oh my God, you have no idea how good it is," she said, imitating sounds of ecstasy.

"Yuck! And I never will."

"Brenda, I so wish you could see the look on this old lady's face standing across from me right now. I'm at Neiman's and the old biddy gave me the most shocked and appalled look when I made those sounds right now. Wit' her nosey ass," she laughed.

"You're eating a corn dog and ice cream while you're shopping? Girl, go sit your little pregnant behind down somewhere before you go into labor," I playfully scolded.

"Oh, shit, Bren," Athena replied intensely.

"What?"

"Your damned ass just spoke it into fruition because...my water just broke."

"No way!" I exclaimed.

"All the way down my leg," she said calmly.

5

Brian

I took a shower, oiled my bullet wounds and transplant scar with Vitamin E, and dozed off for a couple of hours on the bed after Nadia left. I didn't like knowing she was upset with me; especially over a non-issue like whether I loved her or not. But I wasn't gonna jump every time she got her back up, either. She knew what kind of man she was getting when we got together, and now she was trying to wussify me.

She was already getting: handsome, tall, sexy, funny, confident, and smart; not to mention my superb sex skills and cooking. She was just being greedy, trying to get me to be sensitive, too. Shit, the closest she'd get me to that would be me downloading Ralph Tresvant's "Sensitivity" to her iPod.

Still, she and I usually jelled pretty well, and I was surprised that she'd gotten so bent out of shape over a word I'd already said to her previously. I threw on my gray sweatpants, flip-flops, keys, and rolled out of the house commando, with my chiseled chest, out to Nadia's.

I knocked first out of habit, then put my keys in her door and let myself in. She was sitting on her beige leather couch in a white tank top and shorts, next to somebody else that I didn't know. Nadia's eyes grew wide as Lindsay Lohan's gap at the sight of me, and it took me a moment to figure out whether the person to her left was a woman or a man. The hair was cut into a short afro and they were wearing big baggy jeans, a RUN D-MC t-shirt, diamond studs in the ears, and red and white Nike sneakers. After I did a double take, I noticed the boobs, which were probably taped down under her clothes.

"Hey, baby," Nadia greeted me nervously.

"Hey," I replied, with automatic suspicion.

"Brian, this is Tracey. Tracey this is Brian," she said, introducing her with hand gestures.

"Hi," the rugged chick said, looking me up and down.

What the fuck was going on in here?

I put the keys in my pocket and let my hand rest there.

"Am I interrupting something?" I asked coolly, not returning the greeting.

"What? No," Nadia answered approaching me and kissing me lightly on the lips. Her body language and the bitch on the couch's expression seemed to be saying something different.

Tracey's plain-Jane, coco-brown, barely made-up face was twisted as though she'd just gotten a whiff of a fart from an onion. She and I played eyeball hockey while Nadia spoke.

"She's here visiting from DC and popped in to surprise me," Nadia explained with nervous laughter. "I didn't even know that she knew where I lived."

"You joked about the name of your apartment building when you first moved in; you said that Behind Buckhead sounded like directions instead of an apartment name," Tracey stated, without diverting her cold stare from me. "Nadia and I have a special connection. She knows there's nowhere she could ever be that I wouldn't be here for her. So, Brian, you always walk around with your chest out like that?"

"Not always; but since I was intending on make-up sex with my girl, I figured more clothes would only get in the way. Dick is swinging free as a bird, too," I countered, turning my gaze from Tracey to Nadia.

Was her butch friend trying to move in on my territory?

"Brian!" Nadia scolded. "What is wrong with you? Watch your mouth."

"How about you watch my mouth," I said in a low, seductive voice, grabbing her around the waist and pulling her close to me and French kissing her.

Her body tensed up and she broke away from me, turning red.

"Is this show for me? Or is he always like this?" Tracey asked blandly.

"Who is this dyke, Nad? Did I catch y'all about to fuck or something? Why's she cuttin' her eyes at me and sizin' me up like competition? And why did you just stop kissing me? You embarrassed?" I blurted out. Enough of the bullshit already!

Nadia looked like a deer in the headlights.

"No! She just popped up over here! I didn't even know she knew where I lived! I haven't even seen her since I left DC."

"Dyke? I bet this dyke can show you a thing or two. Why are you even bothering to explain to this lame? He got you wrapped around his finger like that, so you can't even still be cool with your exes?" Tracey said, standing up and placing a baseball cap with the Washington Redskins symbol on it on her head. "I see how you're rolling now. Frontin' for this lame-ass dude. But he's never gonna know you like I know you. It's okay, though. You'll find out soon enough. It's time for me to go."

"Ex? What the fuck is she talking about, 'your ex'?" I asked angrily.

Nadia and I had talked a lot about our past relationships, and never once did she bring up having an ex-girlfriend, or even liking girls like that.

"Shut up, Tracey!" Nadia screamed at her. "Nobody asked you to follow me to Atlanta, and stop trying to say shit just to get under his skin. Yeah, you're motherfucking right it's time for you to go."

Tracey rolled her eyes and huffed, making her way to the door at a slow, un-intimidated pace; still glaring at me, of course.

"Bitch, why are your eyes on me? I know you think you got balls like a man, but I am a man. Know your role."

"Bitch? The only bitch in here must be your girl because I don't answer to that," Tracey retorted, stopping and balking up.

"Just get out, Tracey. Just get out!" Nadia shrieked, opening her front door and attempting to shove Tracey out.

Tracey walked, but with stuttered resistance.

"You can kick me out all you want to, but he's not gonna love you like I love you, and he's not gonna make you squirt like I can, either!" she yelled, as Nadia finally succeeded in shutting the door on her.

My mouth dropped. "Squirt?"

* * *

Nadia leaned her back up against the door and hung her head low. I began to recall the feelings of betrayal I had when I realized what a lying bitch Gabby had been in college, and the various times she'd probably been out cheating on me rather than doing what she'd said she was. I took a chance and opened my heart to this woman because she'd shown herself to be genuine. Now it was starting to look like she'd been making a fool of me, too.

"Brian, I know this looks bad, and I know I need to explain some things but..." her words trailed off as tears began dripping from her bowed head. "Just please listen to me before you decide to write me off. Please."

My instincts said to curse her out, toss her house keys in her face, go back to my place and call over another chick to make me forget I ever loved her; but my heart told me to see what she had to say first.

"Can you, just sit down with me for a minute?" she asked, walking slowly past me to the couch.

I didn't answer, but I followed suit, and we sat down in unison. The whole time I was looking at her, one question was ringing in my head.

"So, that bitch made you squirt?" I asked gruffly.

She shutter-blinked and put her hands to her face before looking back to me. "Really? That's what you want to know?"

"Hell, yeah I want to know that! It's not the only thing I need answers to, because obviously you've been keeping secrets, but yeah. I want to know if some female made you squirt but I haven't yet."

Her face turned to the ceiling and she rolled her eyes. "She was just trying to needle you, Brian."

"Well, it worked. I didn't even know you were a squirter at all. That's some shit you should tell a dude. She did it with just her fingers? Or her fingers and her tongue?"

The thought of some butch dyke being able to give my woman more pleasure sexually in bed than I had, really burned me. All this time I was giving Nadia pleasure, she was probably secretly thinking about how some female made her cum harder than I ever could. And why the fuck hadn't she ever told me she was bi-sexual? We could have had some threesomes by now. Not only was she a liar, but she was selfish, too.

Nadia sighed. "Brian, that is uncomfortable to talk about at this moment and it's not important, anyway. What you and I have is more than just sex. Look, I told you I'd broke off an engagement with my ex after he cheated on me. Tracey and I were really good friends back in DC. She was there for me when I was going through it with him, and when I was all broken after it was over. I wasn't myself. I enjoyed the attention, and I got all wrapped up in the things she was giving me and doing for me. I tried to pretend like she was a man in my head, but after four months, that wasn't working. It was a rebound thing. She was in love, I was in lust, she got too serious, and I got my shit and moved to Atlanta. There was absolutely nothing happening when you came in. She showed up at my door saying she wanted to talk, and I was listening to her, since she came all the way from Washington. That's it. That's all. Nothing else."

"You know I already stepped out on a ledge trusting you in the first place because of my history with lying women. Then, I come over here to find you about to tongue down your ex-lick-lover, which you never even mentioned. Right now, I'm feeling like you're no different than the women I—"

"I was not about to do anything with her, Brian!" she interjected. "I never lied to you about anything. I didn't tell you, but I didn't lie about it, either. It wasn't even like it was a secret. I just didn't see the point in bringing it up. You never asked me if I'd been with a woman before."

"So, if I was fucking men in my past, you'd be okay with that?"

She wiped her face again nervously. "No. But it's not the same thing. You've already said you're not into guys and honestly, I'm not into girls. I was into her at the time, and was emotionally confused. It was a one-time thing, and I can't really explain it, so...I just don't talk about it. I never expected to see her again, Brian."

I looked away from her, trying to determine what I thought about what she had to say. When I came in, she looked like my sister every time her dumb ass got busted when she was a teenager doing something she shouldn't have been. Maybe it was just the fact that the girl was here at all, but either way, I was unsettled. Who I thought she was, wasn't really who she was. Or at least there was more to her than she'd let on. Now I wondered who and what the conversation she was having earlier was about.

"Who were you talking to when you came over earlier?"

She scanned her apartment nervously, sighed, and looked back at me.

"I was talking to my friend, Josey, who still lives in DC. Tracey told her that she was going to track me down and do some other things while she was here. She didn't come here specifically to see me though, Brian. She's here to visit relatives."

"Did seeing her bring back up your feelings again?" I asked coldly.

"No!" she protested. "No. I left her because I didn't want to be with her anymore, and because being in that lifestyle ultimately wasn't what I wanted. I love you. You know that. That's why I was so upset at your place, because I worry about keeping your attention. I don't want her, I want you."

Our eyes were locked, and the sincerity in her expression made me believe in her again. Damn. This was so unlike me to be so forgiving...ever.

I exhaled, shuffled in my seat and said, "So, you'd be open to a threesome?"

* * *

Nadia was not game for a threesome. She frowned like I'd just asked her if I could shit in her mouth, and changed the subject.

I don't understand some women. If you want to make sure I don't lose interest and get with another chick someday, why not give me what I want where you can supervise it and keep me happy? I wasn't unhappy with her just yet, and truthfully, other chicks barely garnered more than a couple of boob and ass checks, but it could happen in the future.

My dick got hard at the thought of another woman and Nadia doing me at the same time, watching them kiss, or another chick going down on Nad while she sucked me off; but I didn't like the idea that she would return the licks on a chick. My woman should only be pleasuring me, and that's it. There's nothing enticing to me about watching somebody else get the satisfaction I should be getting.

Then I thought, what if, God forbid, our threesome partner pulled a sex move that made Nadia squirt before I've had the chance to figure out how to do it for her. Fuck that!

"So, are we good?" she asked, moving closer to me with bashful eyes and perky nipples through her tank top.

All the arguing, talk about threesomes, squirting, and the beautiful visual of her pretty round areolas fighting to get out from under those clothes had my engine revved.

"We could be better," I said, shifting my legs so that my now erect penis was notably tenting my sweatpants.

She half-smiled, pulled the elastic band of my pants up over my tool, and descended her warm, hot lips onto it. I moaned and moved my hips with the rhythm of her mouth. She stroked it slow and steady; her lips tight and controlled. I was becoming entranced by the sight of her ample ass rocking ever so slightly from right to left as she did.

She lifted up, pulled her shirt up over her head and exposed her breasts before standing to slide off her shorts. I smiled, realizing she was commando. That better not have been in honor of her ex-butch's unexpected visit, I thought to myself.

Nadia tugged my sweatpants off, then straddled me and inserted my manhood with surgical precision. She was gushing wet and her sexual see-saw had my entire body saluting her command.

She leaned in and kissed me deeply while I tried to mentally restrain myself from cuming too soon. Her hands caressed my chest and torso before grabbing hold of my sides as she thrust her head back in ecstasy. I passionately grabbed the back of her head, drilling upwards into her love box, and when she lurched forward, I saw Gabby's face. Or I thought I had.

The momentary surprise caused me to jerk backwards, and Nadia stopped her erotic dance abruptly.

"What's wrong?" she asked.

"Nothing, nothing. I got a charley horse," I lied.

"Are you okay?"

"It's gone baby, it's gone," I answered, kissing her to mute the questions and get back to the action.

We kept going until we were both too spent to do anything but climax and fall out onto her couch.

"I think my ass is chafed from rubbing against the leather," I complained, lifting and re-positioning myself.

Nadia giggled and stretched her long legs out with her feet in my lap and her head resting on a decorative pillow on the arm of the couch.

"Poor baby, you bruise easy," she replied. Then after a long pause she said, "I'm sorry."

"It's not that serious, girl. No need to be sorry."

"Not about that, about the whole thing with Tracey, and not telling you about that experience in my past. You've shared a lot with me that was hard for you to expose, and I don't want to do anything to make you feel like I'm not doing the same. I was kind of ashamed, and I just hope you won't hold it against me, baby. I know how you can hold a grudge."

I turned my eyes away from her. She was right, I could hold a grudge, but I wasn't sure what significance I was going to give everything I'd just discovered. I was of the belief that all women were innately bi-sexual anyway; most were simply taught not to engage. Still, I wasn't about to be in a relationship with a chick that could flip-flop from pink to penis at the drop of a hat.

"So, is there anything else you need to let me know? How do I know you won't switch back to the other team on me? There's not a strap-on in your closet, or an orphaned dildo that's gonna come back to haunt you, is there?"

She threw the pillow from behind her head with a playful smile and said, "You are a fool. No more secrets. I'm straight, I tell you! Now anyway. I promise, I've gotten any desire for women out of my system."

The angle of her face highlighted her cheekbones and dark eyes, which made her deeply favor Gabby.

Damn it! Why couldn't I get Gabby out of my head all of a sudden? Nadia didn't look a damned thing like her, did she?

Gabrielle was looking as good as ever at the restaurant, though. The short haircut certainly gave her a sleeker look than she had in college. I wondered if she'd ever told Trent what she'd done, or how I eventually made her pay for her sin against me. He seemed like the nice, gullible type. I guessed she needed someone she could snow if she ever decided to cheat again, if she wasn't already.

"Brian?" Nadia called, nudging me with one foot.

"What?"

"Did you hear me?"

"No. What did you say?"

"I asked if there was anything about your past or present that you haven't shared with me, or maybe just didn't think was important, that you want to share now."

I thought about telling her how my sexy as fuck ex-girlfriend, that I hated to the core of my soul, was married to my new restaurant partner and that I'd been seeing her face instead of Nadia's for the last 30 minutes...but I wasn't stupid.

"I'm an open book," I said smugly.

6

Julian

"No, I will not," I told Paul, as I reviewed my fingernails for signs that I may need a manicure.

"Please, Julian. I need you to talk to your sister and see if you can get her to take back what she said, mon. She can say she was confused, or that...I don't know. I've been thinking on this all day, and you have no idea how bad this is for me," he pleaded through the phone.

'And I don't care' is what I wanted to say, but thought better when I recalled Tia's warnings that he may go ballistic.

He sighed deeply, and there was silence for a handful of seconds.

"She drove up to Rhonda's job to tell her, Julian. Rhonda's left me four voice messages and sent me three texts cursing me out. I bet Brenda's already told my boss, too. I might even be fired right now."

Waaa Waaa Waaa, Blah Blah Blah...who cared? Brenda spoiled my little blackmail scheme before I was even able to get it fully underway. Oh well. It was fun trying. I enjoyed the four sweat sessions Paul and I shared previously, even if the last one was cut short. C'est la vie.

"Fired for what? Being gay? That's not a crime. Wait...actually, we're in Georgia. There's no telling what old sodomy laws are still on the books here," I chuckled, as I turned the silver swan head faucets off over my tub.

"It's nothin' funny about this, mon!" he yelled. He sounded like a wild dog, and I imagined the spit foaming around his mouth as I turned both chrome swan handles, which spouted my bath water, off. "I could lose everything because of this! I have a 12-year-old daughter to think about as well! And I'm not gay!"

Not gay? He sure fooled me when he had his lips and hands all over my man parts. I had no sympathy for closeted cowards at his age, which was 32, unless they had prestigious jobs that warranted such secrecy. This wasn't 1965, for Christ's sake, and we lived in Atlanta, the new black homosexual capital. Sad to say for Paul, mechanics were not high on my list of prestigious occupations.

"Why didn't you tell me that Brenda was your sister?"

"What difference would it have made? We are virtual strangers to each other. Furthermore, why didn't you notice my family resemblance to Brian? Even when I saw him, I thought we looked like two sides of the same person. I only met them once," I rebutted, annoyed. How dare he blame his poor decision-making choices on me.

"I've only seen the guy twice, maybe t'ree times before, Julian. I don't pay no man attention," he whined. I dared not laugh aloud, but I did on the inside. 'I don't pay no man attention'? He sure as hell paid me attention.

My other line beeped, and Aunt Linda's name flashed across the screen.

"Paul, I've gotta take this call," I said quickly.

"I don't know what to do right now, Julian. I don't even want to go home. Can I come to your place? Just to think?" he begged.

"No. That is not a good idea, and I have to take this call. I'm sorry, Paul. Good luck," I said coarsely, as I clicked over and took the other call.

Nick would Lorena Bobbitt me if I ever pulled a stupid stunt like bringing a booty call to stay with us! Not that either knew of the other one, but I knew. No way, never!

"Hello?" I said, letting my bathrobe fall to the floor, stepping into the warm tub water and sitting down slowly with the phone to my ear.

"Boy, I almost hung up the phone because I thought the voice mail was gonna come on," Aunt Linda complained.

"Well, it didn't come on. How are you?"

"I'm agitated because my nephew is screwing everything that moves all around Atlanta, just like his father did," she continued.

"Tsk tsk, Brian. Where are your morals?" I said, playfully scolding him. From time to time, she'd complain about Brenda or Brian's antics that she'd discovered third hand, since they rarely dealt with her directly. I simply assumed this was one of those times.

"Brian? I'm talking about you, mister. Brenda just called here wanting your phone number and wanting to get to the bottom of why you were taking it in the bottom from her best friend's fiancé! What in the body of Christ the Lord my Savior have you done now?" she scolded.

I rolled my eyes at her theatrics and wished I hadn't lost my Bluetooth in the house earlier so that I didn't have to hold the phone while I soaked.

"Well?" she prodded.

"Well what?"

"Well, what do you have to say for yourself?" she hollered back.

"What is it that you want me to say for myself, Aunt Linda? I'm a grown man, doing grown things. Nobody forced him to do anything. How was I supposed to know he was engaged? Especially to Brenda's best friend? It's not like I've spent time with them and gotten to know their friends. Atlanta is just so small that—"

"Who do you think you're fooling, Julian? I know you like I know my own big toe. You screwing around with that girl's man wasn't no accident," she continued. "And now that huffy-ass little chile' is calling my phone demanding things. Well, I'll tell you what...she doesn't have no hold over me. She's just like her evil-assed momma. Thinking everybody owes her something and she can just start bossing me around. Little bitch was mad I wouldn't give her your number, and I told her I'd have you call her instead. I don't have the time for her foolishness. Do you have a pen so you can take this number down?" Aunt Linda complained.

I put my cell phone on speaker and sat it down on the floor by the tub. I really wasn't in the mood for this shit. Here I was trying to have a nice, relaxing bath, and I couldn't because Brenda was kicking up dust with Paul and my aunt.

"Julian!" Aunt Linda yelled as I squeezed the pomegranate liquid soap onto my loofa and began washing myself.

"Yes, Aunt Linda?" I called over the edge of the tub.

"I asked you if you had a pen to take the number down."

"No, I don't. I'm in the tub. Can you just text it to me please?" I said, rolling my eyes and neck all at once. She was getting on my nerves.

"The tub?" I heard her suck her teeth. "All right then, I'll text it to you. Call me after you talk to her and let me know what's going on."

"Sure will," I replied in a phony sing-songy voice before pressing the END button with one suds-covered finger.

Neither one of those bitches needed to hold their breath on my phone call tonight.

I was not in the mood.

* * *

"So, why do I have to stay in here while you guys watch horror movies?" Nick pouted, sitting on the edge of the bed as I pulled my pajamas from the dresser drawer in our room.

"Because this is our thing, and because you don't even like horror movies," I responded in a snarky tone.

"Just because I'm not all into them like you and Tia doesn't mean I can't watch them. Why would you exclude me from something in my own home, anyway? I mean, what's the big deal if I hang with you two?"

"Listen, we don't just watch horror movies. We drink, eat popcorn and play Monopoly while we gossip. That's our thing. It's my bonding time with my best friend. We haven't had one of these nights in almost a year. Why do you have to be so clingy?" I hissed, while buttoning my royal blue Ralph Lauren pajama top.

If I had it my way, he'd be watching TV in his own place; but I hadn't worked up to finalizing that request of him just yet.

"You know I hate it when you say I'm clingy, Julian. All I'm asking is..." he whined, but paused when my cell phone's ringing began.

I could feel his eyes burning holes into my back as I went over to the bedside table to answer it.

"Hello?"

"Is this Julian?" a female voice asked.

"Yes," I replied, a little annoyed at the rudeness of the caller who didn't bother with a proper greeting first. They hung up on me and I looked at the phone with an attitude, as though the idiot who'd just called could see my expression.

"Who was that?" Nick asked.

"I don't know," I answered, noticing that the number showed on my phone as PRIVATE. "Some woman who hung up on me, I might add. Or maybe they just dropped the call, I don't know."

"Really," he replied suspiciously.

I glared at him, grabbed my pajama bottoms from the bed, and put them on.

"Why ask if you never believe what I say?"

"I didn't say I didn't believe you," he claimed, with folded arms.

I slipped on my bedroom shoes and turned to put a clip from the dresser in my hair when the doorbell rang.

"Can you get that, please? Tia's probably got her hands full of popcorn, liquor and Monopoly. I gotta pee," I asked, heading towards the bathroom.

He sucked his teeth, but got up to do as I asked. Just as I began to release myself, I heard Nick shriek and a loud thump.

"Nick, you okay?" I called, frowning, as my stream continued. He didn't answer.

A few more drops came out; I shook and put myself back into my pants. "Nick, what was that noise?" I called again, as I ran my hands under the water and dried them quickly. Silence.

I left the bathroom, grabbed my phone off the bed, and went downstairs to greet Tia and see what clumsy foolishness had Nick all up in arms. Instead, I was struck with fear once I rounded the corner into the foyer. The front door was wide open, and Nick was on his back, with blood spurting from his head and a huge, blood-spattered brick rested nearby.

"Oh my God! Nick!" I screamed, as I simultaneously began dialing 9-1-1.

I was panic-stricken and confused, but I wasn't stupid. I rushed to close and lock the door, and peeped cautiously out the side window-pane to see if I could see who'd done this to him.

"9-1-1. Where are you calling from and what's your emergency?"

"Somebody bricked my boyfriend in the head and he's bleeding really badly," I answered, with tears welling in my eyes looking at his stilled body.

"Okay, what's your location, sir?"

"500 Heatherview Court, Glenayre. I can't tell if he's alive or not," I whimpered.

"Can you check if he's breathing please, sir, or if he has a pulse? I've already dispatched a unit to your address," the operator advised.

I leaned down and put my hand on his neck to check for a pulse. He was still breathing. The closer I got to him, I could actually hear his ragged breathing. "He's breathing, but he's unconscious."

"All right. Can you tell me what happened? Is anyone else there with you?"

"No, it's just us. Somebody rang my doorbell, and he went down to answer. I was in the bathroom; I heard him yell, a thump, and when I came downstairs, the door was open, and he was lying on the floor with blood coming out of his head."

"Was he shot? Or stabbed? Can you tell how he sustained his injuries?"

"I told you, somebody bricked him!" I reiterated.

"What do you mean, they bricked him? They hit him with a brick?"

"What else would I mean? Yes! Yes! Somebody hit him in the head with a big brick!"

"Okay, sir. Calm down. Do you know if they're still there? Or if anyone has a weapon on the premises?"

"I…I don't think they're here. I don't have any weapons," I said, looking cautiously around the corner back towards the stairs and the entry to my living room. What if they'd ran past him into the house? I hadn't thought of that.

"Do you know who hit him in the head with the brick?"

Was this bitch brain dead? I just told her what I knew! Not a God-damned-thing! All kinds of things ran through my head. I was scared.

"I just told you what I knew, lady! I didn't see what happened!" I exclaimed, as the sound of police sirens blared up my driveway.

I just hung up on her. Who I needed, was here now.

I opened the door and two officers trotted up to my doorstep, with a paramedic truck pulling up closely behind their vehicle.

"He's right there," I said, pointing to Nick as though he wasn't the obvious victim. I was so discombobulated I didn't know if I was coming or going. What had just happened here? Why would anybody want to hurt Nick?

I saw Tia's lime-green Scion pulling up to the curb as an officer went to check Nick's vitals and the other stopped to question me.

But I didn't know anything!

* * *

Police canvassed the neighborhood while the paramedics rushed Nick to Northside Hospital. Two officers detained me at the house for about 15 more minutes while they took my statement, and I walked them through everything I heard and saw. After they found out how little I had to offer, they let me leave with Tia to follow Nick.

"What happened?" Tia asked, while driving with her brunette dreads piled on top of her head in a bohemian head wrap, and her thin-rimmed glasses teetering on the bridge of her nose.

"Girl…" I said, taking a deep breath and letting my seat back as far as it would go in her tiny car. "I honestly don't know. He went to answer the door for you, and the next thing I know, he's knocked out and blood is everywhere."

"For me?"

"Well, yeah, we thought it was you ringing the doorbell; but it must've been whoever attacked him."

Tia nodded and put her right hand on my knee. "Are you okay?"

"Yeah, I'm fine," I answered, leaning my head back against the headrest. "I'm just trying to think of who would do this, and why? Nick's a pain in the ass to me, but other than that, everybody loves him."

"What about you?"

"What about me? I wouldn't have hit him with a brick and then—" I began defensively.

"No, no, Julian. Not, for doing it. What if they meant to attack you and not Nick?" she clarified.

I stared at her blankly. The thought hadn't crossed my mind; but why would anyone want to hurt me? But then again...

"Like who? Paul?" I contemplated, thinking aloud.

Tia nodded, and the many bracelets on both of her wrists jingled as she turned the steering wheel.

"Or your sister," she added, before circling the parking lot of the hospital a couple of times looking for a space. I didn't even know what to say. Sure, I was used to dealing with Nick's drama and the hassle of dodging his cheater radar, but this had become dangerous. Maybe Brenda and Brian were used to the stakes going up to deadly force, but I wasn't; and I didn't want any part of it.

"Come on," Tia ordered, snapping me from my temporary fear-induced trance and grabbing her huge purse from the floor behind my seat. "I actually hope it's none of them. Maybe something like a mistaken identity."

"Me too," I replied more sullenly.

We went in through the ER entrance and Tia headed straight to the check-in desk.

"Hello, ma'am, my brother Nicholas Dempsey was brought in by ambulance for a head injury, probably about 20 or 30 minutes ago. We had to stay behind and make the police report. Do you know what room he's in or where I can find him?" she asked politely.

The woman looked up from her computer screen at Tia and back with a sigh before answering disinterestedly, "Let me check the computer."

I guess she hadn't noted that Tia was white, and Nick was Puerto Rican, but then again, she might not have even seen Nick. I wasn't shocked at Tia's approach, though. It was much easier to get information when you were a relative.

I looked around with arms folded at the scores of weak and wounded waiting in the ER. A teenager sat crying in one corner with what looked like a broken leg, a scantily clad black chick was on her knees tossing up cookies in a garbage pail by the door while another braless female rubbed her back, and a white-haired old man moaned loudly as an equally old woman consoled him. "Just hang on, sweetheart. I'm sure someone will help us soon."

A chill went up my spine at the thought of the many germs floating in the air, and I was suddenly very aware that I was standing in the ER of this hospital dressed in my pajamas and bedroom slippers. Oh my God! Just as I was turning to say something to Tia, I heard my name.

"Julian?" Brenda said, like my name tasted bad in her mouth.

What the hell was she doing here? I thought, as she approached me from the elevators with Lane behind her.

"I definitely need to talk to you," she demanded, with the neck roll of an experienced shit starter.

"Girl, back up off me. My man's life is in danger, and I don't have time to cat fight with you," I replied, raising my hand to her and stepping back.

"Your man? Who, Paul?"

"Bitch, he is not my man."

"Bitch?" she repeated, stepping into my face. "So you're a homewrecker and a cheater?"

"Hey, man, watch your mouth," Lane warned, pulling Brenda back and stepping forward.

I did not need some 6' 4" hunk of muscles getting in my face in defense of my big-mouthed sister. Why were their asses here anyway?

"You tell her to stay out of my face and my business then!" I responded, not backing down.

"Hey, hey! Knock it off!" Tia exclaimed, inserting herself between Lane and me. "His boyfriend was just assaulted. Just leave him alone."

"I just want to talk to him for a second," Brenda told Tia with a snide once-over. "What happened to your...boyfriend?"

"Somebody came to my house and threw a brick at his head. You wouldn't know anything about that, now would you?" I questioned, with a neck roll of my own.

"No! Why would I know anything about that? I don't even know where you live or who your boyfriend is."

"What are you doing here, anyway?" Tia asked calmly.

"My friend is having a baby, if that's any of your business."

We stood there looking at one another without a word for a few moments until Tia broke the silence.

"Well, the lady said Nick was awake when they brought him in," Tia said, turning her back to Brenda and Lane. "But that's all she knows right now, other than that he's back in one of the rooms being treated. She'll call us back up to the desk when she knows more."

I sighed in relief that he wasn't dead or in a coma as I'd feared.

Brenda's expression softened and she said, "Umm...I'm sorry about whatever happened to your boyfriend. I hope he's gonna be okay."

I was surprised to hear it, and I'm sure my expression said so.

"Since we're both waiting anyway, can I talk to you for a minute? Civilly," she asked, with palms to the air.

I had nothing but time to kill anyway.

"Fine," I said, rolling my eyes.

7

Brenda

I couldn't believe Julian was in the ER waiting room in blue silk pajamas when Lane and I got off the elevator. We were going to get some snacks and charge my phone in the car. The ER was fairly crowded, and there were only a couple of empty seats available, but they weren't together.

"Wanna talk outside?" I asked, observing his frowning face as he scanned the sickly and their drivers.

Julian nodded as Tia sat down in one of the empty seats.

"I'll wait here," she said in a British accent. I wondered what her role was in Julian's life. Was she a beard?

Once we got outside of the ER doors, Lane gently put his hands on my shoulders.

"Baby, I'm gonna wait over here for you until you're done. I'm not comfortable leaving you here with him alone," he said, glaring at Julian.

"I'm gonna be fine. Go ahead and get everybody's stuff. And can you please put my phone on your charger?"

He sighed and brought me closer to him, planting a soft kiss on my lips and handing me his phone.

"Call your phone number if you need me. I'll have it charging in the car," he said, handing me his cell and walking away slowly with a look of warning to Julian across his face.

Julian rolled his eyes in response and exhaled through his nose.

"He's a little overprotective now, isn't he?"

"Not at all. Plus, I'm sure he's not taking too kindly to the fact that you and his employee were screwing on his supplies," I replied smugly, folding my arms the way his had been since he'd seen me.

He rolled his eyes and switched his weight from one leg to the other. Oh my GOD! It seemed like he rolled his eyes like I blinked my eyelashes...every fucking second! I was already becoming annoyed.

"So, what do you want to talk to me about, Brenda?"

"I want to find out what your deal is. Me and my brother never knew you existed for all of these years, but now since we found out about you, it's like you're everywhere," I complained.

He smirked and leaned against the side of the building.

"I've always been around. Maybe you and your brother have just been too self-absorbed to notice anybody but yourselves. I've sure as hell seen you and Brian out before. At Music Midtown one summer I saw you and your girlfriends, and a couple of times at restaurants. I usually see Brian at after-six bars whenever I see him, and once at the grocery store."

I was surprised to hear that my brother's gay doppelganger had been in both of our vicinities on other occasions, yet no one, including us, mentioned their uncanny resemblance to us.

"So, how long have you been seeing Paul?" I cut to the chase. "He's engaged to my best friend."

"I don't concern myself with other people's engagements. I have my own relationship to tend to, if you haven't noticed. Obviously, he was looking for something other than what she could give him, and I gave it to him. We've only screwed, as you put it, a few times. I definitely wasn't his first taste of male tail though," he smirked.

Damn, this guy was definitely an Andrews at heart. Even if his last name was Parkes. He cut me down like a stick of butter and didn't even break a sweat.

"Did you know he had a connection to me?"

"Do you think my world revolves around you?" he snapped back. "Are you worried Lane is next on my list?"

"I don't know. Are you worried you're gonna be the next one to get a brick to your head?" I shot back angrily.

He gasped, and I didn't flinch. Who the hell did Julian think he was talking to? He was the one who had overstepped, not me.

"You bitch!"

"You're the bitch!"

"Bite me!"

"Fuck you!"

"Slut!" he yelled.

"Bastard!"

"Cunt!"

"Dick!"

Then he did something completely unexpected. He started laughing. I stared at him as he unfolded his arms and held his hands up in hysterical...laughter.

"What is wrong with you?" I scoffed.

"Girl, we are standing out here screaming names at each other like two potty-mouthed fools. The two people that just went in the ER behind you had a kid with them and chile'...they looked like their heads were gonna explode if we said one more curse!" He continued laughing.

I was baffled and amused at his ability to switch gears so quickly. Weren't we arguing? I didn't join in the laughter, but surprisingly, I really wasn't angry like I had been 30 seconds earlier.

Once Julian composed himself, he wiped some dirt from his pajama top sleeve and looked into my eyes.

"Honestly, Brenda, I don't give a shit about any of this. My boyfriend is in the ER, and I need to figure out who put him there. I don't know what you want me to say about Paul, but he was nothing but a pastime for me. I'd bet my Prince Albert I'm not the only one he's cheating on your B-F-F with, either."

"Your Prince Albert? You have a penis piercing? T-damned-M-I Julian!" I cringed with a giggle. If nothing else, he was a character!

"Humph. Don't knock it till you try it. Well...I guess you can't actually try it but...never mind. Anyway, are we good? Because it's starting to get chilly out here and my pajamas are not protecting my freshly lotioned skin from these harsh winds."

Despite wanting to dislike him, I kind of already did. He was a lot like Brian, except with more sass and an apparent ability to move on from an issue easily. That was definitely not like my older brother at all.

"Yeah, okay," I said, as we walked in through the sliding doors, back into the loud world of chaos.

* * *

I could see the apprehension in Tia's eyes as Julian and I approached her seated at the end of a row of chairs.

"Neither of you are bloody, and you both have all your limbs, so...everything is okay?" Tia asked, darting her eyes between him and me.

"Girl, she's got a mouth like mine. Wasn't nobody about to stand outside looking like a hood rat arguing with her. I got cold," he said, grinning and squeezing as much of his butt onto the edge of her seat as he could.

She grunted and shifted tightly in place as he crunched her in with a frown.

"Julian. Your lard ass can't fit on this little seat with me. Move."

He rolled his eyes and stood with a huff.

Lane walked in through the ER doors with a big brown paper bag nestled in one arm and holding a Sprite 2-liter soda. When we made eye contact, he stopped and waited for me to approach.

"Well, I'm about to go back upstairs to maternity to check on my friend. I hope your boyfriend is okay," I said sincerely, before turning to walk to my man.

"So, did you want to talk in a less depressing setting next time?" Julian asked, posing his phone as though he were ready to take my number. "Or are we done now?"

I smiled. Something inside of me was pleased to know he wanted to keep in touch. I was curious about his relationship with my substitute father, and I had a lot of questions I wanted to ask him. Besides, he was kind of cool, and I felt like we were clicking.

"Yeah, that's cool," I replied, rattling off my digits to him as he typed them into his cell. "Nice meeting you, Tia," I added, and she nodded.

Lane watched me with dubious eyes as I reached him and we both headed towards the elevators.

"You look like that went well," he spoke, after a side chew of his gum.

"I think it did. He's...different than I thought he was gonna be."

"Different how?"

"I don't know. Both times I met him were under shady circumstances. If you want to count catching him with Paul as meeting him; but he wasn't as bad as I thought he would be. I kind of liked him."

Lane's eyebrow rose when we stopped at the elevators.

"What?" I asked with guilt, although I had a good idea what he was thinking.

"You think Rhonda is going to be all right with you hanging with that guy now that you told her what he did?"

"He said he never even knew about her. He's got a boyfriend himself. That was on Paul to protect his relationship. Not Julian. I was just mad because I thought he knew."

"Really," he replied unconvincingly.

The elevator doors opened, and the three people bunched into the small box moved in enough for Lane and me to fit. I didn't like how he said that, or the scolding look he wore as though his raised eyebrows were mocking me. We were silent until we got out on the maternity ward floor and I picked the conversation back up.

"So, what, you think he should take all of the blame for it?" I asked with attitude.

"I think you should have minded your business in the first place, and then this wouldn't be a dilemma for any of us. You're singing a different tune than you were before you actually talked to him."

I balked and stopped in mid-stride.

"I did what any good friend would do in my place. What the hell do you mean I should have minded my business?"

"Come on, drama queen; we've already discussed this. It's done," he replied, cutting the corner and into the maternity ward waiting room.

How the hell did I become the bad guy in all of this? Everybody seemed to be taking pot shots at the messenger!

I sucked my teeth and followed behind him with arms crossed and my lips forming a perfect pout until I was again stopped in my tracks by the sight of Rhonda talking to our friend Belinda. It made sense that she'd be there, given the depth of our friendship with Athena, but I still hadn't expected to see her.

When our eyes met, she sneered and shifted so that I was soon looking at her back and consequently, her ass.

Bitch. She could keep her stank attitude and her undercover dicklover boyfriend too, for all I cared!

I was so focused on Rhonda and her cold shoulder that I didn't hear whatever Quamé said when he walked in behind me.

"What?" I asked, turning to face him.

"You're a godmommy! Qur'an Garrison was born five minutes ago at 10:02 p.m., weighing 5 pounds and 11 ounces!" he exclaimed with a grin that seemed almost as wide as his face.

The room was then filled with resounding congratulations and banter as I gave the first joyous bear hug on him.

"So, everything is okay?" I questioned, since the baby was a few months early.

"He's fine. A little underweight, and he's gonna have to be monitored, but he's fine, she's fine..." he trailed off as his gray-haired, 5 foot nothing grandmother bowled me over like I was a feather.

"I have a new great grandbaby!" she exclaimed, hugging and kissing him.

"Yes, Grandma. I just wanted to come tell everybody. I gotta get back in the room," Quamé said, after smacking a few hands and hugging friends and family who approached to congratulate.

I sashayed over to Lane, who was leaning against the wall with our food and soda on a table next to him. Surprisingly, he held out his hand

and pulled me in close instead of withdrawing from me like I'd expected.

"Come here, godmommy, and put a smile on your face instead of stressing yourself out," he said softly, placing a kiss on my lips and my forehead.

Wasn't he just mad at me? Lane was definitely a different type of animal, but I preferred what I was getting over what I was expecting. I smiled and rested my head on his chest, just before catching Rhonda's screw-faced stare.

"Get a room," she said nastily.

"Get yo' life," I returned.

The next thing I knew, she was charging me like a bull.

* * *

Lane immediately turned me away from her and shoved Rhonda back so hard that she stumbled over an end table and fell onto the floor.

"What is wrong with you? Act like a lady instead of a stupid high school kid!" he yelled at her, while I peeked out from behind his 6' 4" frame with a smirk.

Clearly, Rhonda had temporarily lost her mind, because I'd seen her fight before, and that wind-milling shit she did was gonna get her beat like an old dusty rug trying to fight me! Lucky for her, my man cut her off at the pass.

There were approximately ten other people besides myself in the room, and I was sure the three that were not there for Athena or Quamé would rather not be in the middle of our Maury Povich Show moment.

"Hey, y'all take that hood stuff outside!" Athena's 5' 10", big and busty older sister Stephanie said, with her hands on her hips.

"Yeah, let's do that!" Rhonda screamed at me once she was back on her feet.

"What happened? Why are you trippin' on Brenda?" Belinda asked, cupping Rhonda's shoulder before she was quickly shaken off.

"Get off me!" Rhonda hollered at her. "She knows what this is all about."

"Leave!" Stephanie yelled, while her husband Greg held her off.

"Yeah, get outta here," Lane interjected, still shielding me.

"Why don't you stop addressing me and let your girlfriend speak for herself? This is between me and her!"

Rhonda zipped up her black sweat suit jacket, looked nervously at Stephanie and then back to me.

Rhonda and I had both been present the day Stephanie beat up two girls in front of her family's house when we were in college. She'd been washing her car, wearing cutoff jeans and a tank top with no bra in the driveway, while Rhonda, Athena and I sat on the porch talking.

Two rail-thin twenty-something girls wearing too much makeup and skin-tight clothes were walking past the yard and one of them, a blood-red-haired light-skinned girl yelled out, "Only skanks gotta wash their own cars!"

"Yeah, big Samoan slut skanks!" the other brown-skinned girl with a ponytail weave chimed in while they chuckled and glared at Stephanie.

Without missing a beat, Stephanie dropped the wet sponge and ran down the driveway like someone shot off the gun during a relay. The red-headed girl was the first one tackled and from there, Stephanie slung them around and into each other repeatedly while shouting, "I'm Filipino!" I think they were too surprised and shaken to get composed enough to defend themselves. I barely remember either of the other girls landing a punch.

Stephanie was not the one we wanted to rile up.

My expression didn't change, though; I held my ground and looked Rhonda directly in the face, saying, "You're looking really stupid right now. Don't be mad at me because my man likes women. Take that problem to the source."

Score! Rhonda's chocolate-brown complexion flushed, and I knew I'd delivered the cryptic Floyd Mayweather-style body blow to her ego that I'd intended. She should have known that I would take the gloves off once she turned on me.

Lane shot me a disapproving look, and Belinda's eyes widened like saucers.

"What in the world are y'all fighting about? You guys are best friends!" Belinda yelled.

"She ain't my fuckin' best friend," Rhonda mumbled, walking slowly towards the exit while maintaining menacing eye contact with me.

"I wish I would've known that before I wasted my time trying to save you," I hissed.

She shot me the bird and pushed past one of Quamé's friends near the door, turning the corner.

Suddenly, all eyes were on me.

I pivoted to face Lane and deadpanned, "She started it."

"Well, I'm going to go see about my great-grandchild. You all need to act a fool somewhere else," Quamé's grandmother said, leaving the room and heading towards Athena's room.

Belinda advanced on me with micro-braids swinging in her face and an irritated expression. She didn't say anything to me, but we stood eye to eye for a number of seconds before I spoke.

"Ask her what it's all about."

"Why won't you tell me? I've never seen y'all so mad or at each other's throats like that before," she answered.

Lane retreated to where our food was and began gathering it. He looked like he'd had enough of the shenanigans for the day.

"Hey, this is all about Rhonda and her personal business. All I tried to do was be a good friend to her and..." I began before the uncontrollable urge to vomit overwhelmed me. I quickly covered my mouth and attempted to rush out to the ladies room, but puked through my fingers in the hallway before I could make it.

"Baby, what's wrong? Are you sick? You feeling all right?" Lane asked, catching up to me and resting a hand on my back as I stood hunched over, the contents of my stomach now in full view on the floor.

"No," I muttered, thinking his entire line of questioning sounded stupid. How often do well people throw up?

Two nurses dashed to my aid: one carrying paper towels, with the other focusing on me.

"Come on, honey, and sit down over here," a sweet-sounding white woman, who I was only viewing from the legs down at the moment, advised, as she led me towards a chair in the hallway. "Do you feel like you already know what's wrong with you, or do you think you might need to see a doctor?"

I was shaking my head "no" as I looked up at the pleasant face of the nurse who reminded me of a brunette Edie Falco from The Sopranos.

"Are you sure, hun? Is it maybe morning sickness? Could you be pregnant? Contrary to popular belief, it doesn't always happen in the morning," the other nurse said, standing over the paper towels she'd dropped to cover the evidence of my innards revolt.

Pregnant?

8

Brian

Gabby stood in my office doorway, gazing at me with a smirk, and one hand lazily resting on her hip. Her green tailored dress with snake-skin patches and matching money-green reptile pumps perfectly projected the personality trait I associated with her now. A snake.

"What do you want?" I asked, cutting my eyes at her briefly before focusing my attention back to the menu selections I was viewing on my laptop.

"I want…" she said, approaching my desk with a slow, sultry stride, "…for you to stop treating me like I have the plague. I realize I hurt you, but I've apologized for that, and it's not like you didn't return the favor."

I chuckled at her ignorance.

"So that's how you see it, huh?" I asked, leaning back into my chair and clasping my fingers together on my lap. "As far as you're concerned, we're even?"

Gabby's eyebrows raised, but her expression wasn't transparent.

"Sounds like you disagree."

I momentarily fantasized The Hulk grabbing her and thrashing her around like he did Loki in the Avengers movie.

"Brian; I can't rewind time and un-do the hurt I caused. All I can say is I was young, reckless, and stupid. I sacrificed our love for a momentary lapse in judgment," she professed, resting her ample bottom on the edge of my desk, crossing her legs, and leaning closer towards me. "How much longer are you really planning on holding this grudge now that you're partnered with me?"

"I'm partnered with your husband; not you."

She looked towards the doorway, then back to me with a crafty smile, and spoke with a breathy quality, "You're partnered with us."

So, her cheating ass wanted to make amends for cheating on me in college, by cheating with me while she was married?

She obviously hadn't changed, and as far as I was concerned, she could take her shabby olive branch and replace her tampon with it!

"Woman, why don't you knock this bashful girl bullshit off and get to the meat of what you want? You obviously waited until Trent left to come in here strutting around like Joan Collins on Dynasty, so spit it out."

"I just want us to start over. We used to have so much fun together. I just wish we could get back a sliver of that friendship that we used to have. I didn't realize how much I missed you until I started seeing you again. It's been so many years since that whole thing, Brian. Can't you just forgive me and move past it?"

I heard every word she spoke, but my attention was on her movements. If anybody knows what flirting looks like, I do; and this was no innocent conversation she was having with me. What concerned me about it was the fact that I wasn't repulsed by it as I'd anticipated. The crossing and uncrossing of her legs was beginning to serenade my mini-me to attention.

"So, are you open?" she asked, leaning into me and exposing a closer look at her nested bosom.

"Are you trying to seduce me?" I asked, feigning disinterest.

"Is that what you think I'm doing?" she grinned.

"Gabby, I'm not that naive little idiot you used to date anymore. I don't play games, and I don't like bullshit bitches; thanks to you. So stop wasting my time with this coquettish performance, and do whatever the fuck it is you actually do here, before your husband walks in and sees that his wife is still the same slut she was in college," I spat, sitting up in my chair and bringing my face to hers. "Beat it."

She recoiled, leapt off of the table's edge and quickly headed towards the door.

"You're an asshole, Brian."

"Thank you," I snickered, focusing back onto my laptop screen.

"You know what your real problem is?"

"I thought you were leaving," I huffed.

"Your problem is that you still love me and you're fighting it every time you look at me. I know you, Brian, and I could always tell what you wanted, even when you denied it. I hurt you badly, and I get that; but you wouldn't still be holding onto all of that anger if you didn't love me. I see how you look at me. Hell, I saw how you were looking at me just now. It's stupid to waste your time hating me when you could be loving me instead. You'll come around. Believe me," she proclaimed. Then she was gone out the door and down the hall.

I was glad her view of my pants was obscured by my desk, because my dick was stiffly betraying my confidence. I didn't know if I hated her more for what she'd done in the past, or for knowing me well enough to know that I probably would have fucked her right then given enough time and opportunity. My attraction to her was undeniably stronger than my disdain for her, which really agitated me.

I blindly stared at my laptop screen and massaged my budding five o'clock shadow. I couldn't let her control me. I was a relationship guy now, and the last thing I was going to do was let the devil who turned me at origination, destroy what I was building with Nadia.

'You'll come around. Believe me.' Her words rang in my head again.

Smug bitch.

* * *

My cell phone rang and I answered swiftly while shutting down my laptop computer and preparing to leave.

"Hello?"

"Hey, Brian, I've got good news!" Lauren, my real estate agent replied.

"Shoot."

"The house on Pharr Road accepted your bid, so all that's left to do is the paperwork."

"Well that is good news," I grinned, exiting my office and talking to Lauren via Bluetooth. "So, how soon can we close?"

"As early as this Friday, if all goes well. See, I told you I would get it done."

"That you did," I replied, passing Gabby, who was doing something on her iPad and nearly collided with me.

She was startled by the near miss, but quickly re-focused on what she was doing, continuing her stride.

"You'll come around," she said, turning into Trent's office.

Lauren had just made a comment, but I didn't hear it because I was paying attention to Gabby.

"Right?" Lauren inquired.

"I'm sorry, right what?" I answered, leaving the restaurant and heading toward my newly purchased Range Rover HSE. I hadn't been driving much since my incident and recovery from my kidney transplant, but when I woke up, I wanted a change. I traded in my Escalade and upgraded to a black Range, with tinted windows and nearly all of the amenities. I was tired of relying on other people to get me where I wanted to go.

"I was just saying how great it would be if your friend and his wife found a home in the same subdivision as you."

"What makes you say that?"

"Just because, I've seen the wife and her agent at that yellow house I showed you last week, at least three times this week."

"Is that typical?" I asked suspiciously.

"Well, I guess it just depends on the person. Usually, a buyer wouldn't make so many visits, especially in the same week, but..." Lauren's uneasy pause lent to my skepticism. "I guess this one likes it so much, she just keeps coming back around the same time...every day. A lot of his clients seem to have similar feelings."

I knew women well enough to know when they were dying to gossip but needed the right motivation to make it seem "accidental."

"So, you think there's more going on in there than just viewing the house?" I questioned, now sitting in my car.

She nervously sniggled, "I don't want to insinuate anything, but, I know her agent, and he has a reputation for bedding some of his clientele. I'm not saying that's what she's doing, because I don't know her, and I know she's married to your friend, but...I haven't seen him with them any time."

Lauren was a previous lay-mate who'd been to a few events with me and consequently, she'd met Ike and Tara at one of them. Lauren mentioned to me that she saw Tara at a Ladies of Atlanta brunch a few weeks ago, and offered her services when Tara said she was looking for a home.

Tara, being the mega-bitch she is, brushed her off and actually said, "Sorry, sweetie, but I don't deal with women in business. I like to get my way, and men bend easier."

I laughed when she relayed the story to me with an obvious contempt for Bitchzilla's business philosophy. Evidently, Lauren was still a bit perturbed by the incident, and she didn't intend on missing this opportunity to stick it to her.

As much as I hated my best boy's wife, though, I didn't want to believe she'd cheat on him again, with less than a year of marriage under their belts. I'd already proven her to be untrustworthy in college when I personally ram-rodded her one weekend to show him the type of chick she was. He was angry at both of us; but, over time, we were forgiven.

I could understand why he would forgive me, since I was just trying to show him who he was dealing with; but her? A foolish mistake I was sure would come back to haunt him when he married the wench. Still, it wasn't my problem to brew over, and Ike would never believe it without proof anyway.

"All right, well, get back with me when we have a definite closing date so I can make plans to move."

"Uh... o... okay." Lauren replied. I'm sure she expected me to continue investigating Tara's possible indiscretions, but my topic turn caught her by surprise.

I hung up and speed-dialed my sister, Brenda, but it went straight to voicemail. I'm sure it was because the knucklehead's phone was either dead or dying somewhere outside of the vicinity of wherever she actually was.

I turned the radio up and thought about my encounters with Gabrielle that day. I wondered if she had another angle other than trying to lure me into banging her back out over my office desk. I felt a little twinge of satisfaction knowing that, regardless of the fact that she cheated on me, she still wanted to feel me inside of her again. I knew it couldn't have been my sex game that made her cheat, anyway; clearly, I'd just been blind to her early stage sluttery at the time.

Pulling into the parking lot of my apartment complex, I smiled, thinking about finally moving into another place. As I parked in the space in front of my unit, Nadia was exiting hers, and paused outside of it when she saw me.

"Wow. Is that yours?" she asked, wide-eyed, once I exited the car.

"Yes, ma'am. It was time for an upgrade," I gloated, approaching her as she posed with hands on her hips. I was loving the way that baby blue sweat suit hugged her curves, but knew I'd like her better out of it. "Where are you headed?"

"Going to jog a couple of miles and back," she answered, raising her iPod and earpieces with a sly smile and peck on the lips.

"You're doing the wrong kind of exercise on your day off, lady. Come with me. I know a better way you can work out those legs."

I grabbed her hand and pulled her towards my apartment.

"Later, baby. Let me get this jog in, and I'll come back to your place to shower and get my cool down," she coaxed, tracing my lips with her index finger.

"You know I don't like being told no," I countered, as I unlocked and opened my apartment door. I began unzipping her sweat suit jacket, exposing her pretty pink lace bra. "Yes is better."

I'd already been aroused once without gratification. It wasn't about to happen twice.

"So spoiled," she proclaimed, closing the door behind her and removing her jacket completely.

Yes, I was.

* * *

I felt dehydrated after our sex session, and went to the kitchen for some water while sleeping beauty lay sprawled across my bed. The message light was flashing on my cell phone, so I brought it with me and listened to it. My sister, Brenda, had returned my call, and asked me to call her back, which I did as I poured myself a pitcher of water.

"Hello," she answered.

"What's up, chick? How'd your meeting with the wicked bitch of Atlanta go?"

Brenda sighed, "In comparison to everything else that has happened in the last 24 hours, relatively well."

"Everything like what?" I questioned, making my way to the couch with my drink and getting comfortable.

"Okay, let me start from the beginning. I went over to Mommy's place, and she told me that her, Jenny, and the guy she's been dating, Avis, drugged daddy's drink and pushed him into the water."

I would have been shocked if I hadn't already predicted it. I figured my mother was the culprit in that asshole's death anyway; I just had no idea she'd had accomplices. Jenny, my mother's faithful sidekick, was always a fair bet in any situation, though. She already looked enough like my mother to be her body double sometimes, but she was my mother's biggest cheerleader. "Well, that's what we both suspected all along anyway, right?"

"I mean, yeah...but still. Confirmation that she killed him doesn't make you feel some kind of way?"

"Look, I've been stalked, shot and held hostage. It's gonna take more than hearing that my mother killed her abusive, cheating husband to make me uneasy," I joked, while turning on the TV with the remote.

"Well, I was still a little taken aback by it. Then she proceeded to tell me that Avis was a private investigator she'd hired to trail daddy when you were two years old. She had an affair with him, too and..." she now audibly wept.

"What? Why are you crying?"

"He's my real father."

"Your real father?" I repeated, dumbfounded.

"Can you believe her? That's probably why daddy was extra tough on me. He probably hated me, knowing all of those years that I was the product of her screwing around on him. And hell, my real daddy was no angel, either. His ass was married, with a 3-year-old daughter at home. Two adulterous peas in a pod."

A lot of thoughts ran through my head. I never expected anything like that to come out. Yes, it did seem that my father's side of the family had strong genes; therefore, most of us had hazel eyes. But Brenda not having them didn't mean she wasn't his. There were lots of subtle hints in hindsight, but I still would never have guessed. Wow.

"Now his wife is dead, they claim from cancer, and obviously his daughter is grown, so he wants to get to know me. Our mother is a real piece of work, I tell ya."

"So do you want to know him?"

"I don't know. Yes. I think I do. I don't know," she said, clearing her throat. "It's a lot to process, knowing the facts of how I was conceived, and with all the resentment I felt towards daddy; the daddy I knew. Then, on top of all that, now I know he's a freaking murderer, too? I mean, really? Who else would this crazy shit happen to but me?"

"Yeah, that is crazy."

"Oh, but wait..." she said, pepping up. "So, I go over to Lane's auto shop to tell him everything, right; so he wasn't there, but I caught Julian and Paul in the supply closet gettin' it in."

"Who the fuck are Julian and Paul?" I frowned, wondering why she thought I wanted to hear about some homo love.

"Paul! Rhonda's fiancé and Julian, our brother!"

"Get-the-fuck-outta-here," I slowly articulated. "That ja-fakin' ass Negro was fucking our homo half-brother? Aww, shit. Now I done heard it all. This dude been incog-negro for over 20 years, and now he's making rounds outing random people we know? You gotta be kidding me," I said in disgust.

"I couldn't believe what I was seeing, but I ran and told Rhonda, because she's supposed to be my best friend, right? So I go all the way up to her job to tell her, and the bitch snaps out on me like I'm the one cheating on her!"

"Your little snitch ass," I chuckled. "But that's one violation I probably would have told on, too. Why's he gonna marry a chick when he knows he likes dick? It's dudes like him that spread disease, and doesn't he have a kid or something? Plus, Rhonda's old thirsty-for-a-man ass probably didn't want to know because she'd do anything to be a wife."

"Yeah, he has a 12-year-old daughter. Well, whatever her motivation was for being mad at me, she was directing it at the wrong person. I was just trying to look out for her, and she turned on me. Even when I saw her at the hospital she was trippin', trying to fight me and whatnot."

"The hospital? What were you at the hospital for?"

"Athena went into labor, so me and Lane went down to Northside Hospital. Get this; Julian was there, too."

I huffed in disbelief and shook my hands in the air.

"For fuckin' what? Was the guy stalking you or something?"

"No. He was there because somebody hit his boyfriend in the head with a brick. Yeah...old boy has a boyfriend. We actually talked for a little while, and we're gonna talk again later."

"You talked for a little while? So, now you want this fool in your life when he's obviously trying to bring drama to it?" I protested. "Why the hell would you even bother to deal with him?"

"Because he is our brother, and I kind of want to know him."

"Actually, he's not your brother, based on what Mommy said, if we get technical. His punk ass has been invisible from you and all of us for this long. Fuck him."

"All right, we can debate about that later. I have one more thing to tell you," she said flatly.

"Shit, you weren't lying when you said a lot had happened in 24 hours. Okay. What?"

"I'm pregnant."

9

Julian

I sat in the kitchen looking at the floating sponge and bucket filled with blood-tinged water. I'd had a hard time cleaning the stains from the foyer floor, and to my further dismay, there was some splatter on the door and walls as well. I couldn't believe someone had been so evil as to commit such a heinous crime against a harmless man like Nick. Even more disturbing was the thought that the tossed brick might have been meant for me.

I pulled the sponge out, opened the back door and tossed the water from the bucket out onto the backyard grass. As grief stricken as I was about the incident with Nick, I was happy to have the place to myself. It seemed I rarely had any time away from him anymore, and I reveled in the hours few and far between his nagging.

The front door chimed and moments later, Tia walked into the kitchen with a couple of Waffle House bags.

"My God, they were slow as a snail at that place. That's the last time I let you send me on a breakfast errand. I think listening to all of that native jibber jabber gave me a headache of sorts. I couldn't wait to get back to your flat," she complained.

"Oh, chile', please. You are the most stuck-up food critic I know."

"I'm probably the only food critic you know and thank goodness I'm not critiquing these grease vat dishes."

"True, but Waffle House makes the best scattered, smothered and covered dishes. Call it my guilty pleasure, but if I could eat it every morning for breakfast, I would," I stated, as I took my food from the bags, now resting on the kitchen counter.

Tia rolled her eyes, withdrew her food from the bags, and we both sat at the kitchen table.

"So..." she began, before taking a bite of her eggs and chewing. "What time do you want to go pick Nick up?"

"I'm not. His mother called me and said she's going to pick him up and have him stay with her for a week or more."

"His mother?"

"AKA his best friend," I discharged. "Are you really surprised? The only person he keeps more tabs on than me is her. Truth be told, girl, I'm glad she's going to get him. I'm going to enjoy a few days of solitude. It would be nice if he would just move his needy ass back in with her full-time, but I know that's not gonna happen."

"Seriously, I think you should just stop stringing him along and tell him you want him to move out. You've been miserable for months being with him, and it's turning you into a sneaky bloke," she scolded. "And as your friend, I have to be equally sneaky to help cover your tracks. My memory's not good enough to do this for too much longer."

"I know, I know. I just don't know how to do it, and I know he's gonna make a big scene and tell all of our friends what an asshole I'm being to him. But, Tia, if I'm being honest with you, girl, my dick doesn't even get hard for him anymore. His mouth is always complaining or accusing. I'm over it."

"Okay, so how long are you going to keep this facade up then? He has a right to know if you're done with him, Julian; so he can move on... and move out."

We both chuckled.

"Girl, Lord knows I don't like to be cold-hearted but, I might have to break it off while he's over at his mom's recovering. Then he won't have any reason to come back except to get his stuff."

"I know you don't think it's going to be that easy. What about his job at the salon? Are you gonna let him keep working there? And you know he's not going to just get his stuff and go." She side eyed me.

No, it certainly wouldn't be that easy. I'd actually attempted to break it off with Nick last year, and not only did he refuse to leave the home or stop reporting to work at my salon, but he brought a fresh bag of tears to cry rivers every day. It was exhausting for me to combat, and eventually I just gave in.

Not much had improved since that incident, except my sex life, of course. That's when I started getting it elsewhere.

"So, we didn't talk much about your conversation with Brenda. You two sure seemed more like buds," Tia stated, finishing her breakfast and putting her trash into the garbage.

"Well, yeah," I answered, fingering my ponytail, which was hanging towards my chest. "She's got a lot of our family fire in her. Could you believe the little trollop started off talking to me crazy?"

"Uh, yeah! What did you expect, after what she saw? Man, I was just glad you didn't get to scuffling around in there, because I've never had a fight, and I never want to."

"Like this pretty face likes putting itself in harm's way," I countered, with a quick roll of my eyes. "Chile', you know I prefer yaps over slaps. But she didn't want any." I finished with a neck roll.

"So, what'd she say?"

"She was asking how I knew Paul and why I was with him. I told her it was just a coincidence."

Tia's expression turned stern.

"I know that's not exactly the truth, but hell, I don't owe her the truth just yet. I just really met the girl."

Tia sucked her teeth.

"Well, I'm done plotting against them anyway now, so what does it matter?" I argued defensively with her non-response.

She just shook her head from side to side with a scolding half-smile and leaned back in her chair.

"Why do I feel like I was just interrogated by a mute?" I asked.

We both laughed, hard.

* * *

Tia left me to my own devices at about 2:30 p.m. I called Raul late last night and explained what happened, so he cancelled or rescheduled all of my appointments for the next couple of days. He assumed I'd be taking care of Nick, and I didn't correct him.

I sat in my backyard by the pool in the buff with my copy of Essence magazine, a pitcher of iced apple martini, a huge martini glass from my last Mardi Gras celebration, my phone and my favorite Gucci sunglasses. As I flipped through the pages, a fly buzzed past me and into the pool, where it seemed to die instantly. Thoughts of how horrible a drowning death must be flooded my mind. I wondered if my father was even aware he was drowning when it happened, or whether he was so passed out that he never woke up.

I wished I had tears to shed for him now, or even at the funeral, but none fell. Although my father had spent some time with me throughout my life, it wasn't enough, in my opinion, to mourn the loss of a man who barely acknowledged me. I attended the funeral because it was my God-given right as his son to be there, and I knew my Aunt Linda wanted me to; but there wasn't a lot of sorrow on my part.

My phone rang and when I saw it was Paul, I hesitated so long to answer that I almost missed the call.

"Why are you calling?" I asked smugly.

He spoke slowly. "I'm asking for your help."

"I told you yesterday there was nothing I could do for you. And by the way, do you know where I live?"

"No, give me your address and we'll talk about this face to face."

I laughed mockingly. "Chile' please! I wasn't asking so I could tell you where it was. I'm asking because I'm trying to find out if you were the lunatic that was on my property last night or not."

"I don't understand what you're talking about, Julian, but I need you to 'et least call Rhonda fa' me and explain to her that I thought you were a woman. I thought it through, and I talked to her last night and I think she believes me. I just need you to back up my story to her," he pled.

I had already backed my ass up enough for him in the past, and now that those days were going to be gone, I wasn't going to be backing up anything else. His excuse was the dumbest I'd ever heard and if she believed him, she was as much of a moron as he was. I didn't want any part of that foolishness. No thank you.

"Paul, I know that I am very pretty for a man, but nobody, including your fiancée, would believe that you thought I was a woman from the front. Especially once my dick was out. Now, if you somehow found the only cow in the world to believe such an idiotic tale, then you've got a keeper, and good luck to you; but I'm done here."

"This is no laughing matter! I'm over here fucking panicking because I'm losing everything for one slip in judgment. I can't even go home and face her or my daughter for the shame! Now even my boss is calling me, because I know his bitch of a girlfriend told him to! She's trying to destroy me to everyone and it's your fault!"

"What? My fault? Uh...how do you figure that?"

"You're the ras-clot that coaxed me to the back room! I told you it was too risky and..." he continued yelling until his accent became so thick that I could barely understand what he was saying. Not that I was listening anymore anyway.

I hung up. I was too old to be arguing about something that no longer concerned me, with a man that was never really my concern in the first place. Clearly, I was going to have to find another auto shop for my little purple beauty, but that could be arranged without so much as a blink.

He called me back immediately, and I decided that he was going to force me to block his number if he tried me one more time. I'm too smart to be harassed. I simply don't answer the phone call, or I hang up when they start speaking. He'd soon get tired of harassing me. This wasn't a problem I was going to be able, nor was I planning, to waste a minute of my time to solve for him.

There's an old saying, 'If you sleep with dogs, you wake up with fleas.' Well, my saying is, 'If you sleep with a man, you wake up gay. Believe it.'

I laughed out loud thinking about it.

I was done caring what anybody else thought about me, or wanted me to do. Nobody else was worried about satisfying me, paying my bills, or who was possibly out to hurt me. I could have been the one in the hospital, or worse, from an attack last night. To hell with what Paul, Nick or anybody else who wasn't God wanted.

Truth be told, even God might have to stand in line since, according to the church I used to attend religiously, my lifestyle is considered an abomination. Oh, how they hurt me the day Reverend Faulk and some other members I respected in the church planned an "intervention" by approaching me with the idea of praying out my homosexual desires.

I was so surprised and wounded, but I stayed in that church for over a year attempting to banish my desires through prayer. Then I wised up and decided that I wasn't going to let them make me hate myself for being who I've always known I was. If God didn't want me to be this way, then he shouldn't have let me out of my mother's vagina, because it was too late now! Julian Parkes was nobody's mistake, and I could see that every day in the mirror.

I put my copy of Essence down on the table, got up, and dove into the deep end of the pool.

* * *

I was just getting comfortable in my bed, ready to take a nap after my swim, when my cell phone rang, and I begrudgingly answered.

"Hello."

"Julian, you gotta get down here, now!" Raul screamed through the phone.

It sounded like he was in the middle of the mall with all of the noise, but I knew that couldn't be, because he'd called from the salon line.

"What the hell is going on?" I demanded.

"There's some guy down here raising hell and knocking things over. He said he's not leaving until he sees you, and that you'd better make it fast."

"Well, did you call the fucking police?" I questioned, springing from the bed and searching through my drawers for something to wear.

I was livid that anybody would come into my shop demanding I do anything!

"Not yet, I called you first, but I'm going to call them next. He's in here acting like a straight fool! Scaring the customers and me. I'm in the back office because once he started knocking things onto the floor and getting in my face talking reckless, I got the hell away from him. People are crazy as a loon these days, chile', and I love this shop, but I'm not about to die for it," Raul whined.

"Stop being so goddamned dramatic! Who is it?"

"Some Jamaican man, how should I know? He came in here angry."

Paul! That bastard! I was seething at the thought of possible damages to my salon and you'd best believe I was gonna press charges on his black ass; and believe me, his ass was black!

"Raul, get your ass off the phone with me and call the police. I'll be there in 10 minutes!" I barked.

I quickly dressed in jean shorts, a purple button-up shirt and my brown Kenneth Cole loafers. I gave myself a brief once-over in the bathroom mirror, brushing my hair back into a perfect ponytail, and put some Carmex on my lips.

I made sure to set the alarm before leaving and put the top down on my Mercedes as I left my driveway. There was no reason why I couldn't still be fabulous en route to the bullshit which was my life, was there?

Acknowledging as many traffic rules as were absolutely necessary, I was there in less than nine minutes. I parked haphazardly in my spot, got out, and strolled past the flashing lights of a Fulton County police car parked in front of the salon. There was utter chaos going on inside. Clients were scattered about with wet hair, towel-wrapped heads, and fresh scowls on their faces while watching Paul and Raul ranting to the officer.

Fulton County's finest kept one hand on his gun, while speaking and gesturing with the other hand for both men to calm down and slow down.

"Oh, thank God! There's the owner right there," Raul said, pointing at me with an exasperated twist of his neck.

"I was just trying to come and see him!" Paul shouted, attempting to approach me before the officer backed him up. "He's avoiding me when I need him to—"

"Sir, you need to calm down and stay where you are, or I'm going to have to cuff you," the average-looking white officer commanded while turning to me. "Do you know what's going on here?"

"All I know is that this fool has been told that I cannot, and do not, want to help him. The next thing I know, my employee was calling me saying there was a strange man in my salon threatening people, trashing the place, and driving my clients away," I responded with folded arms, while staring at Paul.

I had Paul by at least 3" in height, and I could look pretty intimidating when I wanted to, if I do say so myself.

"So, this is a lover's spat?" Officer average asked.

"No!" Paul, Raul and I responded in unison.

"I'm not gay!" Paul insisted.

I sneered at that blatant lie, causing him to lunge towards me, and the officer to force him back against the wall while retrieving his cuffs.

"All right, well, you can explain yourself down at the precinct. I got a call that there was a disturbance and that you were vandalizing this salon. From the looks of all of the stuff on the floor, eyewitness accounts, and your own admission, you are the trespassing vandal."

"No, no! I'll calm down! I'm sorry, I'll calm down!" Paul now appealed, to no avail.

"It's a little late to make these decisions now, sir. Now stop resisting, or it's gonna get ugly." Paul complied. "Did you want to press charges?" I was asked.

I stared into Paul's pleading eyes, scanned the small amount of damage he'd created, thought about how desperate he must've felt to come all the way down to my shop and make such a scene, and said...

"Yes."

I wasn't about to show mercy to the asshole who'd come to my home and threw a brick through my front door. Fool me once, shame on you. Fool me twice, no more acting nice.

"Julian! No! Why would you do this to me? You know I'm desperate for your help! I'd never hurt you. This is not necessary!" Paul cried, and I do mean literally, as the officer dragged him towards the door.

"Desperate, yes, but I can't help you with that. You think I don't know you're the one who threw that brick? But your stupid ass missed me. You could have killed him!" I taunted.

He looked bewildered as tears began streaming down his cheeks and the officer led him further to tuck him into the backseat of his cruiser.

"Mister Parkes, I'm gonna need you to come down to the precinct to formally press charges and to make a statement," the cop advised, handing me a card with his name and the precinct info.

"Not a problem," I said, before walking to my back office.

Nick was the salon manager, but since he was out, Raul's scary ass was the best we had. The other hair techs barely wanted to pay their booth rent, let alone manage it.

"Oh my God, Julian! What was that all about?" Raul asked, bowling into my office behind me.

"Will you stop saying that!"

"Saying what?"

"'Oh my God.' You've said it like 100 times since I got here. Just shut up already and stay out of my business. The salon isn't gonna run itself," I ordered.

He rolled his eyes and pouted. "Well, I would stay out of your business if you would keep your business, out of your business," then he sashayed out of my office, slamming the door behind him.

Drama queen!

10

Brenda

Three weeks had passed since I found out I was pregnant. I couldn't believe I was not only gonna be a mother, but an unwed mother at that. I was relieved that Lane was happy about it, but at the same time, I was afraid. I had no idea what kind of parent I was gonna be, and my examples hadn't been anything to brag about. Besides, there was the elephant in the room that I hoped I'd never have to address...what if Lane wasn't the father?

I stood in my underwear in front of the full-length mirror on the back of the bathroom door, studying my profile. My belly was sticking out more now, even though I could still fit in most of my clothes. I closed my eyes in silent prayer that this bundle of joy I was carrying was the heir to Lane's throne, and not the product of my last night with Teddy before Lane and I got together. There were some weeks in between my interludes with both, but and I was using condoms with Lane in the beginning. Still, nothing is full proof.

Lane appeared in the bathroom doorway and leaned against the frame.

"You getting used to the idea of being a mommy yet?" he asked with a smile.

"Umm, not quite. I'm kinda nervous."

"About what?"

"About everything. Aren't you?" I asked, with both hands akimbo on my hips.

He shook his head and pulled me into him. "What's to be worried about? We live in a nice house, I can support all of us, I love you and you love me. Right?"

"Of course," I blushed. But would you love me if this wasn't your baby? Please God, don't make me ever have to find out!

"So, tell me what exactly you're nervous about?"

I looked away. "What if you change your mind about wanting the baby, or wanting to be with me? Hell, I haven't had a real job in months, and I'm not sure what I really want to do after this book is written. What if you get tired of me living off of you? Even you're always saying I'm a trouble magnet."

He frowned. "First off, you're not living off of me. We're living together. Yeah, we did kind of speed past dating and straight to living together, but," he shrugged, "that's just how it happened. I like having you here with me, baby. And I know you're not some slouch wanna-be Housewives of Atlanta-type chick. You went through a traumatic situation. If you need a break from a nine-to-five in order to get yourself together, or figure out what you want, I'm fine with that. It's not like I'm struggling to keep a roof over our heads, and if you're a gold-digger, you're horrible at it, because you rarely ask for anything. Stop worrying so much. Nobody has a crystal ball telling them what's gonna work and what's not, Brenda. We just gotta live."

Easy for him to say. Even as he gently kissed my lips, my anxiety hadn't subsided much. Aside from my fears about our relationship, our baby and true paternity, I was still stressed about my nearly non-existent friendship with my so-called best friend Rhonda.

When Athena found out how bad things had gotten between the two of us, she tried to bring us together to make up, but Rhonda wasn't so eager. Even with Athena agreeing that it was ridiculous for her to hold a grudge against me for trying to be a good friend, she was still acting funky. We ended up having a 5-minute screaming match at A's house last Sunday, where we both got some friendship gripes off of our chest that had apparently been festering for years.

Rhonda claimed I was selfish and that I always thought I was better than her because of my family's money and my lighter skin complexion. What? I was floored. What kind of "house nigger" vs. "field nigger" shit was she insinuating I subscribed to? That must've been her own insecurities or jealousy, because I never acted like, or thought I was better than her...until I heard her say that!

Oh, we screamed, all right, because I had my own complaints. Thanks to her giving intel to that jealous ass stalker, Gwen, even after she was popping up like Where's Waldo everywhere we went, my brother and I were terrorized and damn-near killed by that psycho bitch. Rhonda acted like I didn't want her to be just as happy with Paul as I was with Lane. It didn't even make sense for me to be trying to sabotage her relationship. I'll be damned if she was gonna use me as the scapegoat for her backdoor boyfriend blues!

Athena managed to coerce an agreement to be civil between Rhonda and me, but our friendship was far from being mended. The meeting ended with a feigned smile exchange and both of us giving Athena the 'We'll talk later about this bullshit' look.

I leaned my head against Lane's chest and inhaled his masculine cologne scent.

"Don't worry so much, honey. I got you covered," he assured me with a kiss on my neck.

I smiled and turned to kiss him deeply. It had been a really long time since I'd felt this secure with a man...if ever. Before Lane, I was so wrapped up in whatever crumbs of affection I was getting from Teddy that I'd stopped expecting anything more.

"What time is your mother coming?" he asked through pecks.

"At one, one o'clock."

"So, we have more than an hour," he said, slowing his voice to a sexy tone while beginning to unsnap my bra.

"Lane," I whined playfully, and squirmed from his grasp. "No! I just took a shower."

"We can take another one together," he grinned, grabbing me back into his arms.

Aw, what the hell. I needed to get it in as much as I could now before I was too fat and too tired to get any at all. I unsnapped my bra and let it fall to the floor, then pulled my thong off.

Lane was already shirtless, and when he pulled on the drawstring of his pajama bottoms, they easily dropped to the floor, exposing his erect manhood.

He picked me up and sat me down on the bathroom counter, haphazardly knocking the toothpaste and our toothbrushes into the sink.

His mouth was back on mine before I could say anything, and one of his hands was forcefully cupping the back of my head while the other caressed my box to ensure I was excited enough. He slipped one, then two fingers inside me, and that was all that was required to open the floodgates. I moaned, shifting my hips into position so he could enter me.

"Uh! Uh! Yes!" I squealed, with my legs now wrapped around his waist and leaned back, using my firmly planted hands to work in rhythm with his drive.

His face was twisted like he couldn't believe how good our sex felt. An expression I'd become accustomed to.

Soon, little bursts of light exploded before my eyes as I climaxed, but my bottom was starting to feel sore from the sexual pounding I was taking. He must've sensed my discomfort, because he lifted me higher off of the counter without breaking stride.

His muscles, gleaming with sweat, were flexing in motion as he stared at me intensely, and I could see that his orgasm was coming right behind mine.

"Oh!" he uttered, tensing as I felt the surge of his soldiers gushing into me.

We were both drenched in sweat and he collapsed forward, burying his head into my chest.

Kissing my collar bone he said, "Marry me."

* * *

Marry him? Was he being serious? Marrying him was definitely what I wanted, but his proposal left a lot to be desired. I mean, who proposes to somebody right after they bust a nut and expects anyone to take them seriously?

He slowly lifted his head up with a smile, but once he saw me, he looked perplexed.

"What's wrong?"

I watched him, waiting for him to backtrack on the proposal and say how he didn't mean now, just someday, or something of the sort.

"Did you hear what I said?"

"Nothing's wrong," I replied meekly.

He stared at me. "I asked you to marry me. Did you hear that?"

Oh-my-God. He meant it?

"Yes... I... Yes."

"Yes, you heard me, or yes you'll marry me?"

"Yes! Yes, I'll marry you!" I yelled, hugging him like a crazed teenager.

This was really happening!

He chuckled, our naked bodies embracing.

"For a second I thought I was getting a no."

I kissed his cheek and hugged him tighter.

"I know this isn't the proposal you were expecting, but I was caught up in the moment. I'm serious, though," he promised, pulling back to look me in the eyes. "I want you to be my wife."

"And I want to be your wife."

We kissed, and then I eased him off of me and hopped off the counter towards the shower.

When Lane got in behind me, we got physically reacquainted one more time before finally washing up, drying off, and getting dressed.

The doorbell rang just as I was zipping up my jeans, and I soon heard the automatic chime go off when Lane went downstairs and opened the front door. Primping my hair and straightening my white tank top as I took a last glance into the mirror, I felt butterflies in my stomach; or maybe it was just the baby. This was the first time I was going to meet my real father face to face.

I could see my mother hugging Lane as I descended the stairs, and his surprise was obvious in his awkward posture.

"It's so good to finally get to meet you in person, Lane. I've heard lots of good things about you," my mother beamed, as though I'd been discussing him with her at length. Clearly, she was planning to play the role of the doting mother today. Oh, brother.

"Hi, Mom," I said, coming down the stairs.

As usual, her butter-brown face was perfectly made up, her newly dyed black hair was brushed back behind her ears and she was over dressed for the occasion. Her ankle-length coral dress was embroidered with a sequins and bead collar that matched the beading on her 4-inch sandals.

Avis was tall, stocky and brown-skinned, with sunken eyes and short salt and pepper hair. His beige button-up shirt was sloppily tucked into his jeans and he wore a brown fedora that matched his loafers.

"Hi, baby," he said, openings his arms for a hug.

"It's a little too soon for 'baby' and all that, don't you think?" I snapped.

I actually surprised myself a little with how curt I sounded, but he really was pushing his luck so early in our meeting.

His huge smile faded, and both Lane and my mother frowned at me.

Sashaying past them into the living room, I sat on the far end of the couch with the three of them following suit behind me.

"You have a lovely place here," my mother chirped, rubbing her hand against the seating of the plush couch.

Lane thanked her for the compliment and leaned forward with his elbows on his knees, with his hands clasped together.

I hadn't taken my eyes off of Avis yet. So this was supposed to be my real father, huh? Humph. He was handsome enough, but so far, I couldn't point out any notable resemblances.

When he noticed me staring, he held my gaze confidently.

"So, congratulations on the baby," he said, looking back and forth between Lane and me. "When's the due date?"

"February 15," Lane answered before I could.

Dear old dad seemed really anxious to jump right in and assume the role Robert Andrews had previously botched. I mean, I did want to get to know him, but he needed to ease into it. Besides the fact that he'd let another man raise me all of my life, he was also an accomplice in the murder of that man. Not quite the warmest and cuddliest reputation that one would hope their father to have.

"I was so surprised when Brenda told me she was expecting. Not that her biological clock hasn't been ticking louder than the Liberty Bell, but I never expected her to have a family before she had a ring," mom hinted, batting her eyes coyly at Lane.

Really? Did my battle-axe of a mother just do that?

"Olivia," Avis scolded with a playful tap.

"What? I'm simply saying that it would be nice if the baby could be born into a full-fledged family setting. I mean, you are sure this is your baby, right? You should want him or her to have your last name since you two already live together so—"

"Mom!" I yelled. "What the hell?! Are you insinuating I've been sleeping around on him?"

"No, darling. I'm simply confirming that we're all on the same page. Honestly, Brenda, you did skip from that Freddy fellow over to Lane pretty quickly, didn't you? Of course, I wasn't in the bedroom with you, but if you're at all as reckless as Brian is with his sexual activity, anything is possible."

If I could have hit her upside the head with the nearest frying pan I would have.

"I was not sleeping with Teddy at the same time. I may be your daughter, but I'm not you. I guarantee you that I won't have to introduce my son or daughter to their real father after almost 27 years!" I spat.

She shifted her eyes between Avis and me, never breaking her pompous grin, and slowly challenged me. "Is that so?"

"Yes, that's so!"

"You might as well tell her now," Lane whispered softly in my ear.

I turned my venomous look toward him now. "Tell her what?"

Now his facial expression mimicked mine as I realized he was referencing our engagement.

I nearly laughed but didn't dare, although I'm sure rolling my eyes didn't convey my response any better. There was no way in hell that I was going to tell Elizabeth Taylor's black bitch twin that I was engaged without a ring to show. Not in this lifetime!

"Wow," he said audibly, and leaned back on the couch dejectedly.

"Olivia, why are you starting a mess? Just let them do it in their own time," Avis scolded.

"I didn't start anything. I'm just saying what the rest of the world would be thinking. She's my daughter, and yours. Of course, I'd want her to be married before having a baby. Who but some hood rat's mother would be ecstatic to know their child is having a—"

I cut her off. "Mom! Stop!"

* * *

My mother later apologized to Lane over dinner for anything she may have said to offend him, but conveniently overlooked any apology to me.

Hello! She was obviously offensive to me!

"Anyway, I'm just excited that I'm gonna be a new Glam-ma."

"Glam-ma?" Lane questioned.

"Yes, Glam-ma. Grandma is such a matronly title, and I'm anything but matronly." She stood, giving us a runway twirl for emphasis. "I'm way too fabulous to be anybody's grandmother. But I do want a sweet little bundle of joy to cuddle and spoil."

My mouth agape, I turned to Lane and rolled my eyes.

He stared blankly at me, and then looked back towards my parents. Damn! Somebody was still pissy.

"So, Lane, why don't you show me around this nice, big mansion while my daughter and her father catch up?" she coaxed, coming around to where he sat and grabbing hold of Lane's right arm.

"Sure," he acquiesced with a sigh.

He trailed her as she ascended the stairs; obviously intending on orchestrating the direction of the tour.

Avis and I sat in silence, gawking at each other from across the table.

"So, do you want to go back into the living room and talk?" he asked politely.

"Sure," I answered, getting up and leading the way.

We sat on the couch in close proximity to each other.

"So, I know me being your father was kind of sprung on you, but I'm hoping you're open to getting to know me like I want to get to know you."

I sighed and shuffled my position to face him more precisely.

"What I want to know is why you all of a sudden care about getting to know me? Is it just because you're back in the saddle with my mother now or what?"

"No, not at all. It's not actually all of a sudden, either, Brenda," he stated, straightening his fedora. "I've always cared about you and I've kept tabs on you over the years. I checked in with your mother and received some updated pictures from her over the years." He pulled out his wallet and showed me a school picture my mother must have given him of me in the ninth grade.

"Yeah, but you never contacted me."

"It was complicated. We were both married. My wife didn't know about you, and Robert was raising you as his own daughter."

"And that was good enough for you, huh? Knowing what kind of man he was. Knowing that your biological child was growing up in the house with a womanizing abuser was okay with you?" I lashed out.

"No," he shook his head rigorously. "No it wasn't okay with me. But your mother and I were both prisoners of our own bad decisions, and neither of us was in a position to change them. Believe it or not, baby girl, I was there for you, protecting you, even when you didn't know it."

"Is that so? Well, I would like to see the videotape of those times, because I damn sure don't know about any. Robert Andrews did what and who he wanted to do. When did you ever protect me from him?"

He exhaled and leaned forward, with his hands resting on his knees.

"I did what I could, Brenda. You know your mother called me once when you were a teenager. Maybe about 15 or 16, and told me that he broke your shoulder in some kind of argument. I wanted to snap his goddamned neck. Believe me I did." He made eye contact with me then. "She never really told me about the abuse part before that night. She just said he cheated on her all the time and talked down to her. In all my investigations of him, I never came across any domestic abuse charges or anything like that. I told her to leave him. I was ready to leave my wife and be with her and take you with us, but...she didn't want to. My daughter had just started college, and I didn't have anything holding me back anymore, but your mother didn't want to tell you. She didn't think you'd be able to handle it, and she kept saying that we needed to wait until you were out of school. Hell, she and I got into a big argument about it."

"And that's your example of protecting me?" I sucked my teeth.

He straightened his fedora again. I guess that was his nervous tell. "I waited for him at Magic City the next day. Even though it had been more than 15 years since I'd investigated him for your mom, men that frequent strip clubs the way he did usually stuck with old habits. When I saw him, I got up in his face, threatened to beat the shit out of him and have some of my underworld buddies see to it that he came up missing, if I ever heard he'd hit you again. We argued, I got physical, and tried to stomp him out by the stage. Probably would have been arrested if I didn't know a couple of the security guys there. I just got kicked out, but he understood that I meant business. As far as I know, he never put hands on you again. Did he?"

I should have known it was too good to be true. All these years I'd convinced myself that he'd restrained himself from hitting me again out of guilt or remorse, but it was really because he'd been threatened with retaliation. Raising another man's daughter, especially one who was still keeping in touch with his wife, and sometimes popped up to whoop his ass must've been difficult for him. I chuckled at the thought, and wished I'd been there to witness that pummeling.

"So I suppose you were just making good on your promise when you helped my mother to kill him, huh?" I asked smugly.

"Does ol' boy know?" he whispered, checking over his shoulder to see whether anyone was within earshot.

"Yes," I replied, shifting again.

His eyes hardened, but his face still seemed curiously relaxed.

"Who else have you told?"

I adjusted my posture upwards and swallowed hard.

"Why?"

"Well," he paused. "If too many people, especially the wrong people get wind of what you know, we might all be vulnerable to some consequences that none of us want. Too many people, knowing too much, can be dangerous, and be what an old hit man friend of mine used to call, 'Grounds to expedite death by natural causes.'"

He followed with a sinister knee-slapping laugh, straightening his fedora again and abruptly quieting.

I felt a chill.

11

Brian

This had been a hectic week. Eat Your Art Out was busy every night since the grand reopening, and I was working my ass off both in the kitchen and outside of it. I was also still settling into my new house, and had barely unpacked anything that wasn't of immediate use. Nadia was coming over almost every day after work and helping me organize, but I was too tired to do most of that or even to do her, most nights. I was exhausted, partly due to the new 11:00 a.m. to 11:00 p.m. Monday through Saturday and 10:00 a.m. to 8:00 p.m. on Sunday scheduled open time changes we made.

One of the highlights was that my signature dishes, Honey Braised Pork Chops and Sweet and Sour Tilapia, were garnering exactly the flattering foodie reviews I had anticipated. Being partners in the restaurant wasn't as easy as I'd thought it was going to be, though. My tolerance level for bullshit is already in the basement in general, and to me, it seemed like a lot of our waitstaff, who were college students, were majoring in bullshit.

I got in an argument with some scrawny Urkel-looking kid that Trent hired before we partnered. Not only was this punk placing orders and not charging his equally as broke friends, but he was caught drinking on the job twice. When I confronted him, he denied everything and got loud in front of other staff, and tried to pit me and Trent against each other.

Lucky for him, Trent is an even-tempered kind of guy, because I was ready to slap the taste out of that youngster's mouth before Trent calmed the situation down. Of course, that pipe cleaner ass kid got his walking papers after that.

When I got to Trent's office, he was partially lying all six feet of himself across the beige sofa lining the wall of his office. I knocked on the open door and he waved me over to a chair adjacent to the couch.

"Yo, I think tonight might have been our busiest night so far," I said, leaning back in the chair.

"Gabby has really been hustling the business in here from the AUC, Georgia State and Georgia Tech. It's turning into the hot, artsy, college hang-out spot."

"Yeah, well, we don't wanna just cater to broke-ass college students. We need to bring in the upper 20-something crowd and people with full-time jobs."

He laughed. "We got them in here, too; I'm just saying that we're buzzing with the college crowd right now, which is a good thing. Business is good. Lighten up. We're turning a profit already, even after the renovations and added staff. You made a good decision partnering with me."

He was right, to an extent. Trent was actually a lot like Ike; dark-brown, upbeat, financially driven, and naive. I almost felt bad for the man, because he had no idea how trifling his wife really was. Gabby's advances were less subtle and more frequent since the first day she came strutting into my office in her reptilian business attire. Most recently, she'd taken to lingering in my doorway in provocative poses, or calling me on the office phone and my cell to ask insignificant questions.

"Well, let me get the hell outta here and go pick up my brother from the airport," Trent said, standing up and stretching with a yawn. His tangerine orange shirt hung just below the waistline of his black pants and was now wrinkled where he'd previously sat on it. "And don't forget, we have that food critic from Morsel Magazine coming in to do a spread on us tomorrow."

"Yeah, okay. Same bat time, same bat place," I said, standing up to dap him and exiting toward my own office. My cell phone rang as I approached the chair behind my desk. I picked up, recognizing Ike's number on my phone.

"What up, I?" I answered.

"Shit, nothing good. You game to hang out tonight?"

"I guess so. What's the problem?"

"Man, I just need to get out of the house for a minute and blow off some steam before I end up doing something I'll regret."

"Trouble in paradise?" I poked, leaning back in my leather chair.

Ike groaned. "Yeah, and you're the last person I'm gonna tell about it too."

"Aww, Negro, please. You know damned good and well you're not about to hang out with me, drowning your sorrows in Hennessey and Coke without spilling your guts. You might as well just tell me now, bruh. What did the Wicked Bitch of the Southeast do now?"

He went silent, and I unbuttoned my chef's coat to get comfortable while anticipating his news.

"I don't want to talk about it, dude. You trying to roll out with me tonight or what? I need a designated driver. I'm planning to get trashed."

"Yeah, okay. I'm still at the restaurant though, so you gotta give me some time to lock up here, go home and change. You thinking Jaguars, The Man Trap, one of the other spots? What?"

"The Man Trap. The way I'm feeling, I need some tits and ass in my face to remind me what they look like."

"What the fuck you mean, 'what they look like'? Ain't you married? That's supposed to be 24/7 tits and ass. On call tits and ass!" I mocked.

"Yeah, well, Tara must've missed the memo on that. She's been holdin' out most nights and we've been arguing nonstop for weeks. I'm working a lot of overtime at my job and she's been complaining about that; but she's the one trying to move into a goddamn mansion!" he squawked into the phone.

I knew he'd tell me what was up sooner or later. In my opinion, that bitch Tara was the root of all evil in his life, but he was too blind to see it.

"What mansion is she trying to move in to? That house she's been checking on is only in the two hundreds." Hell, it wasn't even worth that much from what I saw. Ike's lazy ass should've gone to see it with her.

"What house are you talking about? Her picky ass has been looking at almost a house a day, and I don't have time like that. I work my ass off so she doesn't have to work, so I just stopped going and told her to pick what she wants. I'll be happy as long as it has a basement and his and her sinks. I can't stand all of that damned weave hair around where I brush my teeth."

"My agent said she thought Tara and Teddy were looking at a yellow house in my subdivision," I said, eyeballing Gabby, who was now leaning against my office door frame staring at me.

Her hair was starting to grow out, and her bangs now draped lazily over half of her face, exposing one eye, which she used to conjure a beckoning stare.

"In your new subdivision? I didn't know she looked at any of them by you. Like I said, she's got Teddy out on the hunt with her almost every day. Anyway, fuck all that. Hurry up and come get me so I can get outta here and burn off some steam."

"I'll call you when I'm leaving my house. Later," I told him, hanging up as Gabby advanced.

* * *

She'd already unzipped her glove-gripping royal blue dress down to her belly, exposing her balloon-like breasts that held my attention like a hypnotist. Her 6-inch ribbon-strapped stilettos slowly click-clacked across the floor as she sauntered around my desk and up to where I sat in my chair.

"What the hell are...?" I began, before she leaned down and grabbed my face, tongue kissing me like I was the master of all passion. She knew me well.

I was stupefied by her boldness, but turned on instantly.

"Don't talk. Just fuck me. You don't have to forgive me," Gabby begged, lifting her dress and straddling me, exposing her neatly shaven snatch.

I could hear R. Kelly's voice in my head singing, "My mind's telling me noooo...but my body...keeeeeps telling me ye-e-e-es! Baby!"

I still despised her, but all of her advances in the previous weeks had begun to weaken my disdain and increase my attraction. I didn't want to be with her, but I did undeniably want to fuck a fibroid out that pussy. She knew dirty talk would put my mini-me at attention, and he was absolutely saluting her.

"Get up," I commanded, putting my hands around her waist, ready to lift her off of me.

But she swiftly pulled her breasts out and thrust them into my face, simultaneously grinding her womanhood onto my lap.

"Nobody has to know. Just this once," she pled lustfully, leaning in and fondling my right ear with her tongue.

I was on autopilot. My lips went directly to her nipples and licked one, then the other, eagerly. She smelled so good, and those titties felt just as ripe in my mouth as they always had. She was right; nobody had to know, and I was getting tired of avoiding her advances. It was time she got one last taste of the dick she'd once cheated on for that baboon-looking half-wit all those years ago. I was going to beat that pussy up like Rodney King, and then discard her like yesterday's trash afterwards. I deserved this revenge.

I hoisted her off of me and sat her down on my desk, then buried my face into those luscious titties while I unbuttoned and unzipped my pants. She shrieked with pleasure, grabbing my head and pulling me in.

"Yes!" she called, then jerking my face up to hers and Frenching me again.

Once my dick was out, I plunged it into her with the force of all the anger I'd stored up. She was as wet as a Slip 'N Slide, and I felt her vaginal muscles sucking me in with every thrust.

"Is this what you want, bitch? You want me to penal-ize-this-pussy?" I emphasized with each pump in and out of her.

"Oh, yes!" She cried out. "Penalize this pussy!"

The more I fucked her, the less I wanted to see her face. I hadn't forgotten my commitment to Nadia, but my urge to release this pent-up energy between me and Gabby was stronger than my desire to be faithful. Still, just as I'd been hallucinating Gabby's face while sexing my girl, I was now seeing Nadia's face on the whore I was fucking before me.

I pulled myself out of her, yanked her off of my desk, forcing her to plant her feet on the floor, and flipped her around so that she was bent over, ass up. She cried out when I rammed myself back into her wet box and pumped so hard that my desk lifted up and down with every blow. Oh my God, she felt so good inside. She started yelling something about cuming, and that brought me closer to erupting. I pulled out, splashing all of my unborn seeds onto her ass and onto the back of her dress.

Breathing hard, I stepped back, holding my deflating manhood in one hand and looking at Gabby's limp body lying across my desk.

"Brian, what the fuck are you doing?" Gabby complained. "Not on my dress; damn!"

I snickered, pulling my underwear and pants up, noticing the time on the clock by the door. I needed to head home to shower and change to go out with Ike. Shit, since Gabby was still here, I could bounce out and let her lock up.

"Can you at least get me a tissue or something and wipe your mess off of me? I can't go home with my dress looking like Monica Lewinsky's," she whined, leaning stiffly in front of me. I handed her the box of tissue on the far end of my desk and she grabbed a handful, reaching back awkwardly with one hand and wiping the remnants of our activity off of her.

When she was done, she threw the tissue in the garbage, pulled her dress down, put her breasts back inside her bra and zipped her dress up. I draped my chef's coat across the back of my chair and grabbed my keys and wallet from the top drawer of my desk. Gabby swiped at the wrinkles in her dress and then posed with her arms crossed, staring at me.

"I gotta go, can you lock up?" I asked her blandly, walking around her and heading out.

She whirled around toward me with an agitated expression. "Really? That's all you're gonna say?"

"What the fuck you want me to say? You been begging to get fucked and you got what you wanted. Now you can go about your merry way." I paused, giving her a nonchalant once-over, then continued my stride. "I gotta go."

"Motherfucker!" she called behind me.

* * *

When I drove up to Ike's house, I honked my horn and sat back listening to a 50 Cents CD. A few minutes later, Ike flung the front door open and was exiting with Tara hot on his heels.

"So it's okay for you to go out with your scumbag friends and spend money on strippers at the club but not for me to spend money on shoes!?" she hollered behind him.

She was wearing a blue tube top, a lot of jewelry, and blue leggings, and trailed him hurriedly in bedroom slippers.

"Hell yeah it's okay, because I'm the one bringing home the money that's getting spent! I go out every blue moon, but you're shopping every damn day like you married Donald Trump!" Ike retorted with his face twisted in fury, walking towards my car.

"You agreed that I didn't have to work. Now you're resentful because I want the life you promised me? If you really cared about this marriage, you'd be staying home tonight to talk about this instead of going out with this douche bag," Tara argued, glaring at me through my open windows.

I smirked at her, knowing it would piss her off, and sang along with a 50's song, "I don't know what you heard about me, but a bitch can't get a dollar out of me, no Cadillacs, no perms you can't see, that I'm a muthafucking P.I.M.P."

"Tara, go back in the house!" Ike yelled, getting into the passenger's seat and slamming the door behind him.

"Okay. Fine! So much for happy wife, happy life then, Isaac. Because I am definitely not happy!" she screamed, turning her Holly Robinson Pete-looking ass around and storming back into the house.

"You sure you wanna go with me instead of going back in there with the Dragon Lady? It might be worse later," I offered.

As much as I hated them as a couple, I didn't want to get blamed for yet another rift in their bullshit marriage later.

"Just drive," he ordered, reclining his seat and turning up the volume on my radio.

Once we arrived at The Man Trap and found seats at the bar, Ike immediately ordered us two rounds of Hennessey and Coke. His thin-rimmed glasses were atop his head, and he pitifully slouched on the stool in his dark blue T-shirt and perfectly creased straight-legged jeans.

"So, you ready to talk yet?" I coaxed him over the booming music.

He didn't answer, he just took another swig of his drink, and looked back towards the heavily made up, long-haired stripper who was making her booty clap in a way worth a thousand applauses.

"All right then, I'll start. She got me," I confessed to him after I ordered a Corona.

"Who got you?"

"Gabby," I sighed, watching the stripper do a split and then snake her body across the stage.

Ike frowned. "She got you how?"

"She waited till Trent left and started taking her clothes off in my office." I sucked in air, shaking my head from side to side. "She came at me with her pussy out and everything, man. Tongued me down in my chair and started begging me to fuck her. I couldn't take it anymore. I gave her what she wanted," I told him, as the bartender placed my beer down in front of me.

His jaw dropped and he leaned onto the bar, bringing his hand to his mouth.

"Naw, you didn't."

"Yeah, I did," I replied, smiling. "I can't front. That pussy was still good, too."

"What are you doing, man? You fucking shitting where you eat? I thought you hated her?"

"I do. Well, I did," I laughed. "But shit, she was throwing that sexy ass up in front of me one too many times. I hate to do Trent like that, but…" I broke off, shaking my head.

Ike stared at me straight-faced. "That's fucked up, B. Yo' ass hasn't changed at all. What about Nadia?"

"Man, this ain't got nothing to do with her. That was just something we had to get out of the way before we could move on. It's not like I'm gonna be fuckin' Gabby every time I see her. Nadia is 10 times the woman Gabby is, and I never cheated on her before. This was an understandable slip. Right?"

I was getting sick of Ike and his purity lectures. While he was being faithful; her scandalous ass was probably out sucking the skin off of Teddy's dick in a vacant house somewhere.

He shook his head in disagreement. "Nah, man, I don't understand it or you; but shit, I ain't gotta live with the decision. You just better hope Nadia never finds out and that your partner never finds out. Your dumb ass fucked your partner's wife, in the restaurant you own together," he continued, shaking his head as he drank the last of his drink and ordered another. "But I guess if you would fuck my girl when we were best friends, I should never really put anything else past you."

I scowled. I should've known that Negro was still holding a grudge against me for fucking his easy-as-Sunday-morning-ass wife. She threw it at me just like most women did! Just like Gabby had just done! Dudes wanna be mad at me because God didn't bless them with hazel eyes and model looks like he did me. Blame your average to ugly ass-looking parents for that!

"That's low," I told him, gulping down more beer.

"Yeah, it was," he laughed. "But I'm over that shit. You wouldn't do that shit to me now though, right?"

He was side eyeing me like he really thought there was a possibility that I would be screwing his wife again.

"Wow. Are you really asking me that on the serious tip after how she just talked to me?"

Ike didn't answer. He just stared in obvious wait for an answer.

"Man, I don't want your fucking wife. I didn't like her then and I really don't like her now. I was a different kind of fucked up back then, and I'd never do you dirty like that again. I've apologized to you for that already, man. Don't keep holding my feet to the fire for that one bad mistake, Ike."

He looked towards the stage where the next stripper was being announced and stared for a brief moment, then turned back to me. "I think she's cheating on me, B. I don't know with whom, but either she's cheating on me, or she's losing interest in me already. We haven't even been married a year and already she's acting completely different. I don't know what I'm gonna do if I find out she's betrayed me again."

If I didn't know better, I would think he had tears welling up in his eyes. I wanted to tell him what my real estate agent revealed to me about her everyday visits to the house in my subdivision, but decided against it. I didn't wanna be in the middle of their bullshit, and I didn't have any proof. Besides that, the dude she was probably fucking was also my sister's ex. There were just too many pitfalls for me to fall into if I said anything to implicate that dirty, lowdown bitch.

I shrugged and swiveled my stool completely around to view the sexy, dark-brown, buxom chick with micro braids on the stage who was standing on one leg, with the other kicked straight up into the air.

"I don't know, man. Trust your instinct," was all I offered.

Ike's eyes were as glued to the stripper as mine were.

"That's the problem. I do."

12

Julian

His abs were so tight and defined that I wanted to spray the whipped cream I had in the refrigerator over them and lick it off. Unfortunately, there was no time for me to do all of that because my Latin lover was going to have to go.

The clock read 10:04 a.m. and I'd planned to go into the shop today. My first appointment wasn't until two o'clock, but since Nick was no longer the salon manager, I needed to be there to ensure operations were going as expected until I found a new one.

"Good morning, honey," I said, shaking the 5' 7", olive-colored cutie I'd met at Bulldog's the prior night and brought home to my bed. Marco was a Dominican who grew up in Harlem, New York, but now lived in Atlanta. He and I had flirted on several occasions in the past year, but never consummated our meeting the way we both wanted to. Nick had posed a bit of an obstacle for both of us previously, but that obstacle was no longer in the way.

Marco stretched his short but toned limbs out and turned towards me with sleep in his eyes and a smile on his face.

"Good morning to you. What time is it?"

"A little after 10," I advised, getting up from the bed and strutting in all my nakedness into the master bathroom to relieve myself.

"Oh."

"I've gotta get ready and get out of here," I called from the bathroom. "Do you need to be dropped off somewhere, or do you want me to call you a cab?"

He was silent. Once I finished up and washed my hands, I exited to find him dressing and despondent. "What's wrong?"

"Nothing. Yes, I would like a ride to the Dunwoody Marta Station, if that won't be too much trouble for you," he replied, buttoning his jeans and slipping his black mandals on blindly.

"Okay," I said dubiously, standing in the bathroom doorway watching him. "Have I upset you?"

He sighed and eyeballed the ceiling before turning to me. "I guess I was just hoping we could spend more time together. We've been flirting so long, and I guess I just thought...I thought that last night meant something."

Marco's almond-shaped eyes were pleading for reciprocation that he wasn't going to get from me. His dark hair was closely cropped to his scalp, exposing the gorgeous face it sat upon, and his chiseled body would make any Calvin Klein model flinch; but his use had expired as soon as my eyelids opened at 10:04 a.m. I was not looking for another steady, or a clingy booty call. Maybe Marco didn't want to be either, but I didn't care to find out what he wanted at all. What I wanted was for him to get his shit and leave me with as little drama as possible.

"Marco, baby, you do understand that this was just sex, right? I picked you up in the club, I brought you home and we fucked. That's not exactly the stuff fairytales are made of," I chided, swishing my long mane from one side over to the other. "Perhaps we will see each other again soon, but right now, I've got to go to work. Do you work?"

He continued to dress, buttoning up his checkered shirt and rolling up the sleeves to his elbows. "I'm a ballet dancer, but my dance company is on hiatus for the month."

"I see," I replied, pivoting back into the bathroom and starting my shower. "I was going to say that you could join me in here if you wanted to, but you were getting dressed before I could make the offer."

Curse my star quality love-making skills. It seemed no man, or woman, wanted to let me go after they'd had one romp with me. I'd dabbled in females one year out of boredom, but their breasts were such a nuisance during sex, and I always preferred their chocolate star to that baby-making abyss anyway.

Just as I was about to step into the shower, I heard the alarm go off and I stiffened with panic. Did somebody just break in my house? Why would anybody be so stupid as to do it while someone was home? I breathed heavily, nervous that it would be either a burglar, or Paul coming to exact revenge against me for my refusals and his brief incarceration. I frantically scampered into the bedroom just before the robotic alarm voice enunciated, "Alarm, disabled."

I froze, and Marco stared cluelessly into the hallway from the bed.

"Julian?" Nick called, as he ascended the stairs.

Marco glanced at me, then back toward the hall as though he was expecting all hell to break loose.

When Nick entered what had previously been our bedroom, he halted in the doorway and darted his eyes back and forth between my stark-naked ass in the middle of the room and Marco seated on the bed. He gasped and turned to me, dewy-eyed, "How could you?"

Both of our eyes were suddenly drawn to the used condom which lay beside Marco's feet by the bed and Nick slowly blinked, releasing a single tear from his left eye as he brought both hands to his mouth.

Marco was staring at Nick like a two-headed dragon; but that may have partially been because Nick's black knit skull cap seemed to be harboring an abnormally large head that was probably due to thick bandages. The gold Ferragamo sunglasses that rested atop his cap matched the gold lamé short-sleeved shirt he wore with his black linen pants and thong-toed sandals.

He looked a hot fashion mess!

"What are you doing here? You weren't supposed to come get the rest of your stuff until tomorrow," I chastised, crossing my arms in front of me.

There was no point in trying to get dressed now. Neither of them were virgins to my nudity anymore at that point.

* * *

"You wretch!" Nick squeaked, flailing his arms in front of himself. "In our bed? You didn't even have the decency to screw your piece of ass outside of our home?"

"This is not our bed or our home anymore, Nicholas. We've broken up. Remember?" I countered, knowing the use of his full first name would further infuriate him.

"I never confirmed we've broken up!" he shrieked. "We're separated! But at least I guess I should thank my lucky stars you bothered to use a condom!"

Marco now looked miffed.

"Listen you Project Runway fashion reject; I know you're not insinuating that I'm diseased, are you?"

Nick swiveled his neck long and far as he arrogantly planted a hand on his hips. "I wasn't even addressing you, Mister Oscar De La Hoya, so you might want to shut up and stay in a side whore's place."

Now that he mentioned it, Marco did resemble the boxer, but I was sure that Nick only knew who he was because of De La Hoya's good looks; otherwise, the most he knew about any sport was that he wasn't a fan.

"Side whore?" Marco balked, jumping up from the bed. "Keep talking like that and I'm going to beat you like Oscar De La Hoya."

"Please," Nick sucked his teeth, waiving Marco off. "So, did I interrupt you and your little harlot before you could have shower sex, too? Huh? Is he why you want to break up with me?"

"I broke up with you because you can't even get it up anymore without a blue pill, and because I'm sick of your nagging and whining all of the time. Happy now? I said it. Now since you brought your ass over here early, you can kindly leave my house keys and get the rest of your stuff. It's all neatly packed up in boxes in the guest bedroom," I proclaimed, dismissing him with a wave of one hand and heading back into the bathroom.

Suddenly I was wildly hurling forward; my knee hit the top edge of the tub and my hands splayed out in front of me just before my head collided with the tiled shower wall. I was being punched about my back and head as I twisted around inside the tub, attempting to escape my attacker and the force of the shower water in my face.

"You heartless son of a bitch!" Nick hollered, still delivering blows to me before Marco grabbed him from behind.

"Don't put your hands on me! Don't touch me! I have a head injury! I'll sue your ass!" Nick then screamed, backing away from Marco the second he was touched.

"Then get the fuck outta here if you don't want to be touched! You're the one getting violent, you idiot! Are you fucking crazy or something?" Marco snapped, lifting my bruised and contorted body from the shower where the water from the shower head was attempting to drown me.

"This is my life! Who are you to tell me to get out of my own house? Why don't you get out and leave us to work out our problems?" Nick stood his ground, with his Puerto Rican face flaring up.

"Get the fuck out of here, Nick!" I shrieked. "It's over! We're over!"

I was furious, and my right knee felt like someone had come after it with a bat. I just wanted him to get his temperamental ass out of my house!

"Go!" Marco yelled at him as he led me, hopping on one foot, over to my bed and sat me down.

I regretted not getting dressed now. My knee wasn't the only place that was sore. My ribs, butt, head and dick also felt like they'd been run through a kneading machine.

Nick remained in place, sobbing loudly and uncontrollably. He was making some sort of plea, but I couldn't understand most of it through his blubbering. Finally, he slithered out of the bathroom with a tear-drenched face and started toward the spare bedroom.

"Are you okay?" Marco asked, giving me a grimacing once-over.

"No, but I'll be okay," I answered, flopping back onto the bed as he left me momentarily and turned the shower water off.

I took several deep breaths, mentally cussing myself for not getting Nick's key back from him a week earlier when I saw him at his mother's and broke up with him face to face.

"Are you sure these are all my things?" Nick appeared again in the doorway of my bedroom holding two large shipping boxes. I'd brought everything else of his that would fit into my car with me and left it at his mom's when last I saw him.

"Yes! And leave my keys, too, goddamn it!" I growled.

A new stream of tears ran down his face as he silently set both boxes down on the carpet, removed the ring of keys from his pocket and began working my house keys from it.

Marco glowered at Nick in a rigid stance that made me think he was gonna bust out into a plié instead of projecting intimidation.

When Nick had both keys off of the ring, he tossed them onto the carpet in my room with all the vigor of a 4-year-old girl.

I giggled then and he leered back at me.

"I can't believe I ever loved such a hideous human being," he scoffed, picking up his boxes and descending the stairs.

A few moments later I heard the front door open and then slam shut behind him.

I panted as a sharp pain shot through my kneecap when I sat up and peered at Marco, who was looking at me like he 'pitied a fool.'

"Guess you'll be calling out today, huh?"

I really hated to cancel on my clients, but I was no longer in the mood to be standing on my feet when it felt like my spleen was going to bust out of my side. Raul set my appointments up with Selene and Gary, who were the best stylists in my brood, other than myself, of course.

Given my newly injured state, I took a half-hour to soak in the tub, and Marco was good enough to both bathe and service me while I unwound. A couple of hours later, I dropped my boy-toy off at the train station and headed to meet Tia at Eat Your Art Out on a food review excursion.

I wondered how Brian was going like that.

* * *

I wore beige linen pants with a baby blue button-up Ralph Lauren shirt, blue Josef Seibel sandals, and my hair in a sleek bun at the back. As I put my wallet in my pocket, I checked the time on my silver Cartier Santos watch, a gift from a former lover, and grabbed my Versace sunglasses for another road trip.

One thing was for sure, no one could ever say I wasn't stylish. I always believed you had to look like money to attract money; and that went for whether you made it on the job, or on your back. I hopped into my car parked in the driveway and made a mental note to myself to start parking in the garage again. Now that Nick and I were no longer together, there was no car-blocking issues to worry about anymore. Besides, I didn't want to leave my purple people-eater exposed to a possible drive-by keying, or worse.

When I arrived at the restaurant, which was located smack dab in the heart of Buckhead, the parking lot was already pretty packed. It looked like an eclectic smorgasbord of artsy, college, and cultured Atlanta patrons above the drinking age.

It was 4:30 p.m. on the dot, and I knew Tia would already be inside because she was the type that felt being on time, was being late. Now I was a stickler for punctuality, but she was a downright tyrant when it came to her time. Clearly, I was now late.

A pretty young Julia Roberts look-a-like (save the horribly bleached blonde hair which I absolutely loathed), greeted me, and I intended to politely pass her a business card to Hair To The Throne before I left.

"Hello, sir. Party of one?" she asked with a huge smile.

"No, I'm meeting a friend here. She's probably already seated. Oh yeah, there she is," I said, spotting Tia sitting at a table near the live band and heading toward her. It almost looked like a museum, with statues, paintings and other unique pieces displayed on the walls and between tables. It had definitely been redone since my last visit before Brian was a partial owner.

On my way I saw numerous people getting their portraits drawn with chalk or pencil, either at their tables or in an area near the live band where people waited to be drawn. Most were reveling in their finished portraits, or in their food.

Tia had her dreads wrapped up in another one of her signature head scarves, this one with a yellow and black print. She wore a yellow strapless sundress that reached just below her thighs, and black low-heeled sandals that wrapped around her legs up to her calves. She smiled when she saw me, showing all of her pretty white teeth through her lightly painted pink lipstick. Tia was a natural beauty.

"Hey, punkin'," I greeted her, as I leaned in and kissed her on both cheeks before sitting down. "Don't you look pretty."

"Well, don't you look handsome? Handsome and late," she taunted.

"I am not late, clock Gestapo."

"It's 4:34 by my clock, Mister Julian. You're...late," she smirked, taking a sip from the straw in her water glass as I skimmed the menu. There was a nice selection.

Tia always let restaurants know she was coming, but never the time, and sometimes, not even her name, if she thought they'd flag her. The crazy Brit even disguised her voice when calling so her accent wouldn't be a dead giveaway upon her arrival.

Tia and I ordered, ate, got our portraits drawn, and yammered about both of our hectic days. Some ugly, freckle-faced, light-skinned waitress with Pocahontas-style pigtails approached, looking all in my face.

"Excuse me; Hi," she grinned, with more teeth in her mouth than a killer whale. "I'm Tricia. Some of my co-workers and I have a bet; are you by chance our chef's twin brother? Because y'all look almost identical."

"No, we're not twins," I stated, taking a sip from my watermelon martini while eyeing Tia.

"But you are related?"

"He's my brother. Yes."

"I knew it!" Pippi Longstocking exclaimed, like she was waiting for us to hand her a brain surgeon degree. "See, I told y'all!" she shouted to two other waitresses hovering by the bar.

"Well, since you're here, can you please see if Chef Andrews is available? I'm Tia Brewer from Morsel Magazine."

"Oh, yes of course," Tricia answered, her expression changing to one of concern as she quickly scampered away to the kitchen.

I braced myself for his arrival. I was hoping this encounter would be better than our last.

Brian's direct ogle on me and phony grin as he approached our table verified that he'd been forewarned of my presence.

"Ms. Brewer, I'm Chef Brian Andrews. Nice to meet you. I hope you enjoyed your meal and our ambiance," he said, taking her outstretched hand and cupping it between his before sitting in a chair between us. "Brother," he addressed me before turning to Tia.

She was smiling like Denzel Washington had just introduced himself, and at every pause during their conversation from that point on, she giggled. She was recording his responses to her questions and comments via her iPad, and I wondered if she'd notice how coquettish she sounded during the playback. As an eyewitness, I wanted to vomit in a The Exorcist style upchuck at their nearly 15-minute conversation of public frippery.

When her interview concluded, Brian finally acknowledged me for the second time. "So, Julian, was it good for you?"

I felt heat rush to my face. Was he talking in code about my escapade with Paul? Or did he mean the food.

"Yes. Live band, good decor, good lighting, and good food. Look at our portrait," I rambled, pulling up the thinly framed chalk drawing of Tia and me.

"Terrific. Can I talk to you for a moment?" he asked with an unidentifiable tone.

I glanced at Tia, then back to Brian, bewildered. "Uh...sure."

"Excuse us," Brian asked of Tia, rising from his chair. "It was a pleasure to meet you, and I hope your review will be as radiant as you are."

Tia beamed once again, and I rolled my eyes. Was that charming? Pu-lease!

"Right this way," Brian said, before leading the way.

"If I'm not back in 10 minutes, call 9-1-1," I half-joked with Tia as I followed Brian.

13

Brenda

I hadn't slept well at all, and the uneasy feeling I had prior to going to bed lingered all day. After meeting Avis, I'd almost wished I hadn't. He continued to probe me about my life and future plans, as should have been expected, but I was skeptical about sharing any of it with him after he made that comment about "expediting death by natural causes."

I damn sure wasn't going to admit I'd also told my brother, after he made that not so subtly camouflaged threat. By the time Lane finished showing my mother the house, they were bantering like old buddies, but I was now as paranoid as an FBI snitch. My mom waited until dinner to drop another atomic bomb on me, though.

"I gotta be honest." She started shaking her head as the scolding was brewing. "I still think you kids should get married, since you're about to have a kid yourselves. It just makes life so much easier. You don't have to have a big wedding if you don't want to, Brenda. Avis and I are just gonna go to the Justice of the Peace."

I nearly choked on the spoonful of saffron rice I'd just put in my mouth. Lane pat my back incessantly until I signaled that my airway was clear, and I was okay. Avis watched me coolly while my mom leaned across the table to pat my hand.

"Are you okay, honey?" she asked.

"How you gonna marry him when he hasn't even met Brian yet? Plus, you don't think that's gonna look suspect to the police and everybody else?" I admonished, with dramatic hand gestures towards Avis.

"Brenda, we're not getting married tomorrow. Calm down. Of course, Brian's going to meet him first. We were thinking more like next week, Friday," she assured. "There's nothing for the police or anybody else to say about it. Robert had a girlfriend, and probably a harem of hussies when he died, Brenda. Nobody could blame me for moving on and getting a little some-thin' some-thin' for myself. He's dead! I'm perfectly free to do what I want to do now, aren't I?" She was actually laughing through the last statement, and playfully slapped Avis on the thigh beneath the table. "Listen, girl, at our age, you gotta stop living for everybody else and just do you. I've done what other people wanted me to do for most of my life. No more. Life's too short. Here today, gone tomorrow."

"You can say that again," Avis chimed in, draping his right arm across the back of my mother's chair.

I eyeballed Lane, hoping for some assistance, but he'd barely said two words to me since my earlier declination to announce our engagement.

"Oh my God," I said in disagreement, focusing back on my dinner plate and shoving a fork full of string beans in my mouth.

"It wouldn't hurt you to visit his house every now and then either, instead of just calling his name when you need him," my mother added.

I shot daggers at her and replied, "Didn't help you much. You certainly didn't waste any time waiting on the Lord to solve your problems this time now, did you?"

We locked eyes briefly before she broke off, picked up her plate and took it over to the sink.

"Well, this was lovely, Lane," she said, reverting back to her Clair Huxtable voice. "I think it's time Avis and I call it a night, and maybe your girlfriend's pregnancy hormones will be calmer the next time we see her."

I rolled my eyes...hard.

I sat with a pretentious smile plastered on my face that mimicked my mother's when she and Avis said their good-byes. Later that night,

Lane and I talked about how the evening had gone and ended up in a huge argument once we got on the subject of his impromptu proposal.

Now, as I drove to Athena's to see my godson, I was tormented by the sum of it all.

Athena told me that she and the baby would be in the back yard, so when I arrived and parked in her driveway, I walked around back. My baby bump seemed to have grown into a baby ball overnight, and therefore, I forewent the jeans and crop top I intended to wear for a casual, black, knee-length baby doll dress. I heard my godson's cries and began to speak as he and Athena came into view, until I saw Rhonda.

She watched me, stone faced and Athena held Qur'an in the air facing me while cooing at him. "Hey, godmommy!" she called as I walked up.

I didn't answer, but came up to where they sat on the patio chairs and took Qur'an from her hands.

"Hi, sweetie pie!" I said sweetly, and an insecure smile began to spread across Athena's face. "Look at godmommy's fat tummy, baby," I continued, sitting in a patio chair on the side of Athena, furthest from Rhonda.

"You're really starting to show now, girl. Rhonda, look at how big her belly is. How far along are you again, Bren?"

Rhonda and I exchanged glares, but no words were spoken.

"Fourteen weeks," I told her, lying Qur'an tummy-down across my lap and rocking him. He looked like he was two seconds from conking out to sleep, and as tired as I felt, I envied him.

"Well, when are you gonna find out the sex?"

"I don't know. Soon."

Athena looked back and forth between Rhonda and me, her long, wavy tresses flinging side to side, and contorted her face.

"So y'all just gonna act like the other one doesn't exist, huh? Nobody's gonna say nothing?" she chastised.

Rhonda fingered the edges of her slicked-back mane and pursed her glossy lips with a neck roll.

"Really, guys? Still? I thought the two of you agreed to squash this mess the last time we were together."

"We did," Rhonda and I unintentionally retorted in unison.

* * *

I averted my eyes from Rhonda's cold stare to rest on my godson, who was now sleeping peacefully.

"C'mon, girls. We've been friends too long for you two to keep this rift going. I thought we said we'd never let a man come between our friendships," Athena began solemnly.

"Listen; don't talk to me about our friendship. Talk to your home girl here who got the bright idea to humiliate her so-called best friend at her job," Rhonda replied.

"What? You act like I got on the PA and announced it to everyone at your office. Knock it off already. Nobody humiliated you at your job. I'm sorry you found the information humiliating, but it was gonna be that, whether I told you at work or in your living room. He was the one cheating on you, but you're mad at me? See, it's twisted reactions like this that keep women from sticking together!" I shrieked.

"Oh, is that what keeps us from sticking together? Or is it your selfish-ass tendency to rub other people's misfortune in their faces? God forbid I have a happy relationship and get married before you do!"

"Whoa, whoa, Rhonda. Now hold on. Brenda has always stuck by you through whatever you've gone through. Me too. So where's all this coming from?" Athena interrupted.

"Oh my God, are you possessed by Gwen? Or better yet, maybe she was brainwashed with your bullshit jealousy in the first place," I accused.

"Jealous? Jealous of what? A grown-ass woman who chased a dude that only wanted you for your cookies for three years? A chick that almost got killed by another random dude she gave coochie coupons to because she was lonely? So now you think you're hot shit because you're pregnant with one of two possible suspect's baby? Nah, no thanks. You can keep your life."

I flinched from the sting of her words.

"Plus, I apologized for whatever role I played in Gwen's craziness towards you a thousand times already. Don't blame me because she couldn't stand your bitchy ways."

"Fuck you, Rhonda. How dare you disrespect me and my pregnancy like that! Maybe your fiancé couldn't stand your bitchy ways anymore, so he turned to a man!" I cursed her.

"Fuck you!" she hollered back, about to rise from her chair.

"Stop it! Stop it!" Athena yelled, holding up her hands to ensure we kept our distances. "This foolishness and swearing out here around my son ain't gonna happen. Why are y'all fighting when Paul is the one who messed up? Rhonda, I'm not taking sides but...girl, you're taking your stuff out on the wrong person. Now yes, I agree Brenda should have told you at a different time, but damn, she was trying to be a loyal friend. You can't see that?"

"Hell, I wouldn't have told you at all if I knew you were gonna blame me for seeing it," I added.

Rhonda thoughtfully looked to the sky, then back to me on the verge of tears. "I'm just so angry about it. You basically told me that my whole life was falling apart in a place where I couldn't escape to deal with it. How was I gonna keep it together at work after hearing that? And then to find out it was your brother? It felt like a setup."

"A setup? Setup for what? Setup how? I'd only met Julian once before that day. What would my motive even be?"

She brought her hands up to her face and sobbed. "I don't know. I guess it doesn't make sense. I just didn't want it to be true. I thought I was gonna spend the rest of my life with Paul and Paulette. I was gonna be a wife and a mommy one minute, the next I was back to looking at being a spinster."

I felt horrible, but would she really rather I didn't tell her? I hoped not.

Athena put her arms around Rhonda and comforted her as she cried, and soon I was also weeping.

"I'm so sorry he did this to you, Rhonda. And I'm sorry for handling it like that," I wept, patting Qur'an on the back lightly when I felt him stir a bit. "I was trying to be loyal."

Rhonda brought her hands down from her face, came over to my chair, and all three of us hugged as I sat in the chair with Qur'an over my lap until Athena picked him up and brought him inside to Quamé.

"So you swear you and Lane didn't know anything about what Paul was doing before that day?" Rhonda asked, wiping her wet eyes and smudging her eyeliner.

I was baffled. "No. I really don't understand why or how you think I'd do that."

There was a pregnant pause. "Well, it's your boyfriend's shop. Julian looks just like Brian, from what you say. How's it possible no one at the shop knew?"

"Girl, Lane owns the shop, but he doesn't see every customer that comes in. And plus, remember, he has more than one location. He's not at the Buckhead one every day. Don't you think if Lane had seen Julian in his shop before and remembered, he would have told me? And he sure as shit didn't know Paul was on the DL from how he acted when I told him what I saw. In fact, Lane said Paul never even came back up there to get his check or anything. He just ended up terminating him for no show/no call after the third day and direct deposited his last check."

Athena came back out and sat between us.

"Have you been talking to him?" I asked cautiously.

Athena crooked her neck and we both waited for a response.

"We've talked a few times but...I can't believe anything that comes out of his mouth now, and just the thought of what else he might have been doing behind my back makes me go ballistic. All he's been doing is lying anyway."

"What's he saying?" Athena probed.

Rhonda looked towards the house, then down to the floor like she was embarrassed to speak further.

"About everything for all I fucking know; including loving me. He said he thinks Julian drugged him when they drank coffee together while he was working on his car. Claims he thought he was having sex with a woman through whatever hallucinogen was in the drugs."

Athena and I twisted our lips in disbelief and she let out a, "Umph." Paul was dumber than I thought with that ridiculous story. Fail!

"I asked him if he used a condom and he said he can't remember. Shit, I just packed all his stuff and told him to come get it. I'm done with listening to his bullshit. Brenda, did you see a condom?" she asked hopeful.

I cringed. "I really didn't look that close or that long, honey. I'm sorry, I don't know."

She nodded. "I know. It probably wasn't long enough to see past his stomach anyway."

We all broke out into laughter.

* * *

I lollygagged with the girls for another couple of hours, and then decided to go by one of my favorite Sushi spots out in Conyers on the way home. It was a small, out-of-the way restaurant that my ex, Teddy, and I sometimes frequented whenever we visited the horse park. Typically, I would never have bothered to drive so far on the other side of town simply for some sushi, but this baby, boy or girl, wanted what it wanted!

I pulled into the shopping plaza, grabbed my bag and sunglasses from the console, and then made a beeline to the object of my affection. Food!

The restaurant was set up with buffet-style stations and a hostess podium at the front where you were to receive your seating instructions from whichever employee was paying attention to you upon entry.

"Good afternoon," the petite Japanese woman wearing black pants and a white shirt greeted me.

"Good afternoon."

"Lunch for one?"

"Technically, yes," I nodded, rubbing my stomach.

I think my inside joke was literally, an inside joke between myself and the baby, as the waitress smiled uncomfortably and led me towards an intimate booth close to the kitchen. I truly couldn't have cared less where I was seated, because the only thing on my mind at that moment was the major chow down I'd planned commencing like I was a professional eater.

I left my bag in the booth, grabbed a plate from one of the stations, and began piling various types of sushi onto it. As I made my rounds, a woman's flirtatious laughter rang out and I looked in her direction with a smile. It usually made me happy to see couples having a good time...until I recognized the tramp and her cohort.

I watched them as my face reddened and disgust built up in me like newspapers in a hoarder's house. I could see his hand under her skirt beneath the table; probably fondling her vagina highway as she readily spread her legs open and leaned her barely covered bosom onto the table for him to ogle.

Those sneaky motherfuckers!

I rested my plate down on the counter and marched my fuming little ass over to give them a piece of my mind.

"Well, isn't this cozy," I stated more than asked when I arrived at their table.

Tara jerked back so quickly than I'm surprised she didn't pull a neck muscle or two.

"Brenda," Teddy replied as cool as a cucumber, leaning back against the booth chair and clasping both of his hands on the table. His smile grew wide and his black opal-colored eyes gleamed as he spoke. "Long time no see."

There was a time when I would lovingly look into those dark eyes and do everything in my power to make him mine. But now, he disgusted me.

"Same shit, different bitch," I said, eye-balling Tara and then turning to him with one hand on my hips.

"Well, that's nothing for you to worry your pretty little head about anymore, now is it?"

"Yeah, I'm just having lunch with my realtor, so what's your beef?" Tara chimed in unconvincingly.

"Really? Is he helping you find a house or your G-spot? Because from where I was standing, sushi ain't the only fish his fingers been touching today."

"What?" she protested, looking panicked at Teddy.

"Aw, calm down, girl. I don't know what you think you saw, but that's not what I was doing at all," he responded with a huge, typically charming smile.

But this time, his charm was 100 percent ineffective. Not only was I pissed off that Tara's bum ass was cheating on my brother's best friend with my ex-boyfriend, but this slimy bastard didn't even have the decency to take her somewhere that didn't desecrate my memories here with him.

"You're overreacting, Brenda. Don't go spreading any bullshit rumors about what you saw here, either, because you don't know what you're talking about right now," Tara interjected.

"Bitch, please. Don't tell me what I saw or what to do. You got guilt written all over your face, and he has your nasty-ass pussy smell all over his fingers," I taunted.

She blanched as I shifted my weight from one leg to the other, glaring at the both of them.

"Don't make a scene, baby. Why are you so concerned with what's happening over here, anyway? Don't you have a man to get home to?" Teddy questioned smugly.

"I'm not your fuckin' baby," I grumbled, giving him an irritated head to toe once-over.

"No, you're not. And that's not my baby that you're carrying. So why are you concerning yourself about what's going on over here? Why aren't you checking up on your baby daddy?" he snapped.

It was a verbal body blow to my ego and my heart. I yelled an internal silent prayer to God. 'Lord please don't make this man my child's father!'

"Carry on, sluts," I finished, waving them off and abandoning their lying asses. I returned to the station where my plate lay to finish composing my meal, breathing with the anger of a dragon.

What else was left to say, anyway? Right now, it was more important for my child and me to eat than for me to interrogate their two-timing behinds. There really wasn't any further point in it, anyway. It was clear as glass what was going on.

Once I was seated back in my booth, I scarfed down my food like a lioness devouring her prey, and contemplated what I was going to do with my newly discovered information. The last time I'd snitched on some shady business I witnessed, it backfired on me and almost brought my B-F-F and me to blows. I knew Brian hated Tara more than the thought of crow's feet, but I also knew he was always telling me to mind my business. I was sure Lane would probably second that emotion as well if I ran the idea of telling past him.

After I'd sucked up everything but the sauces on my plate, another Japanese waitress came to my table with a water refill and the bill. I left payment on the table and got up to leave, scanning the restaurant for Tara and Teddy, but as expected, they were nowhere in sight. They probably hadn't wasted too much time burning rubber from the time I confronted them.

I decided to sit on what I knew for a while after all. There was no reason to insert myself in any unnecessary drama at this point in my life.

On my drive home, I received a text message from Lane asking if I was on my way home. I was glad that he even bothered to check, and even happier I hadn't left my cell phone in the house like usual. Hopefully his question meant he was no longer upset with me.

"Yes," I texted back quickly while at a red light.

He replied with a smiley faced icon.

14

Brian

The previous night, I'd seen Julian with the critic from Morsel Magazine and I instantly got my back up. That jealous bastard better not have planned to taint my restaurant review. I wasn't too keen on the fact that he was inserting himself all around Brenda and me in unlikely places, and I planned to get to the bottom of things with his gay ass. Not literally, of course.

I called him back to my office so that I could speak freely, and so we'd be out of earshot of everyone.

He sat cross-legged in the chair in front of my desk, and I sat in mine on the other side behind it.

"So, what's the deal?" I asked, resting my elbows on the desk and clasping my hands loosely together.

He looked puzzled and shifted in the chair. "I beg your pardon?"

"Look, we never saw or heard of you until the funeral, next thing I hear; you're fucking my sister's best friend's fiancé. Where? At my sister's boyfriend's auto shop. Then you end up at the hospital the same time as she did; now you're at the table with a food critic who's critiquing my restaurant. Coincidental? I think not. So, I'm asking you, what's up with that? We never saw your ass one minute of our lives before the funeral and now you're everywhere."

He grinned and swiped his upper lip with his index finger before speaking. "Well, Brian, stranger things have happened, I'm sure. I can't explain why you'd never seen me before, because I certainly had a lot of friends telling me how they 'saw my twin' somewhere before we actually met. As for Paul, well, he is to blame for both those times our sister saw me. I think he's the one who hit my ex-boyfriend at my—"

I wasn't looking for him to give me an in-depth description of his booty banging history. I just wanted to know why the fuck he was everywhere we looked these days; so I interrupted. "I don't want to hear about your lover's spats. Just be straight with me," I chuckled. "Okay maybe not straight, but honest."

His face twisted into a scowl. "Can you please be mature enough to stop with the gay jokes already? I don't know why who I sleep with is such an issue for you, but I didn't come here be judged or to fight with you. Of course, if you're gonna keep insulting me, that may change."

"Man, save those empty threats for your bitch-made boyfriends. Are you here with the lady from Morsel Magazine to try and sabotage my review?"

He crinkled his nose. "Oh my God. Is that why you've got me back here interrogating me? Tia and I have been friends for years. Boy, nobody is up here trying to wreck your little food critic review."

"So, you expect me to believe you didn't know this was my restaurant?" I questioned, placing my hands flat on the desk.

"No. I didn't say I didn't know it was your restaurant, but I hadn't been here since it reopened. Actually, I wanted to see the changes because if I liked them, I was gonna consider it for the place to have my birthday dinner next weekend. I'm not gonna lie, I might have thought about a plot or two on you before, but I've got too much going on in my life right now to worry about destroying yours. Besides, from what I've seen on the news, you're already doing a bang-up job at that, all by yourself."

This motherfucker had a smart mouth that I didn't like. I remembered that somebody, either him or Brenda, said he owned a popular hair salon, though. Having his dinner party at E-Y-A-O could create more of a buzz about our place, and maybe some influential people would be in the mix. I was still skeptical about him, but I wanted to keep our business running in the black.

"How many people are you talking about?" I asked, less rudely.

Circumspectly he answered, "About 20 or 30, maybe."

We eyed each other for a few moments.

"We do look a lot alike. The more I look at you, the more similarities I see," he confessed, looking me up and down.

"If you were straight, maybe. We have a lot of the same features, eyes and facial structure, but your...mannerisms are way different. Is that a weave?"

He gasped and clutched his throat like Rue McClanahan probably would have clutched her pearls on The Golden Girls. "A weave? Hell no, this is all my natural hair. And P.S. You live in Atlanta; don't you think your hatred, especially here, is dated these days? Who are you trying to convince? Me or you? Because it's you overly aggressive homophobic types that end up in the bed with one of us as soon as opportunity knocks. Umm hmm. Just like Paul," he chastised, while petting his hair, and commenced to another re-crossing of his legs.

"I don't hate gay men. I just don't understand wanting to cuddle up with another dude's hairy ass, especially when you got these Andrews good looks; but hey," I said, throwing my hands up. "This ain't a conversation I want, or need to have with you. What day are you looking for? We have a couple of party rooms near the second bar towards the back where we can accommodate up to 30 at a table in one room and up to 60 banquet hall-style in the other. I could let you have the smaller one this Saturday from eight o'clock with a 3-item, sampler-sized portion for everybody; 2 dessert choices; 2 bottles of wine and 2 complimentary group drawings for $1,200. We've already booked the other one."

He raised an eyebrow and smiled. "Well now, little brother, that sounds very doable. I can definitely round up 29 of my friends, and Tia is going to help me."

I peered at him as I rose from my chair and he popped up like a tart in a toaster. I didn't like that 'little brother' shit.

"You just make sure your Morsel Magazine friend gives us a great review."

He nodded femininely and followed behind me to Trent's office, where Trent was looking in a desk drawer.

"Yo, T," I said, rapping lightly on his open door as he noticed us. "This is Julian Andrews—"

"Parkes," Julian interrupted snidely.

"Oh, excuse me, Parkes. He's gonna have a birthday dinner party here Saturday night; 30 people in party room A at eight. Can you set him up for me?"

"Sure. Gabby just booked the other room for some ball player's party Saturday, too. Nice to meet you, Julian. Twins?" he said with a huge grin, standing from behind his desk to shake Julian's hand as he entered.

"No, definitely not. Just set him up," I uttered, dashing off toward the kitchen.

* * *

I woke up next to Nadia snuggled up against me and the incessant ringing of my cell phone. I knew by the ring tone that it was somebody I didn't want to talk to; my mother.

"Hello?" I answered blandly.

"Good afternoon, Brian. You're not just waking up at this time in the day now, are you? I didn't think you'd be keeping the same lazy hours you had when you were a bartender now that you're a restaurant owner," she began.

"Why are you calling?" I retorted, not bothering to explain that I'd been up for hours already and was simply now waking up from an afternoon sex-induced nap.

She paused, cleared her throat, and continued, "I really wish you'd stop being so ugly every time we speak. It's completely unnecessary and disrespectful."

"It's impossible for someone as handsome as I am to be ugly, Mother. I hope you're calling for a reason, and not just to get on my nerves."

She sucked her teeth. "I'm calling because I'd like for you to meet Avis. I'm sure your sister has already filled you in on the news."

"What news?"

"That we're getting married. I thought that the two of you should meet before he became an official part of the family."

I was caught off guard, and my laughter came out as a snort as I sat up in the bed, removing my arm from under Nadia's head. "Are you fucking serious?"

"Brian! You know I don't like you cussing in my presence," she scolded.

"You're over there, and I'm over here. I'm not in your presence. You didn't waste any time getting boo'ed up now though, did you?"

"It's been months since Robert passed away. Five, to be exact. At any rate, I've known Avis for years, as you know now, so it's perfectly reasonable that he'd be my next choice. I'm sure Brenda has filled you in on his history. I'd really like it if the two of you could meet, maybe get to know each other a little."

"Yeah, she did, and that was a pretty shitty way to break it to her I might add. You've had this girl in the dark about who she really is all this time and now you spring the missing link on us like we're supposed to embrace him? C'mon, Mother. You were probably seeing this dude before dad died, Mom, and y'all been shacking up in that house for months. Why do you give two shits about when I meet him now? I've got a busy life, and I don't have any free time to give," I told her, rolling over in the bed.

"So you've got the whole thing figured out, huh? Could it be that I wanted you to meet him earlier but you've never been available? I thought we'd grown past this constant attitude you have with me when I helped nurse you back to health. Now I'd like the two of us to try and have a better relationship, and I don't want Avis to feel unwelcomed by you."

"First of all, we did grow some after you helped get me back on my feet. I'm not denying that you put in some time trying to redeem your previous poor parenting; but my life doesn't stop because you're rushing. Shit, this is a better relationship. Five months ago you would have gone straight to voice mail. Hell, four months ago you would have gone to voice mail. Don't let me stop y'all from hitting the Justice of the Peace. I don't think I have time for no meet and greet with Brenda's bastard father," I chuckled.

"Bastard father? My God," she mumbled under her breath. "Are you ever going to stop being such a cynical ass? I'm serious."

"Okay. What day are you getting married? What's the dude's last name?"

"Friday, and his last name is Warren."

"All right, well, you go be Mrs. Warren, and I'll try to make some time to have drinks with you on the following Sunday, or you can come down to the restaurant. That's my best offer."

"We're going to be going on our honeymoon that weekend. He didn't tell me where yet, but obviously it won't be local. Can't you come over to the house after work one evening?"

"No, I can't. Well, call me when you come back. I'm not making any special trips to meet this dude."

"You are intolerable. I know you well enough to know that you're gonna hang up on me any minute now," she said snidely. "So anyway, we're getting married Friday afternoon, so if you change your mind and want to come over to the house afterwards, we're having drinks and everything with some friends to celebrate."

"Nah, Friday nights are busy. Send me a picture or something. I'll be there in spirit, and I'll see you when you come back. Anyway, I gotta go."

"Okay, I guess that will have to do. I'll talk to you soon, Brian."

"Bye," I said, hanging up.

I'd promised Brenda that I would not let my mother know that I also knew about her old folks murder gang and I hadn't, but it actually made me respect her a little more. At least she'd finally decided to stand up for herself for a change.

I stood in front of the full-length mirror on the back of my bathroom door and admired my muscular physique. Bullet wounds, kidney removal scars and all, I still had a body most women would pay me to lick. I hadn't been working out much since my recovery, especially with the demands of the restaurant, but my naturally stunning looks were still holding up under pressure. I shaped my fingers like a gun and pointed at my hazel-eyed reflection with a big smile. Life was good, and I was finally getting what I deserved.

"Was that your mom, honey?" Nadia called from the bed.

"Yeah," I replied, jumping into the bed next to her and grabbing her playfully around the waist.

"Oh, cool. I haven't seen her in a long while. How is she?"

"Getting married to Brenda's dad."

She looked confused. "Uh, but your father died, right?"

"Yeah, my father did. My mother just sprang on Brenda that she is the product of an affair and that my dad, is not her dad."

"How long have you known that?"

"A few months," I answered nonchalantly.

"And you never told me?"

"I don't feel the need to gossip like y'all vagina carriers. It wasn't relevant to anything."

Nadia shook her head and flopped back down into the pillow. "You're so damned secretive."

"No, you're just so damned nosey."

She smirked and put her hands over her forehead. "So she's getting married? When?"

"Next Friday. It's at the Justice of the Peace, so no need to start sorting wedding outfits in your head."

Her pretty little lips curled into a frown and I leaned forward, kissing them softly.

"Well, Trent booked some basketball player for a party room Saturday night. I think he said a few celeb guests might attend. So if you and a couple of your girlfriends want to come up, I'll set up a table for you. Plus, my homo brother is gonna have a birthday dinner at E-Y-A-O Saturday night, so you'll probably get to see him, too."

She sighed, "I'd love to come up to your restaurant with my girls Saturday night; but why do you have to call him your homo brother? Who cares that he's gay? And when did you start playing nice with him, anyway?"

I shrugged, "Since it became profitable."

* * *

"You want me to make us something to eat?" Nadia asked, kissing me quickly, then hopping out of the bed.

"Uh, let me think about it. Let's see, I'm a chef, and you're a nurse. Whose food would I rather eat?"

"First off, mister smart ass, I am not a nurse! I am a Nursing Service Manager, for your information," she playfully scolded through her pearly white smile and deep dimples. "But since you're talking, get yo' lazy ass up and make us some vittles then."

She was beautiful, and I knew I was falling in love. I still wasn't tired of looking at her; naked or in clothes, which was a feat in and of itself, given my short attention span. Of course, I could do without most of her rapid-fire questions at times, but I could easily deal with those. I enjoyed her confidence and her no-nonsense approach to most things. Weak women annoyed me, and Nadia was anything but that.

As crazy as it was, this woman was changing me into the settling down type, which I never expected to be.

"You should move in with me," I said, as I got up from the bed and walked past her.

She stood in the doorway between my bedroom and the hallway as I passed her to go downstairs to the kitchen. Her face was frozen, as was the rest of her. I just continued down the steps into the kitchen, and by the time I reached the island, she was on my heels.

"Are you sure I wouldn't be...cramping your style?" she asked with a poorly restrained joyous tone.

"I'm sure I don't like to repeat myself."

I went to the refrigerator and took out two steaks leftover from dinner two nights prior, leftover macaroni and cheese I'd brought home from the restaurant, and green beans in a pot. Once I had them all lined up on the counter, I turned to Nadia, who was beaming.

"Well, you're still my landlord, so, you tell me if I can break my lease."

I smiled back at her. "You can leave tomorrow if you want to, but your return deposit might not be coming anytime soon."

"Oh, really? Believe me; I will get that money back one way or another." We both laughed.

"That's what you think. But seriously, whenever you want to do it, you can. I'll pay for your moving truck or whatever. You know I'm still trying to get this place straight, so having you here full-time would be better anyway."

I put the steaks in the stove and turned it on.

Nadia wrapped her arms around my waist. "So, you're really just looking for me to be a full-time decorator? Because this is a big step for us, and I need to be clear on why you're asking before I pick up all my stuff and move into your space."

"I want you over here with me. I like your decorating and cleaning skills, too," I joked, kissing her on the forehead. "But I want you."

She rested her head on my chest.

I would never admit to a woman making me this soft to any of my boys; especially not to Ike. But this girl had me thinking of having kids with her, and that's not something I'd ever done before. The incident with Gabby was behind me, out of my system and over with. I was actually looking forward to flaunting my newfound love in front of my old lost bitch.

Funny enough, Gabby hadn't been hounding me as much as before I knocked her back out, but she still wanted me, obviously. Trent and I had been spending more time after hours working on plans, implementations, contracts and tweaking menu items, too, so time for her to pursue me was more limited. At least 4 out of 7 days a week were spent in his office or mine till the wee hours.

I squeezed Nadia tightly in my arms, and then broke free to prepare the rest of the food.

"I would have never guessed when I met you out on your balcony months ago, that I'd one day be moving in with you," she cheesed.

"I tried to warn you that day that I was irresistible. Especially after you caught a glimpse of how I was hung under my towel. I knew you wanted me."

"What? Oh my God! No I didn't! I didn't see anything under your towel, you jerk," she blushed. "I did see you trying to poke through it, but I'm a lady, Mr. Andrews. I would never have looked at your naked little ass out there on our first meeting. Even though that's what you wanted."

I grinned and put the dish of macaroni in the microwave.

"I didn't even know you lived there. If I had, I probably would have just come out with nothing on at all."

She laughed, leaned against the island and gazed out of my kitchen window.

"Brian, I hope you know what you're doing by asking me to move in with you."

"I always know what I'm doing," I answered, setting the timer and turning the microwave on.

"I'm serious. I don't want to go through the shit I went through with my ex. Lies, cheating; I don't want to deal with that mess anymore." Her eyes were teary once she turned to me. "Please don't play with my heart."

I brought my hands to her face and kissed her lips, then her cheeks gently. "I won't. I won't play with your heart. You're all the woman I want, and all the woman I need."

"I hope so," she answered, almost in a whisper.

I hoped so, too.

15

Julian

I folded my arms and leaned back in the salon chair in my booth and wished I could take a nap. My newly found single life was starting to take its toll on my ability to stay awake during business hours. My cell phone rang, and I rolled my eyes after glancing at the flashing number on it and set it to rest on the ledge in front of my booth mirror. Sean, one of my salon stylists, side-eyed me and chuckled before resuming roller-setting his clients hair.

Sean was a handsome, 5' 11" dark piece of chocolate that I wished would melt in my mouth and not in my hands. He had a bald head and wore a perfectly lined goatee which accentuated his chiseled features. His thin, gold chain hung just below the collar on his fitted dark blue shirt, but his loosely fitted jeans hid any eye candy from my scouring eyes. His sexiest attribute to me, was the barbwire tattoo that wrapped around the entire length of his muscular right arm, all the way down to his wrist.

Raul was the only prude out of all the women and men in the shop, because the rest of us insisted we'd have bedded Sean for little more than a Coke and a smile; but alas, Sean didn't want any part...of any men.

"And what exactly is so funny?" I flirted, flinging my freshly curled Shirley Temple-styled locks away from my face. So what if he wasn't gay; flirting isn't a crime.

"I'm laughing at your sleepy ass over there screening calls. You've been a busy guy since you and Nick broke up. You'd better slow down and take a nap," he kidded with a bright smile.

"Why? Are you worried about me, Sean?"

His smile quickly turned to a frown and he refocused on his client's hair. "See, now there you go with the bull again."

"What bull?" I asked, coyly crossing my legs as I took a quick look at the clock to ensure my client's dryer time wasn't up yet. I still had time.

"Julian, quit playing, man. I keep telling y'all asses I'm not gay. You wanna hear something funny though?"

"What?" a flirtatious Kendall, our token white boy questioned from his station.

"I'm straight and I do women's hair, but my little brother is gay and he's a bartender. Ironic."

"Really?" Gary perked up, while coloring his hideously dressed client. She wasn't much more overweight than say, an average mother of 3, but her pink jumper looked 2 sizes too small for all that poorly distributed fat. I bet if she'd have farted, the whole thing would have blown off of her. "What's his name and how old is he? You look like your family genes are strong."

"His name's Don. In fact, he just turned 22 a couple of weeks ago, and that's when he came out to our family. I guess he wanted to wait until my parents came to town to drop it on us all together, not that I needed him to say it. I already suspected he was gay since he was little," Sean answered, tapping his client on the shoulder lightly, signaling her to rise and walking her over to the dryers.

"Where are y'all from again? Oakland, right?" Serena chimed in.

"No, no, Oklahoma," he answered, while adjusting the settings on the dryer.

"I didn't even know black people lived there. And he's just twenty-two?" Gary repeated with a scowl. "That's a bit too young for my blood. I only entertain 25 and over. Them young ones are nothin' but trouble."

"Hell, 22 is just right enough and tight enough for the kid," Kendall blurted out while he primped his week-old Justin Bieber hairstyle in his booth mirror.

Sean shook his head facetiously, heading back to his station and leaving his client under a hair dryer.

"So, how'd it work out for him?" Serena probed.

"Can we see a picture?" I asked boldly. Twenty-two certainly was not off of my radar yet, if his brother looked anything like Sean.

"Well, it didn't change anything as far as I was concerned, but it did for my parents. My pops got up in the middle of him talking and went to the car. My mother was crying and hollering about Atlanta being the land of sin and whatnot. In a nutshell; no, it didn't work out." He shrugged as he began sweeping his station. "My brother has always been a quiet kind of dude. Real shy, internalizes a lot, and rarely stands up for himself. I could see how hard it was for him to even get it out at all; he stutters. I'm glad he got it off his chest, though. I don't know what it's like to have to live a secret life or anything, but I know it was eating at him; that's why he left home."

"That's really sad," Serena commented, straightening her black, thick-rimmed glasses on her face and brushing her beautifully curled, kaleidoscope-colored hair back from her neck. "Must've been devastating for him. That's such a cold reaction."

"Can I see a picture?" I repeated. Blah blah blah with the back story. If his brother had prey potential and looked anything like Sean, I wanted the first crack at him.

Sean paused, pulled out his wallet, and surfed through a folder in it before pulling out a small photo and handing it to me.

"That's maybe a year or two old, but he looks pretty much the same now, except he's bald like me," he smiled subtly. "He's been moping around the apartment a lot. Speaking of Don, is it okay if I bring him to your party?"

I tried to mask my disappointment at the specimen in the picture when I handed it back to Sean. "Umm...sure. Yeah, if you wanna bring him, that's fine."

"I wanna see," Kendall's big mouth rang out as he took the picture from Sean's hand.

Sean's brother had a few features in common with him, but otherwise, I was unimpressed. He had a funny-shaped head that I knew had to look just as warped bald. He was also donning a slack-eyed smile that screamed 'country ass dummy' to me. Just our luck, we got the cowardly, bobble-headed brother, while the heteros got Sean's fine ass.

Boo, hiss.

* * *

Thank God Gary agreed to replace Nick as the salon manager so I could take my tired ass home and go to sleep.

I drove my purple baby out of Hair To The Throne's parking lot and dialed Brenda via voice activation on my Bluetooth. We hadn't spoken at all since we saw each other at the hospital, and I still felt an urge to make a connection with her, since I'd now had an unexpectedly civil one with Brian.

"Hello?"

"Hey, Brenda, this is Julian. Your brother Julian," I greeted, as I pulled onto the highway.

"Yeah, hi." She sounded uneasy.

"Did I catch you at a bad time?"

"No, not really. I'm just washing dishes."

"Okay," I answered. There was an awkward silence. "So, I was at Brian's restaurant last night."

"Really? How'd that go?"

"Pretty nicely, I must say. I was there with Tia, my friend you met at the hospital. She's a food critic for Morsel Magazine."

"Oh, is that so? So he kept his cool when he saw you then?" she asked, accompanied by the sounds of dishwater splashing.

"Somewhat. He brought me to his back office and kept making snarky comments about me being gay, but once he realized I wasn't there to cause him any grief with my friend, he lightened up. The food was actually pretty delicious. So much so, that I'm going to have my birthday dinner there on Saturday."

I was still debating whether to invite her out with my friends because I really hadn't quite figured how I wanted to handle a relationship with her yet. For all I knew she was just as shady as Brian was. Please believe, I was not blinded to his potential to flip at the drop of a dime, but admittedly, I had an undeniable yearning to know my siblings.

"Wow, that's definitely better than I would have expected."

"Likewise. Should I be wary of his kindness?"

She cleared her throat. "Well, I don't want to throw my brother under the bus so, I'll just say, don't get too cozy with him just yet. He usually takes his time warming up to people."

"Believe me; I don't warm up easily to people either. Especially people I've already fought."

"Ha! Okay," she chuckled. "So, how's your boyfriend doing?"

"Single, but recovering well last I heard."

"Single?" There was a pregnant pause. "Well, damn. So, are you seeing Paul now?"

"Girl, get yo' life! Hell no, I'm not seeing Paul. I am single, thank you very much." I rolled my eyes at the implication that I would waste further time on her friend's estranged ex after I'd already told her I curbed his ass when we were at the hospital.

"Rhonda broke up with him too, so, I wasn't sure if he was pursuing something more with you or what."

"Chile', stop. He brought his clown-ass up to my salon trying to tear shit up, and I promptly had him arrested. Haven't seen him since."

"You gotta be kidding me! So, he was up there breaking stuff, or just getting loud?"

"Breaking stuff and getting loud. Mad because I wouldn't help him try and get that girl back. You should have seen him crying when the officer cuffed him and took him away with the lights flashing. He was a hot mess!"

I casually cranked the volume up on the radio when I heard Luther Vandross singing "Stop to Love" as she gasped. Oh my God I loved me some Luther Vandross!

"Well, it sounds like you've had an interesting couple of weeks," she teased.

"You don't even know the half of it, girl. But enough about me, I was calling to see if you wanted to come to my dinner party Saturday. I figured it was about time we tried to hang out under pleasant circumstances for a change."

"Well, funny enough, I'm already gonna be at the restaurant that night. My boyfriend's former teammate just got signed with the Atlanta Hawks and he's having a celebration dinner there that night too."

"I thought that tall drink of water you were sporting looked like a professional athlete. Basketball?" I asked, knowing damned good and well I already knew most everything there was to know about Lane. In fact, I would have preferred to let him play with my balls instead of Paul if there'd been half a chance he liked men; back when I was still plotting on Brenda, that is. At any rate, I thought it was better for the purposes of getting to know her better if I didn't mention my prior research knowledge.

"Umm hmm, he played in Spain for a few years before he got injured. So yeah, I'll be there anyway."

"Okay, then you've gotta have some birthday drinks with me and formally introduce me to your guy, little sister."

"Little sister? Ha! You're funny. All right then. I can formally introduce the two of you, but I won't be having any drinks."

"Why? Don't tell me you're one of those non-drinking goody two-shoes kind of gals," I said with another roll of my eyes as I got over to the far right lane approaching my exit. I knew for a fact that the girl drank.

She laughed. "No, I'm not. Still, I don't think it's a good idea for me to be drinking now that I'm gonna be a mommy."

"A what?" I exclaimed. "You're pregnant?"

"Umm hmm. Four months."

Not knowing her well enough yet, I didn't know whether she was happy to have a bun in the oven or not, but for some reason, I was all aglow. I always liked kids, and I knew I wasn't going to be creating any myself, so the thought of maybe having a niece or nephew to dote on was nice.

"Are congratulations in order? I mean, was this planned or..." I trailed off.

She hesitated, and for a second, I thought I'd hit a bad nerve and was maybe crossing a line I didn't know about.

Finally, she answered, "It wasn't planned, but we're happy all the same."

Really? She sounded more like she was being P.C. than genuine but, that wasn't my concern right now.

I pulled up to my subdivision, punched in the code to the gates and eased in as they opened slowly, while slightly focusing on my radio to change the station from the irritating sounds of Two Chainz latest song.

"All right, well, I'll see you Saturday then. This baby is demanding I go to the bathroom," she said.

"TMI, girl. I'll see you on Saturday. Ciao," I told her, then hung up just before my car jolted forward and my phone dropped to the floor.

I threw my car in park and was already fuming as I opened my door, expecting to confront some idiot talking or texting on their phone who accidentally ran into me. Just the thought of a scratch on my purple beauty was enough to send me over the edge; instead, I immediately froze mid-exit as I faced the culprit.

"I want you to remember that this is your fault," Paul said as he approached me swiftly, aiming a gun at my head.

His eyes were bloodshot and rabid. His shirt and jeans were wrinkled as though he'd slept in them for days, and his hair looked like it hadn't been brushed, let alone cut, in weeks. Urine slowly trickled down my leg as he leveraged the barrel within inches of my face.

"My life would still be good if you hadn't fucked it up. Now everybody knows what I never wanted anybody to know. What I never even wanted to be like. I've lost everything, and now I have nothing. My daughter, my woman, my job, my home, my dignity. It's all gone because of you; and you don't even give a shit. This blood is on your hands," he professed, shaking his head maniacally as tears dropped from his eyes and began to well in mine.

"Please…" was all I had managed to utter before he turned the barrel of the gun away from me, and towards his now opened mouth.

A loud boom resounded as Paul's brain exploded from the back of his head on the ground, onto his car behind him, and blood splattered onto my face. His body stood vacantly teetering for a second before it fell forward onto me, knocking me awkwardly backwards into my car.

His limp mass now had me pinned down with my legs partially outside the car and my body wedged between the steering wheel and the driver's seat. As I frantically tried pushing him off of me, my left hand slipped inside the gaping hole in back of his head.

That's when the screaming started.

* * *

I had been in the back of a Crime Scene Investigation truck for what seemed like an eternity, answering a barrage of questions and staring into space as pictures and samples were taken from my body and clothes. I was several feet from where the macabre scene had taken place, now swarming with police officers and stymied spectators; but my mind didn't require sight in order to torture me with instant replays of what had occurred.

Paul's last condemning words echoed in my head as the memory of his brains scattering onto the pavement haunted me. There was dried blood all over me and I stared at my left hand with disgust, recalling the warm and gruesome feel of freshly exposed flesh beneath my fingers. I couldn't even remember how I escaped from under the weight of Paul's dead body, but apparently, a number of people had come to my aid and called the police as well.

I was troubled by what seemed to be accusatory glances from an officer assessing the scene during my earlier questioning. I recognized the short Hispanic cop, who later reintroduced himself as Detective Moreno, from the night Nick was assaulted at my home. Given his icy demeanor while I explained what had transpired, he wasn't particularly sympathetic to my grief.

"So the victim was a former lover?" He interrupted the thin white female officer who'd introduced herself as Officer Foreman, while she took the report.

"Yes," I answered meekly.

"And you said the two of you were estranged?"

"We weren't seeing each other anymore."

"Did he take your break-up particularly hard?"

"He wanted me to help him try to get his fiancée back, but I didn't want anything to do with him. He said it was all my fault that everyone knew what he was now and that he lost everything before he..." I tried to wipe the tears from my eyes before they could fall, "...shot himself."

"What did he mean by that? Had you told his fiancée you were seeing him?" Officer Foreman asked.

"No. We got caught having sex at his job by my sister, and she told his fiancée. It just snowballed from there and..." I didn't want to talk anymore, but I didn't have the luxury of declining to answer their questions.

"Was he supposed to meet you here today?" Moreno asked.

"No. I think he's the one who attacked my ex a couple of weeks ago here too, but he could've followed me home from my salon. I was on the phone coming into the gates and the next thing I knew, my car got hit from behind."

I'd never seen Paul's car before, so it certainly wasn't impossible that he'd followed me without my knowing.

"Then what did you do?"

"I parked my car and got out."

"So, you were aware when you got out of the car that it was Mr. Jelks who'd hit you, correct?"

"No. I barely had a chance to get out when he was coming at me with the gun. I was shocked," I explained, shaking my head and gesturing with my hands. "He started telling me how I messed up his life with the gun in my face, and then he just turned it back on himself and pulled the trigger. He didn't wait for me to say anything back or anything. I thought he was gonna shoot me at first."

Officer Foreman just continued writing, and Moreno nodded with an unreadable stare as though he was in deep thought.

"You have a lot of blood on you for being in front of him," he stated.

"He fell over on me!" I yelled defensively. "I had his dead body lying on me and...I touched his head and...of course his blood is on me!"

"Calm down, Mr. Parkes."

"Calm down? I'm still covered in his blood! I watched a man shoot himself in front of me! I saw things I should never have seen, and you want me to calm down while you grill me?" I cried hysterically, wiping tears from my eyes, unintentionally reactivating the moisture in the blood on my hands and making it wet again. That's when I started dry heaving, and Officer Foreman rushed to my aid.

"Breathe slowly. Inhale slowly, exhale slowly," she coaxed with one hand on my back and the other on my shoulder.

I felt guilty enough without having to recap everything for them to judge my bad acts while I stood covered in gore!

Finally, I was told that I could go home, but that they'd be working the scene for at least another hour; therefore, my car needed to stay where it was for the time being. Officer Foreman assured me that she, or someone, would call me once they were done, and that they'd likely be in touch again afterwards if additional questions were needed. A speech I was becoming all too familiar with hearing from the police lately.

Random neighbors tentatively approached me as I walked through the subdivision toward my home, asking things like; "Are you okay?" "You look pretty shaky. Do you want me to walk you home?" and "Was that your boyfriend?"

I didn't reply to any of them because they were only trying to mask their nosy questions with concern. I didn't owe any of those vultures an explanation.

When I finally got inside my home, I locked the door behind me and leaned my back against it. Who had I turned into? Nick had probably been knocked upside the head with a brick because of me, and now Paul had taken his own life because of a set of events that I started in motion.

Why hadn't I just done what he asked me to do? Not that it would have worked, but at least he wouldn't be blaming me because I refused him. Maybe he'd still be alive right now.

I slid down to the floor and began bawling like a toddler.

I missed my mom.

16

Brenda

I woke up to the very loud sounds of Musiq Soulchild's song "So Beautiful" echoing through the house. I was in bed alone, unless you count Zeus lying against my legs at the bottom of it. He lifted his head and started wagging his nubby little tail when he saw I had risen.

"Good morning, baby," I greeted him, as he trotted up to my waiting hand for me to stroke his head.

Lane and I had patched things up between us since the day my mother visited. We ended up in a heated argument about my concerns for what people thought vs. how he felt and what he was showing me.

He wasn't entirely wrong, but he definitely wasn't totally right. I loved him, and was glad that he wanted to marry me; he should have put more thought into his proposal rather than just blurting it out after sex. There was still some lingering uneasiness about it, even though it had been a couple of days since we'd argued. In reality, I didn't even know if we actually were engaged anymore.

I looked at the clock and wondered why he was still home at 8:07 a.m. on a weekday, let alone blasting music through the house.

As I turned to get out of bed, my toes landed on soft red rose petals and my eyes were instantly drawn to their siblings, which formed a trail from our bedroom into the hallway. My face immediately lit up, and I anxiously followed their lead, self-consciously finger-combing my wild mane and straightening Lane's knee-length white tank top, which was doubling as my pajamas.

I descended the stairs and stared, awe stricken once I reached the landing, at the transformed living room. Furniture had been re-arranged to accommodate Lane's surprise and there was now a huge, white, pink, and red rose petal-created heart covering the floor. Lane, bare chested and sexy as ever, was kneeling down on one black pajama pant-covered knee in back of the display, holding a ring-bearing open box in his left hand.

"Good morning, Miss Andrews," he stated with a knowing grin.

"Oh my God, this is so beautiful!" I exclaimed, also taking in the dozen or so red, pink, and white balloons hovering over long strings tied to colorful weights lining the perimeter of the rose-petal heart. I practically pranced over to him, stopping directly in front, eagerly hopping from one foot to the other in rapid excitement like a poor imitation of Jessica Biel in Flash Dance.

The ring was beautiful! A princess-cut solitaire diamond, at least three or four carats, sat atop a diamond embedded band. Hell, I was so giddy I might even have been drooling.

"I love you, I love our baby, and I would love to make you happy for the rest of your life. Will you marry me?" he asked, as his grin widened, and he removed the ring from the box.

"Yes! Yes!" I exclaimed, bouncing and squealing through my Kool-Aid smile as I dangled my left hand out in front of me for easy access.

He took my hand in his, placed the ring on my finger, then pulled me in close and kissed me long, deeply and sweetly.

Now this was the type of proposal I was hoping for! Not that I'd negated or forgotten his prior motion; I had accepted, after all. But let's just say I was less enthused previously about relaying the event without a ring. It would be different if Lane wasn't a former ball-playing auto-shop-franchise owner, but how would I look claiming I was engaged with no ring from a man who could clearly afford one? They'd either think I was a liar or worse, a fool.

Of course, I was ready to strip him naked, fuck and suck every inch of my new fiancé right where we stood, but after we kissed, he pulled away.

"We'll have time for that later. Right now, you have to pack," he said abruptly, moving towards the kitchen.

"Pack for what?" I called behind him.

"You'll see for what, when we get there. You only need a few sundresses, a bikini, and some sandals," he advised, returning with a small carry-on sized pink rolling suitcase. "I put some of the things I knew you'd need in the bag already. Toiletries, a few pairs of panties, which you probably won't need," he snickered. "And your lion head bedroom shoes."

"Well alrighty then, Mister Hamilton. I like it when you take charge but, uh rum, did you say bikini? Hello, I'm pregnant."

"That's a baby, not a fat bump, woman. Sport my baby with pride!" he ordered, kissing my lips quickly and then heading back into the kitchen. "I made us some bacon, egg and cheese sandwiches already, which I'll bring up to you in a few minutes. For now, go ahead upstairs, pack the rest of what you need and get dressed. We're only going for three days so you don't need that much. It took me longer to put all these roses out than I expected so we're gonna be rushing a little to get to the airport."

Airport! Oh my God, I was about to literally pee my pants with excitement; even though more than a smidgen of that feeling was probably attributed to the baby lying on my bladder. I sprinted to the downstairs half-bathroom and handled my business as quickly as possible, already thinking of what outfits I needed to select.

After washing my hands, I stood admiring my ring over the sink, and singing along with Musiq as he sang, "Baby don't you, baby don't you know you're so beautiful, beautiful..."

I looked down at my budding belly and turned sideways, gazing at myself in the bathroom mirror. My shape was starting to resemble that of a beer belly-toting drunk with boobs. I wondered if I was having a boy or a girl, and couldn't wait for my next appointment to find out the sex.

For a moment, my joy was overshadowed by a daunting thought. What if Lane had only proposed because I was having his baby the way my substitute father had proposed to my mother when she was pregnant with Brian? Was I mimicking her past?

I leaned in and examined my reflection more thoroughly.

Fuck no! I was nothing like Olivia Andrews!

* * *

You probably could have parked a car inside the monumentally wide smile spread across my face. I looked out the window of the airplane as I fastened my seatbelt, then lovingly back to Lane.

"I'm so excited. I've never been to Aruba," I beamed.

"I thought about proposing to you there first, but with our luck, I'd probably lose the ring on the way, or somebody would break in and steal it. I didn't want to take any chances," he smiled back, kissing my lips softly.

I inhaled and glanced back out the window. Was this really my life? Lane had a point; our luck, or at least mine, had been pretty shitty. It was hard to believe that God would let me have a good, honest, financially secure man and a baby all in one lifetime. This wasn't the type of stuff that usually happened to me. Apparently, those nervous thoughts penetrated my dreams, because I had a really freaky one when I dozed off during the flight.

I dreamt I woke up in our bedroom with both my legs and arms tied down. My mother was standing on the right side of the bed looking perfectly made up in a floor-length black dress and holding a cooing baby bundled in a black blanket, but I couldn't see the child's face. Avis, also dressed in black, accented his outfit with a tired-ass black fedora and was leering at me beside her, while toying with the barrel of a revolver. Gwen and Rhonda were glaring at me from the bottom of the bed in their black outfits. Rhonda's eyes were smudged with mascara, just like they were the day I told her about Paul and Julian, and her long, black, box cut weave made her resemble Morticia Addams.

Gwen, now she was scary. Her face was pale and her hair, which was up in a ponytail, was covered in dried blood on one side of her face. She wore the same bullet-riddled black sweat suit she had on the day she attacked Brian, and her gaping wounds were oozing with something that looked too thick to be blood.

My spectators were rounded out by Robert Andrews on the left of my bed, dressed in a black preacher's robe and smirking like the cat that ate the canary.

I was totally freaked out, but the first thing I wanted to know was, "Is that my baby?"

My mother's eyes formed into cat-like slits, "This is our baby. You are an unfit mother, and it is in his best interest to rid you from his life."

"What the fuck are you talking about? Where's Lane? Let me out of this bed!" I screamed with a rage I'd never felt before.

I writhed wildly, but my tied wrists and ankles barely budged from their bonds, and that's when I noticed the blood-stained sheets I was lying on. I must've bled legions of blood from between my legs because the sheets were not just stained, they were drenched, and red covered everything below my waist except the very end of the bed.

"He doesn't want your skank ass now," Gwen offered with a growl. "He left you here, bitch. Did you really think he was gonna settle with your stupid ass? You're so fucking stupid and dumb."

Aren't those the same things? I thought, but didn't say.

Rhonda howled and motioned to my sub-dad. "Robert, show that bitch who's boss!"

At that moment, he punched me so hard in the face that I felt the room spinning.

"Shut up! Say another word and I'll slit your cum-sucking throat!" he spat at me, suddenly producing a butcher knife and holding it to my throat.

The baby began to coo and my mother said in a baby voice, "Aww, look at my little sugar plum. You don't need that mean old liar for a mommy now do you, Blake? No, you don't. Umm umm, Glam-ma will make sure we take care of you."

"Let me see my son!" I begged.

"Nope. But you can see your precious Lane," Avis replied, moving to the side to expose a bigger view of the room.

"There he is." My father pointed in the direction of the chaise by our bedroom window where Lane's long, limp and nude body lay on the floor up against it.

His eyes were wide open and vacant, but I couldn't see any wounds or signs that he'd been injured or killed.

"Is he alive? Lane!" I called, looking through tears from person to person, then back to his slumped form, hoping for a sign of life.

"Bitch, you suck the life out of everybody you touch. Of course, he's not alive," Gwen barked, suddenly hovering over my face. "And now, neither are you."

Avis aimed the revolver in my direction, closed one eye like a sniper, and I heard the gun go off just as I jerked from my airplane slumber.

Lane was watching me with a disturbed expression. "You okay? You're sweating."

I looked around, reassuring myself that I was on a plane and not trapped in some sequel to Whatever Happened To Rosemary's Baby.

"I'm okay. Bad dream," I answered quietly, leaning my head on his shoulder and resting both hands on my belly.

That dream practically scared the shit out of me, literally and figuratively enough that I was sure I would be staying awake for the rest of the flight.

"What was the dream about?" he asked, resting the hand nearest me on my knee and stroking my face with the other.

"I can't remember most of it," I lied, not wanting to recap the memory. "I just know it was creepy, Gwen was in it, and we had a baby boy."

"Gwen? Brian's stalker chick that got killed?"

I nodded and snuggled closer to him.

"Well, whatever happened, she ain't coming back, but I do hope we're having a boy. I've been thinking about boy names already. What do you think about Blake?"

I gasped.

* * *

Aruba was more beautiful than I'd seen in pictures, and Lane pulled out all the stops for our hotel room. It was huge, with a separate lounge area, beautifully carved end and coffee tables, a glass shower with a double sized garden tub, romantic art, a large, plush, king-sized bed draped in tropical orange bedding with huge pillows on it, framed by a balcony overlooking the ocean. I kept a smile on my face for most of the trip while we enjoyed romantic dinners on the beach and in the resort restaurant, snorkeled, sun bathed, went jet skiing and made love every chance we got in between. I was in love and in paradise.

Our last night on the island, we lay together in a large hammock on the beach and watched the ocean waves driving up on it.

"This was the best vacation I've ever been on," I told him, with my head pressed against his chest as the sheer pink beach frock I wore over my pink bikini blew in the wind.

"Yeah, this was nice. I would have planned it for a longer stay, but I promised Doug I'd be back in time for his celebration dinner tomorrow, and Ike would have an aneurysm if I cancelled out and he couldn't go anymore."

"Ike? What's he got to do with that?"

"Well, you know Ike's a big Hawks fan, and there's supposed to be a few celebs and players there too. I mentioned the thing to him on the phone the other day and the boy all but begged to come," he answered nonchalantly.

"Is Tara coming with him?" I grimaced. The last person I wanted to see was that grimy bitch.

"Yeah. You know he doesn't get out much without her. Especially to a joint where celebrities are gonna be."

I looked up at him and rolled my eyes before looking back towards the water.

"I know you don't like her, but Ike's my cousin, and I gotta look past her for his sake. At least for the time being."

"For the time being? What's that mean?" I asked, lifting up abruptly to look into his face and unintentionally rocking the hammock.

"Whoa, whoa," he warned. "You're about to tip us over for some gossip?"

I didn't answer, but remained staring at him so he continued.

"He suspects she's cheating on him. He's been talking about maybe having her followed."

My heart was racing with excitement. "Why does he think that? Does he know with whom?"

"He's not sure. He thinks she's been pretending to go out looking for houses with her agent, but that she's really meeting with some other guy on the side. From what he says, they've argued about it, but he doesn't have any proof and she's claiming he's crazy."

That rotten bitch. Ooh, I couldn't stand her, and I hoped to heaven that Ike would bust her. She deserved to get her ass handed to her with the way she was sneaking around on such a good guy; and with my ex! She knew good and damned well that Teddy and I used to be an item, and she still chose to fuck around with him of all the men in Atlanta? Obviously, the tramp didn't have any boundaries about who she'd fuck with, or over.

"Alright, spill it. What do you know?" He looked at me accusingly, putting his hands behind his head and lying back on them making his chiseled body look even more so.

"What? Who says I know anything?" I shied away and lay back down onto him, with my left hand resting comfortably across his chest.

"I know you, gossip girl. My spidey senses are telling me you know something you're not saying. Ike is my cousin, and you know we're close, so if you know for a fact that she's stepping out on my bruh, you need to let me know."

I contemplated feigning ignorance with him again, but thought better of the situation since I didn't want to risk ending our beautiful proposal vacation with him being salty with me.

I cleared my throat. "Well, the other day I was in the mood for this buffet food I used to go to in Conyers, so I drove up there and I saw her."

"Okay. You saw her doing what?" he probed in an annoyed tone.

I paused, knowing that the mention of the name I was about to drop would instantly irritate him even further.

"She was in the restaurant being fondled under the table by Teddy."

He exhaled hard and shifted a little in the hammock, causing it to rock. "Teddy? Your ex, Teddy?"

"Yes." I waited for the storm.

"What do you mean 'being fondled under the table'? Were they playing footsies or what?"

"He had his hand up her skirt and she was giggling."

He swallowed hard. "Those motherfuckers," he seemed to be saying more to himself than to me. "So, why didn't you tell me about that?"

"Because you keep telling me to mind my own business, and plus...I didn't think you wanted to hear about anything that had to do with Teddy," I whined.

"Oh, so now all of a sudden you want to listen to my advice? You see my cousin's wife out fucking around on him and you don't think to tell me about it? Did you at least tell Brian? Ike's his best boy."

"No," I answered shamefully. How was it that I was trying to follow what he'd told me to do and I was still on the hot seat? I couldn't win for losing!

"And you're sure of what you saw?"

"Yes. I talked to them and he tried to play like I didn't see what I saw, but she just kept telling me not to tell Ike."

"So, what were you going to do with that information?" he asked coldly.

"I don't know," I replied weakly, looking up into his face. "I was just going to mind my business like you said. Let them handle their own shit, since trying to help Rhonda backfired in my face."

His face softened; maybe realizing that I had a good point.

"All right," he said, bringing his arms down around me and wrapping them around my waist. "But I am gonna say something to him when we get back."

I didn't reply, but I was grinning in glory.

17

Brian

"It's interesting that you have the same car as Trent," Gabby said, standing in my office doorway yet again, dressed in a low-cut and form-fitting fire engine red pant suit. "I just noticed it on my way in."

I looked up from my laptop where I was doing some personal online banking, with a scowl. "It wasn't intentional."

"Even more interesting," she taunted, sauntering in as though I had invited her to. "I have a similar taste in men who have a similar taste in cars."

"I'm busy. Go fuck with your husband for a change."

"Why so nasty?" She frowned. "I thought we were past that now."

I exhaled hard through my nose and glared her way.

"You don't take hints well, do you? Notice how I'm looking at you like a pile of dirty laundry?" I asked smugly.

She rolled her eyes and cackled. "Honey, I couldn't care less about your little angry-man faces. We've already fucked and the tension, at least for me, is over. I am simply being friendly, sweetheart. Chasing you is no longer entertaining, and you don't have the only bone I can play with, so stop being so mean." She waved me off and sat in the leather chair on the other side of my desk.

I couldn't decide if this bitch was crazy, or just a glutton for punishment. I was determined to keep my focus on my business and my woman, neither of which I planned on letting Gabby get in the way of.

"So, we've got a pretty big night ahead of us tomorrow, huh? Trent said your brother is having a birthday dinner? I didn't even know you had a brother."

"I didn't," I answered, looking back onto my laptop.

"Didn't what?"

"I didn't have a brother then. He's a new discovery."

She chuckled, and I shot her a dirty look from behind my laptop.

"Whoa, whoa. I didn't mean anything by it," she said, playfully holding her palms up. "I'm just surprised you just found out. If I remember right, you always said how much of a cheater your dad was anyway."

"Yeah, y'all must've been drinking from the same cup."

Gabby cleared her throat and sat back in the chair. "Maybe back then, but I've changed."

"Is that a fact? So, fucking me while you're married isn't cheating anymore?"

"Not when you're allowed to, no," she answered, sanctimoniously crossing her legs.

What the hell kind of riddle was she talking in now?

"Allowed to? So, you're telling me what we did—"

"Was perfectly fine with Trent," she said, cutting me off. "He prefers not to be told about my escapades, and I don't ask about his. As long as we don't let it interfere with our marriage and we don't lie if questioned, there's no tension."

"Get the fuck outta here, woman! So you're telling me that he knows I've been banging your back out right here in his own restaurant and he doesn't give a shit? And you don't care who he's knocking down in the bed?"

She smiled and shook her head.

So, Gabby had finally lucked up on a dude who would let her get her rocks off with whomever she wanted without consequences. Unbelievable.

"He doesn't know exactly what and when we've done it, but he knows we've fucked. I didn't explain our history, which might be a slight violation of our rules, but I'm sure it won't be unforgivable if he finds out."

"Why didn't you tell me about your little arrangement before then if it's not cheating?" I asked skeptically.

"Because some men have caused more problems knowing, than by thinking I was cheating. Plus, you were already acting like such a total bitter jackass that you wouldn't have believed anything I said."

"So what makes you think that's changed now? Just because you say Trent is cool with it doesn't mean it's true," I answered with a raised eyebrow.

"Well, what do you want to do about it then? Ask him? Go ahead," she said, clasping her fingers together and relaxing her face. "Better yet, ask Ike. He knows about it. Hell, Tara tried to convince him to be open too, but he wasn't having it, and now look at them."

She had my attention now.

"What do you mean, 'now look at them'?"

Her easy expression was now tense, and her clasped fingers moved nervously. "I just meant that...that they have their problems."

"She must've told you she's planning on leaving Ike for that guy she's cheating with then," I stated. Really, I was just fishing for a response. I had no proof that Tara was cheating, but I was about to find out if Gabrielle knew anything about it.

"No, she never said that," she said with doe eyes. "I think she's just having fun. You know, the excitement of forbidden places and getting doted on. Ike's such a miser and a homebody, but you know Tara's such a free spirit and..."

Her sudden pause was followed by another clearing of her throat.

"What's wrong?" I asked, closing my laptop.

"You just played me, didn't you?"

"How's that?"

"You didn't already know she was cheating because if Ike knew, he wouldn't still be with her. Fuck," she scolded herself.

"I had an idea. Believe me, she hasn't been hiding that she's fucking around too well. Ike is onto her shit, too. He just doesn't have proof right now. Who is it, anyway?"

"I've already said too much," she replied, with her complexion now almost matching her red suit, and hastily heading towards the door.

"No, she's done too much," I retorted, as I picked up my cell phone.

Gabby's face went pale. "You're not calling him, are you?"

"You bet your ass I am."

She lightly rubbed her forehead and walked off.

* * *

Just as I was scrolling my phone to pull up Ike's number, an incoming call rang from a local number I didn't recognize. I was expecting a return call from a potential new sous chef, so I answered in case it was him.

"Brian? This is Athena, Brenda's friend," she said, sounding a bit frenzied.

"Okay," I replied, wondering how she got my number and why she was calling.

"Listen, I'm sorry to bother you, but is Brenda okay? I've been trying to reach her and she's not returning my calls. I know she almost never has her cell with her, but she usually calls me back once she gets my message."

"Yeah, she texted me. Lane proposed and took her to Aruba. She'll be back sometime today. Where's the fire that you had to call me?" I inquired. Athena was the most level-headed of Brenda's ditzy friend clique, in my opinion, so I expected that whatever was wrong was urgent if she was calling me.

She paused, "Well...I wanted to tell her first but, I guess I might as well tell you in case you talk to her before I do. Rhonda is in jail."

I started laughing. "In jail? For what? Don't tell me she beat the breaks off of Paul's ass?"

"No. I thought you knew...Paul killed himself at your brother's house Tuesday."

I stopped laughing and sat up stiffly in my chair as the noise from the restaurant beginning to open started to penetrate through to my office. I got up and closed the door.

"At his house? Nobody said anything to me." I was all too familiar with crazy motherfuckers coming in your house ready to kill you and die, too. "He just killed himself? Or my brother, too?"

"Uh...well, it was on the news. He followed your brother into his subdivision, crashed his car into the back of Julian's car and then shot himself in broad daylight. I don't think Julian was injured at all, actually. At least not physically."

"Wow. Crazy people stay having guns. That's why I always stay strapped now. So, what's Rhonda in jail for then?"

"When she found out Paul killed himself, she lost it. I'm not really clear on all of the details yet, but they're somewhere between the police finding evidence that she threw a brick into Julian's house, and her turning herself in. Whoever the guy is that she actually hit with the brick, he's pressing charges, so...she's locked up for now," Athena replied, as the sounds of a crying baby began to rise. "Umm, can you please ask Brenda to call me when you talk to her?"

"Yeah, I will," I answered, hanging up.

I stood in the middle of my office, looking around at everything and nothing. Brenda had recapped her run-in with Julian at the hospital the night Athena had her baby, and from her description of the guy she hit, that dude had some pretty severe injuries. So now it made sense that Rhonda and Gwen's psycho ass would have been friends. They were both cut from the same crazy cloth. Bitches.

I logged into the restaurant system from my laptop and searched for Julian's phone number. Once I found it, I dialed.

He answered on the third ring, sounding like a PETA worker who had just backed over their puppy in the driveway. "Hello."

"Julian, this is Brian."

He was silent for a moment. "Hey, you calling to confirm my party tomorrow?"

"Umm, I'm an owner, Julian. Don't you think I'd have a hostess or somebody do that?"

He sucked his teeth. "Look, I'm really not in the mood for this back and forth with you, Brian. What do you want?"

I decided to "play nice," as Nadia would call it. After all, I really was calling to check up on him. "Listen, I've had some real traumatic shit happen to me in the past year. I know what a total mind fuck it can be to have it happen where you live, too. Are you all right?"

"Ha!" he exclaimed. "Am I dreaming, or is my brother, who has been treating me like I have the Bubonic Plague, calling to see if I'm okay? Lord Jesus you can take me to the cross now."

"See..." I laughed along with him. "I knew I shouldn't have called your dramatic ass."

"No, really though, I appreciate you calling. I'm definitely surprised by it, but I'm glad you did because you're right, this thing has messed me up in the head. Thank God it didn't happen inside my house, or I would have really been freaked out."

"Alright, so be straight up with me. What was the deal with you and Paul? I heard his fiancée turned herself in for throwing a brick at your...whatever he is." I couldn't bring myself to actually reference another man's mate as a boyfriend.

He sighed, "It really wasn't that serious. At least not to me. Honestly, Paul was just a toy I was playing with to agitate you and Brenda at first; and maybe scratch a few itches, too. I was only seeing him on the side for about a month. How was I supposed to know he was going to get so attached, and that Brenda catching us was going to be the cause of all of this? I never meant for it to happen this way, Brian. I feel so guilty now, and I can't get the images of him shooting himself in the mouth out of my head. I wake up some nights dreaming that his dead body is still lying on me," he sobbed lightly.

I almost felt bad for the dude, but I hadn't overlooked his comment about agitating me and Brenda. I knew his Honey Nut Cheerios ass was up to something.

"So, you got a new plan to agitate us now or what?"

"No! No! I'm done with that. It wasn't really anything anyway. I was just upset at how you guys treated me, and I was gonna do some petty stuff but, to be honest...I don't have the time, energy or desire to do any of that anymore."

My fingers drummed the desktop as I listened.

* * *

I was beginning to realize that, like most women, Julian was a "Chatty Cathy." I barely said a word while he explained everything from his jealousy of the life he assumed Brenda and I were living with our father, the struggles and decisions he made, to his guilt from committing his mother to an asylum.

"When I saw her yesterday, it was like she was looking right through me. I know they have her highly medicated and everything, but I'm her only son. Her only child! The whole time I was there she kept talking about how overrated the movie Friday is and how it just promoted pot use. That was her word too...pot," Julian said finally pausing.

Surprisingly, mister motor mouth told a good story, and in spite of my initial inclination to cut the call short, I listened. He spoke as though he'd been waiting a lifetime to spill his guts, and he wanted to cough it all up before I hung up the phone.

"So, Nick is hoping they throw the book at that girl, even though she admitted to everything and told him it was intended for me. Of course he hates me even more now, since my cheating was at the heart of everything," he sighed into the phone.

"What, y'all broke up?" I couldn't believe I'd just asked that question when I really didn't want to hear any more homosexual highlights; but before I could retract it, he rushed to answer.

"Yeah, chile', we broke up while he was recovering. It's not like he wasn't already a foot and a half out the door anyway. He just didn't want to accept it. He didn't even want to have sex as mu—"

I cut him off. "Okay, okay, I get it. You don't need to get into all of that. So, you're gonna be okay for the party tomorrow?"

"Yes," he answered with an obvious attitude. Oh well. "So, this is going to be our first family affair as siblings, huh? Me, you and Brenda getting along like three peas in a pod."

"Three is actually too many peas for a pod, but I guess you're right."

"Well, I'm just glad there will be reason to celebrate something. There's been enough craziness in my life lately, and all I want to hear from now on is good news. Like the witch in The Wiz said, 'Don't nobody bring me no bad news.'"

I laughed. This dude really was a character. "I know my sister will be happy to share her good news when she gets back and show off her ring, too."

"What ring is she showing off? An engagement ring?"

"Yeah." He let out a loud squeaky yelp and I pulled the phone away from my ear with a frown. "Negro, if you don't knock that shit off...!"

"I'm sorry, I'm sorry. But I'm just so excited for her! Aren't you excited for her? She's engaged! That's so exciting!"

"Not that excited."

He huffed. "Well, anyway, I gotta go."

"All right. Tomorrow then," I said, remembering that I too needed to get off the phone and call Ike.

In mid-hang up, I heard him saying something else that I couldn't make out, so I brought the phone back up to my ear. "What?"

"I said, thank you again for checking on me and talking to me. I hope we'll do this more often."

"Yeah, okay," I replied, hanging up. Hallmark moments were never my strong point.

I'd received two texts messages while I was on the phone with Julian, so I checked them. One was from Nadia, letting me know she was home from work. The other text was from my mother and included a picture of her and her new bald-headed husband flashing wedding rings in front of the courthouse. She was wearing a flowy white pant suit and he wore white linen pants with a matching shirt. His outfit seemed more appropriate for the beach or an O'Jays concert if you asked me, but hell...it was their wedding. The caption read: Introducing, Mr. and Mrs. Avis and Olivia Warren!

I texted Nadia that I was on my way home, sent a "thumbs up" emoticon reply to my mother, and dialed Ike.

He answered on the second ring. "What's up, bruh?"

"Where are you right now? With the she-devil?"

He chuckled. "I'm walking from the parking lot to the gym, man. Why?"

"Pause outside for a minute. I got something to share," I told him, as I contemplated how I was going to phrase the news.

"What? Is Nadia pregnant? Oh, damn, don't tell me Gabby is pregnant!"

"Stop trying to guess, fool, and listen to me," I said impatiently.

"Well, spit it out already then. You holding me up."

"Aiight, well, I don't know any other way to deliver it than to just rip the Band-Aid off. Tara is cheating on you with Teddy."

Silence.

I knew he'd heard me, but his lack of response after 30 seconds had me on edge. "Ike?" I called.

"How do you know that?" he responded coolly.

"My real estate girl said how she's seen her multiple times visiting an unoccupied home with him and coming out looking like she was doing Zumba, but I didn't want to say anything until I was sure. Well, I was just talking to Gabby, and after she spilt the fact that her and Trent are swingers, she slipped up and said that Tara was 'just having fun' on the side because you wouldn't agree to an open relationship."

"You're being 100 percent serious right now right? You're not just fucking with me?"

"Naw, man, I wouldn't do that shit to you. I told you about that trick after she rode my dick back in college. Skanks don't change their—"

"I don't need to hear that shit from you right fucking now, dude!" Ike yelled into the phone. "I gotta go," he said, hanging up abruptly.

I felt bad for my boy, but couldn't help feeling a tinge of joy in the fact that he was finally going to rid himself of that tramp Tara.

18

Julian

I rolled my eyes and stirred the vegetables in the pan as I sprinkled a little more seasoning on them, and Aunt Linda yammered on and on about Olivia.

"I'm telling you, she was having an affair with him while she was with Robert, Julian. It's barely been a year and they're married now? Really? Already? So much for the grieving wife act, huh? That bitch never was a good actress," she snarled.

"So, what if she was? It's not like she was married to a priest. What's good for the goose is good for the gander," I replied nonchalantly.

"That is not the point! Besides, a real lady doesn't spread her legs so easily. She's gonna learn one day that what's between her legs ain't as golden as she thinks. I'm telling you, she knew he was gonna leave her. I know I can't prove it but I know she killed my brother. I bet her and that sneaky bitch friend of hers, Jenny, had a hand in it too. You know I'm usually right about these things when I get a feeling. Same way I knew you were Robert's son as soon as I saw you with your mother at Kroger's. Nobody had to tell me. I knew."

Well, I couldn't argue with her there. She was pretty perceptive about most things, and even though I didn't always 'fess up to it, she'd called a lot of my shady dealings behind the scenes in my relationships without my confirmation as well.

My mother told me the story of how she'd spoken to my Aunt Linda in Kroger's because she remembered her face from a prior meeting.

When Aunt Linda spotted my 2-year-old self kicking around in the stroller, she later told me that she knew her family features anywhere. My mom said Aunt Linda asked her 20 questions about me before they parted ways and by the next day, my dad was questioning her about how my aunt knew I was his son. Eventually he allowed her to interact with us, as long as she promised to keep it under wraps from his wife. A task she was all too happy to undertake, since she enjoyed anything that made Olivia's life less glamorous and satisfying.

Jealousy could learn from a bitch named Linda. Maybe the fact that she couldn't keep a man to herself made her "cheater radar" more sensitive; but whatever it was, she always had her ears and eyes open for Olivia's dirt.

"Well, Aunt Linda, as enlightening as this conversation has been, I need to get off this phone. I don't cook enough to be running my mouth and making a meal at the same time."

"Wait a minute now, wait a minute. I didn't even get to the meat of it yet."

I sighed and took the baked fish out of the oven. "Okay, well, get to it then."

"I Google researched her Mr. Avis Warren, and he's a private investigator. His wife died not too long ago, too. I couldn't find any details on how she died, though. What if they planned to kill them both and—"

I cut her off. "Aunt Linda, come on now. I am not in the mood to talk all of this murder mystery stuff with you right now. A man blew his brains out in front of me and I'm still dealing with that in my head. I don't need anybody else's shit in my head right now."

She paused and replied sullenly. "I'm sorry, honey. I haven't even asked how you're doing or anything. I've been so wrapped up with...well, it doesn't matter. How are you? I didn't forget, your birthday is coming up."

"I'm doing the best I can under the circumstances. What did you get me since you know it's coming?" I asked, making myself a plate of fish, stir fried vegetables and a cold glass of cognac.

"Get you? The same thing I get you every year," she laughed. "A card is coming in the mail, but I can come take you to breakfast if you want me to."

Figured. I just went through a traumatic experience, and the old trick couldn't at least get a get well soon bouquet or some Edible Arrangements? Cheap broad! But then, I knew that already.

"Okay, Aunt Linda, I'm about to sit down and have me a good ol' home cooked meal and some Yak."

"Yak? You sound like your father," she chuckled. "Robert was always ready for a cold glass of Cognac or a Gin and Tonic. How he went from one side of liquor to the other is beyond me. I can't stand the taste of that strong stuff."

I envisioned her curling her nose as she spoke and pursing her lips as she usually did when she was disgusted by something...which was often.

After we hung up, I ate and drank in perfect silence. At first it was refreshing, but the more I drank, the louder the silence began to get. Suddenly the small, infrequent creaks from the house settling began to play tricks on my mind. What if Rhonda was coming back over here to do damage to me since she got the wrong victim last time? What if I'd pissed somebody else off that I didn't remember burning?

I was starting to miss Nick and the conversations we had when he wasn't hounding me about where I'd been before I got home. I wondered how he was.

* * *

I sat stark-naked in the large, plush white chair adjacent to my bed, sipping cognac in a glass and watching Nick sleep in the moonlight streaming through my window. Perhaps it hadn't been the smartest decision to call him over during my drunken stupor; but I didn't want to bring my birthday in alone, and he was the first person I thought of.

Sure, his initial phone greeting was a bit icy and nasty, but within five minutes of my inviting him over to talk out our differences, he'd agreed to bring his ornery little ass over to see me. It was still true that I didn't think I loved him anymore, and didn't intend on going back on my promise to be a better person, but since when was giving in to carnal desires wrong? I wasn't in the mood to bring another random guy over to my place, and although Nick's sex performance had only been worthy of a 6 out of 10 at best before our break up...he could suck the moon and the stars out of dick. That was what I wanted.

When he arrived with a bottle of Grey Goose and a card which he made me promise not to open until my birthday, things started off as expected. I talked, he yelled, we argued, he cried, I drank. It was just like we'd never broken up...unfortunately. As luck would have it, however, he was looking full-blown sexy in dark denim skinny jeans, an almost sheer green muscle shirt, green loafers and a freshly cut fo-hawk. In the middle of one of his rants, I simply leaned in and kissed his blabbering mouth silent. He was surprised, but kissed me back.

Of course, kissing led to touching, which led to undressing, which led to kissing again. Well, that is, if his lips to my cock qualifies. I glanced at the clock over the mantle in my living room while he was giving me head, and realized it was after midnight. It was officially my birthday.

Looking down at his head bobbing and weaving in my lap as I sat spread eagle on the couch, I decided to bring in my birthday full throttle. I fucked him like he was my personal sex toy; pulling him backwards by his neck while I thrust inside him from behind and talked like a pimp to him.

"Take this dick! Uh huh...you missed this dick, didn't you? Didn't you!" I demanded, as he moaned and agreed.

Eventually, we took our act upstairs to the bedroom, where I wore his ass out some more, and we mutually bobbed and weaved to each other's rhythm. Once he was passed out, I got up and got myself another glass of cognac. Watching him now, I knew this little tryst would soon be regretted once he was awake. He just looked too damned comfortable in my bed, and I had no intentions of getting back together with him. I did, however, want to see if we could make future arrangements to bump uglies again, since his new performance was now at a level 8.

Nick stirred and turned over on his side with his back facing the moonlight. My Rolex read 4:22 a.m. I was a bit excited about my upcoming party, but the reoccurring nightmares I'd had with Paul doing various things to me before blowing his brains out over and over again prevented me from seeking slumber first.

I took another sip of cognac and leaned back in the chair, gazing out the window at nothing and everything. This birthday definitely needed to bring on a better year of luck than the prior one had or I was going to lose my mind.

Apparently, my body shut itself down without my consent, because I woke up from a slumber I didn't even know had taken place, with Nick hovering over me, smirking.

"Good morning, Casanova," he said, walking away from me and sitting on the edge of the bed. He was fully dressed, save his shoes, which he was now putting on. "I've gotta go now. But I thank you for bringing in your birthday with me. I only hope that I've given you a gift that can convey what you really deserve, and how I truly feel about you."

"What gift?" I asked, still groggy and butt-ass naked. My empty glass lay lazily on its side by the chair and I picked it up, thankful every drop of cognac had slid down my throat first.

He smiled, stood, and straightened his clothes and walked towards me.

"So, this will probably be the last time I'll see you, since I'm moving to Miami tomorrow."

I assumed his switching subjects meant that he considered our little romp to be his gift, so I brushed it off and played along. "Oh, the gift that keeps on giving, you mean. So you're moving to Miami by yourself? I'm surprised, since you're so squeamish about traveling."

"No... not by myself, exactly, but I needed a change. There's nothing left in Atlanta for me anyway, and I can't keep leaning on my mother as a crutch. I'm going to go and enjoy life while I still have it to live and throw caution to the wind, like you did," he commented, looking me up and down with an air of insolence I didn't quite appreciate. "You don't have to worry about me being in your hair or your hair salon anymore. I've moved on."

Now it was my turn to smirk. Had he? That was a pretty bold thing to say whilst he was standing in my room after having been fucked like a rag doll to the beat of my every desire; but if that's how he wanted to play it, I would oblige. At least this time there would be no tears and arguing.

I got up and stumbled a bit over to the closet door and grabbed my robe from the back of it. Clearly the Yak was still working its way through my system, so I steadied myself by leaning against the wall.

"Okay, well, I'm just glad we're ending on a good note. I really do just want the best for you," I advised, twisting my long hair into a loose bun and grabbing a couple of hairpins from my dresser to secure them.

"I just want you to get what you deserve, too," Nick replied with a wide grin.

* * *

The day seemed to speed by after Nick left, and I passed out on my bed for more than four hours. I was thankful not to have dreamt anything all the while, though, because it actually felt like I'd been to sleep for a change. My phone rang endlessly through the afternoon, from people verifying the address for Eat Your Art Out, to people confirming times and/or if they would be able to make it. My excitement grew when Tia showed up looking like mighty white Aphrodite with her dreads wrapped up on her head in a black scarf, holding a red and white clutch bag and rocking a form-fitted black mini dress with her back out. It looked like something from the Chanel fall collection.

"Yaaaaaas, Lord!" I hollered when I opened the door and saw her standing there in all her glory. "Somebody's out to snag her a man tonight!"

She was beaming as she click-clacked past me in her 6-inch black Gucci shoes. I closed the door and eyed her over-exaggerated sashay, which was done for my benefit. We always showcased our runway walks in each other's presence when we were dressed up. Truthfully though, if I had been into women, I probably would have tried to talk her out of her panties in that outfit...if she was wearing any.

"Bitch, didn't you say there was going to be some ball players and such at the party? I had to make sure I looked hot enough to grab a party favor if I wanted to," she laughed, wandering into my living room and sitting on my camel skin brown sofa.

"Well, mission accomplished then, girl! I'm almost ready, just let me put on my shoes. We can have a birthday toast, and by then the limo should be here to pick us up," I answered, rushing back up the stairs to finish dressing.

I brushed by the full-length mirror and straightened my white-collared Giorgio Armani shirt and charcoal Armani suit with gray trim. My freshly flat-ironed locks bounced perfectly around my head as I'd trained them to do. I grabbed my gray Versace Anaconda Snakeskin shoes from the spare bedroom, which doubled as my walk-in closet.

"Chile' I drank damn near two bottles of cognac all by myself last night!" I yelled down to Tia.

"Well then what the hell are we going to be toasting with?"

"Bitch, look in the kitchen! You know I always have liquor!"

I heard her laughing as I applied a thin coat of Carmex over my lips and descended down the stairs again, joining her now in the kitchen.

She retrieved two wine glasses from the cabinet nearest my refrigerator and then opened the fridge, scanning its contents. She spied the bottle of Grey Goose Nick brought me on the top shelf and pulled it out enthusiastically.

"Ooh, Goose! I thought Nick was the one who always kept Grey Goose on tap in the house before." When I didn't reply she side eyed me and probed further while opening the bottle. "Umm, hello?"

"What? I heard you," I answered coyly, rolling my eyes and flinging my hair from one side to the other.

"Okay, spill it. What are you not telling me?"

"You didn't ask me anything. It's not like I'm hiding it from you."

"Hiding what from me? Are you and Nick back together?" she gasped.

"Heavens to Mergatroids, woman! Hell no! Even though our body parts got back together last night!" I cackled, tapping one foot like Thumper in the movie Bambi.

We both squealed, and she leaned back with her hands on her hips. "You didn't! Oh my God, why would you get mixed up with him again when it took you so long to get out? What am I gonna do with you?"

"Bitch, calm down. Honey, that man is not even sweating me, believe it or not. Especially after the way I beat-that-ass-up." I air-spanked Nick's invisible ass as I spoke. "He should have been begging to get me back. But he wasn't. Chile', he told me he's moved on from me."

"Oh yeah? I guess he showed us then, huh? What else did he get you?"

"Chile'", some card over there on the table, but I'm sure there's no money in it, because there never is."

"Money in it? What is that, some kind of American tradition? We don't do that in the UK," she stated, as she went to retrieve the card.

"That's because half of y'all are already rich in the UK, Tia. You probably don't need no money in a card. But here in the U. S. of damned A... we need all the cash we can get!"

Tia giggled, put the card in her purse, and playfully tapped my arm before pouring us both glasses of Grey Goose. "Well, at least you got one good parting gift. Straight liquor with no chasers! Anyway, I'll bring the card with us so you can open it at the table with whatever other gifts you get."

We tapped glasses and drank in unison.

My doorbell rang, and I strutted like I was on a catwalk to answer it. Of course, it was the limo driver, coming to drive us to the restaurant. I sent him back to the Escalade stretch, grabbed my wallet and keys from the mantle, and Tia and I walked out arm in arm to conquer the night!

19

Brenda

I felt like a big balloon, but at least I was going to be a pretty one, I thought, blotting my lipstick in the mirror of my compact as I puckered.

"So, were you ever able to get in touch with Ike?"

"No," Lane answered, with an afflicted expression on his freshly shaven face. Suddenly, the blare of his horn jarred me, and I almost dropped my compact. "Sorry, baby, but this freaking guy is driving like an idiot in front of us. Probably texting or something."

I put the compact away and rested my left hand on his knee. "I'm sure he's okay. He's probably just trying to get his head together right now."

I'd spoken to my brother earlier that afternoon and we exchanged intel on the Tara-Teddy-gate situation. Seems my brother got some information from his real estate agent, too. Of course, Brian wouldn't keep that kind of info about his arch enemy from his best boy. I knew she could be trifling, but she was outdoing herself now. She hadn't even been married to Ike a full year yet!

"When Ike goes dormant, something's wrong. He jockeyed too hard to get into Doug's dinner party with me to just go off the grid like that."

"Well...this is his marriage we're talking about, Lane. I doubt this party is at the top of his list right now. But then again, maybe he's still coming."

"Yeah, you're right. My cousin just isn't the kind of guy to block people out, though. That's all I'm saying. He's a talker and—"

My cell began ringing in my purse and Lane paused.

"Go ahead. That's my mom's ring tone," I coaxed.

"No, answer it. I need to get out of this funk and cheer up for my boy's party anyway."

Just like that, he forced a smile onto his somber face and focused on driving.

I pulled my phone from my purse and answered on the last ring.

"Hello, Mother."

"Hello, Brenda. I hear congratulations are in order. Brian told me Lane finally popped the question. Thank God. I do hope you and Lane are planning on tying the knot before officially making me a Glam-ma now, right? I mean, you don't want to bastardize the baby unnecessarily, right?"

Glam-ma was getting on my last fucking nerve, and we hadn't even been on the phone for two minutes yet.

"We're on our way to Brian's restaurant right now, Mom. We haven't even thought that far ahead yet to plan a wedding date." I rolled my eyes while turning to Lane, forming the fingers on my free hand to look like a gun, putting it to my head and mouthing the word 'Thanks' as I pretended to pull the trigger. He chuckled.

"I guess if I want him to meet Avis any time soon, we're going to have to make our way over to that place too."

"Julian's having a birthday party there." I don't know why I felt the need to tell her that, but for some reason I wanted her to know we were getting to know our estranged brother.

"Avis and I are going out on Lake Lanier with Jenny on her new boat. We're supposed to be leaving for our honeymoon tomorrow. Guess where we're going?"

I laughed at her complete disregard for anything that included Julian.

"Isn't Avis gonna get sick of hanging out with Jenny all the time? Y'all just got married yesterday."

"She's not going with us on our honeymoon, for Christ's sake. Avis doesn't have any problems with Jenny or how close she and I are. She's one of my oldest and most loyal friends. No man would ever come between us. Anyway, guess where we're going on our honeymoon I said." She sounded as jovial as a girl on prom night, and despite my typical cynicism, I was happy that she was happy.

"Germany! We're going to spend an entire month in Germany! Avis' stepbrother is a recording artist there, and apparently, he has some kind of huge estate we're supposed to stay at. I've always wanted to go there, and your trifling-ass daddy...Robert would never take me. Even though I heard he took that last home-wrecking tramp he was with all over the world. Well, now's my chance to have fun and do what I want to whenever I damn well please. He controlled..." the phone sounded muffled for a moment and when she spoke again, she was whispering. "I gotta go. I promised Avis I would stay off my cell phone today. He says I'm on it too much. I'll call you tomorrow before we leave."

"Okay," I barely uttered before she hung up.

I tossed my cell back into my purse and smoothed the fabric on my orange and white-striped maxi dress as we pulled into the restaurant parking lot.

"What's your mom talking about?" Lane asked with a smirk that told me he expected to hear about drama.

"Nothing really. Her and my daddy are going out on Jenny's new boat tonight, and then tomorrow he's supposed to take her to Germany on their honeymoon for a month."

"What the hell are they going to do in Germany for an entire month? I played ball there for a couple of seasons and I don't know if I'd want to spend more than a week there as a tourist."

"She said he has some big-time recording artist brother there. My mother would not be down to go if she didn't think it was going to be some over-the-top Kim Kardashian-type experience."

He nodded, parked, and got out of the car to escort me from the passenger's side.

I didn't expect there to be a line trailing out the doors of Eat Your Art Out, but obviously I wasn't aware of how popular my brother's restaurant had become.

I smiled, feeling proud of my big bro, and happy that both of us were finally living the life we wanted.

* * *

Eat Your Art Out was a lot different than the last time I'd visited. The 4-person band played "Somethin' Somethin'" by Maxwell as a lanky, middle-aged chocolate man with kinky hair much like the singer covered the tune convincingly. People yammered, ate, and got their portraits drawn in the large main dining area as waiters and waitresses shuffled about.

"Ms. Andrews?" A short twenty-something Latin brick house with her hair in a bun asked me at the podium.

"Yes," I said, with an eyebrow raised.

"I thought so. You look just like the boss, and he told me you were coming. Follow me, please," she advised, smiling widely and giving Lane a pleasant once-over before leading the way.

I chuckled to myself, wondering if it was Brian's idea for her to call him "the boss" or whether she'd just done that of her own accord.

I spotted a couple of co-workers from my old job—where I was a financial analyst prior to the stalking incident from another co-worker, which caused my resignation and an out-of-court settlement for negligence. They both looked like they'd seen a ghost and waved at me with mannequin-like motions. I returned the fake wave and continued to follow the hostess from the main room into a smaller party dining room.

There had to be close to 100 people sitting in the tables which were wall to wall. Doug and his main guests sat at a large, circular, linen-covered table in the center of everything, which looked to seat 10. We were led to a table where my brother's girlfriend and one of her friends were already seated.

"Hey, lady!" Nadia exclaimed, standing and straightening her form-fitting purple dress and hugging me.

She looked absolutely beautiful. She wore a knee-length mummy-wrap dress with modest pearl earrings, and her hair was slicked back behind her ears. I felt a tinge of jealousy when Lane took her hand in his and clasped it lightly for a brief moment.

"Nice to see you again," he greeted.

"This is my friend, Carmen," Nadia introduced, as her mediocre-looking, expired-curly-weaved friend grinned a buttery-toothed smile at my man.

"Don't I know you?" she continued, as Lane and I sat across from the two women.

"Maybe."

"I most definitely would never forget a handsome face like yours. Do you play basketball too?"

See now, this heffa was about to get cut before I even had a chance to look at the appetizers. She flung her rat's nest of hair from one side to the other and batted her fake-ass eyelashes at him without so much as a hel-fucking-lo to me.

"Carmen this is Brenda, Brian's sister. She and Lane just got engaged," Nadia said in a notable attempt to reel her friend back in.

"Oh, isn't that nice. Congratulations," the smug bitch replied unconvincingly.

I blew her off and looked straight at Lane. "Our waiter or waitress needs to get here soon because the thirst at this table is already unbearable."

Nadia looked around nervously, and her tacky friend glared at me as she took a sip of her water and held the glass limply in her hand, leaning back in her chair.

"Your brother has been running ragged tonight handling the kitchen, girl. Isn't this place fabulous?" Nadia said, tapping my hand lightly with a slight smile.

I really liked this girl. She was one of the only women Brian had dated in a long while that I genuinely liked and felt might be good for him. I just hoped he wouldn't eventually slide back into his old womanizing ways and mess things up with her, too. Just as I thought of the devil, he walked up.

"What's up?" he greeted us, as Lane stood and clasped hands with him momentarily before Brian leaned down to give me a kiss on the cheek and touch my stomach. "Hey, beach belly. You're really starting to poke out now."

I playfully rolled my eyes at him as he stood resting a hand on the back of Nadia's chair with a toothy smile.

"Baby, we haven't seen the waiter in a minute," Nadia advised.

His expression instantly tensed. "Fucking college kid is probably out back smoking again. I'll get him or somebody else to handle y'all in a minute. Did y'all go by Julian's room yet?"

"No, we just got here," I answered.

"I took Nadia over to meet him a little while ago. It's a big fairy fest over there already, but they're definitely turned up to celebrate his birthday. Speaking of turned up, guess who's turned out and at his party, too?"

I thought for a moment as Nadia chided him with a nudge, I assumed for his "fairy fest" comment.

"Dude, with all the characters that have been doing pop-ups in our family, I have no idea. Aunt Linda?"

"Donald. The young bald-headed dude I used to bartend with at Jaguars. Remember him?" He guffawed. "Home boy is full-on flame on over there right now. Blue contacts in his eyes, skinny jeans, and everything!"

I shook my head at how childish my brother always was when it came to homosexuality. I remembered him saying a number of times that he thought Donald was on the DL, or in denial. I guess he was right after all.

"I'm the last brother he expected to see tonight. You know I had to clown him a little bit though, because I knew..." his words trailed as his ex-girlfriend Gabrielle approached our table in a tight, low-cut, copper-colored dress. Her copper six-inch heels had straps up to her calves and oh boy did I want those shoes!

Oh my God, what was she doing here? Brian was probably going to flip out!

* * *

"Hi, Brenda! I thought that was you," she said, stepping in between myself and where Brian stood, immediately leaning down and offering me an awkward hug.

Brian backed away from her fat ass that seemed to have intentionally brushed against him and wiped the fresh drops of perspiration from his forehead.

Nadia caught the instance and shot Brian an irritated look, which he didn't acknowledge.

I was shocked. The last time Brian saw Gabby he tried to kill her, and the mere mention of her name made him snarl these days. Yet he definitely didn't look surprised to see her. He didn't look happy to see her, but not surprised, either.

"And is this your handsome guy?" she continued, reaching out to shake Lane's hand and he obliged.

"Yes, this is Lane, my fiancé. What are you doing here?"

"Oh, fiancée! I had no idea. Congratulations. You know I haven't seen you in such a long while. Oh, Brian and I work together. He didn't tell you?" She coyly looked at Brian, who bit his bottom lip in frustration. "Yes, girl. My husband and I owned this place before we brought Brian in to spice it up."

She did a little shimmy to emphasize the spice in her statement and then...was she posing?

This bitch had an angle. Brian hadn't told me anything about working with Gabby, and from the looks of the beads of sweat on his eyebrows, there was an adulterous reason for it. Given Gabrielle's history with my brother, she wasn't exactly on the top of my Christmas card list either, and she knew it.

"Wow, do you now? Brian neglected to mention that."

"And who are these lovely ladies, Brian? Hi, I'm Gabrielle Sheppard. Are you ladies enjoying yourselves?" Her smile was plastered.

"Yes, they are," Brian answered for them. "Why are you over here?"

"Oh, now you know I like to get around," Gabby replied with a grin.

"I'm Nadia, Brian's girlfriend. This is my friend, Carmen," Nadia said, reaching around Brian with her hand out and gesturing toward her friend.

Gabby politely shook her hand. "You are absolutely lovely. Brian has always had good taste, but he's always been rude, too. What on earth are we gonna do with our guy here? He's such a trip. You'll probably have to spank him when you get him home. I'm sure you'd like that, huh?" Gabrielle said, turning her attention back to Brian.

"Is this bitch high?" Carmen interjected.

"Your ass better be drunk. Remove yourself from our area right now before I lose it," Brian barked.

She answered his anger with a wide grin and continued talking, "Well, it was a pleasure finally meeting you, Nadia. I just wanted to say hello, and to let Brian know that he's needed in the kitchen. It seems my job is done. Enjoy the rest of your evening." Without waiting for a reply, she pivoted on her heels like Erica Kane in a scene from All My Children and sauntered off.

Lane and I exchanged 'Holy shit!' glances, and Carmen commented, "Ol' girl came over here to make a point, Nad. She's obviously been fucking your man, or she wants to." She crinkled her nose as if she'd just sniffed something stinky.

Nadia was glaring at Brian.

"Did you just call her Gabby? As in the Gabby you dated in college?" Her pretty face was now twisted into the ugliest of angry expressions and she sat up as stiff as a board.

"Come on, baby, let's go say hi to Doug," Lane said quietly in my ear grabbing my hand under the table.

I looked at him like he'd sprouted two heads. Who was this man who thought I was going to leave this live reality show action? I wasn't going anywhere right now! I shook my head and eyed my brother to see what clever way he'd get out of this one.

"Yeah. Listen, everybody, I got to get back to the kitchen and see what these mofo's are up to." He attempted to walk off, but Nadia grabbed his hand tightly.

"Yeah, what? Yeah, that's the same Gabby?"

"She's married to my partner, Nadia. She was probably drunk. We can talk about this later," he replied coolly before gesturing to me and Lane. "Go check out Julian in the other room. I think they're gonna cut the cake soon."

She let his hand go, sucked her teeth, grabbed her purse from the table and stood.

"See, this is that very bullshit I was afraid of with you. Always on my ass about being a cheater and a liar, and here you are playing hide the sausage at work with this bitch. Come on, Carmen."

"Okay now, don't trip and do something you'll regret. Where are you going?"

"Don't you have to get back to the kitchen? Go follow behind that bitch and bang her on the stove for all I care. I'm done with you and I'm leaving."

Brian surprised me. He actually looked and sounded panicked. "This is crazy. I'm not fucking that woman. You're overreacting, and you're not even giving me a chance to explain."

"Girl, he thinks you're stupid," Carmen heckled behind Nadia. "That ho was way too comfortable. Take it from a bitch who likes to mark her territory. She's fucking your man."

As much as I disliked Carmen, she was right. Gabby's entire display was out of order, and Brian looked guilty as sin.

"Carmen, shut the hell up with your no-man-having ass. You're just instigating some total bullshit here."

She crooked her neck and looked at Nadia for a response.

"Brian, get out of my face. I'm not about to do this here. You've clearly already made a fool of me with your lying ass."

"Nobody's making a fool of you. What are you talking about? I'm working. Stop overreacting. You know I love you!" He grabbed both her arms and looked into her iced-over face.

Nadia stood with her hands akimbo and a look of chagrin. "So now you can say you love me? Stop overreacting? Why don't you stop acting like you're not fucking that woman? I'm not stupid, Brian. The jig is up, motherfucker. Your cover has been blown. Now let me past you."

A tall, handsome, dark-brown man in a black blazer, pants and shirt seemed to appear from nowhere and put a hand on Brian's shoulder. My brother turned as though ready to fight, but simmered when he saw who it was.

"Hey, man what's going on? We need you to put out a fire in the kitchen. Not literally, but you know what I mean."

"All right, I'm coming," Brian huffed, and drew back to Nadia, who was obviously boiling from the inside out.

"Excuse me. Move out of my way!" she said, raising her voice enough to faintly pierce through the music and attempting to shove Brian aside. It wasn't until then that I noticed some of Doug's guests watching the commotion at our table. Doug was busy taking pictures with a woman that I assumed was his wife and other guests, but I doubted it would be too much longer before the foolishness at our table got his attention.

"Wait a minute," Brian demanded desperately through clenched teeth. "Don't do this. You're fired up and don't even know the facts yet."

"I know your ass didn't bother to share any facts about you working with your ex-girlfriend with me and you've had plenty of chances. I know that little show she just put on accomplished exactly what she intended. I now know you're fucking her. That's all the facts I need."

"Working with your ex? Who's your ex, one of the girls on the floor?" the tall man asked Brian as he visually scanned the room.

"Oh, you don't know that his partner's wife, who he's probably screwing, is his ex-girlfriend? Well, at least I'm not the only one in the dark about it."

The tall man's hand fell from Brian's shoulder and his expression turned stern. "What's she talking about?"

Brian shut his eyes and slowly opened them again. "Trent...look, she's just upset. Fuck it. Nadia, let's go talk."

Trent? Wasn't that his partner's name?

"Yeah, right. I'm done talking to you! You're full of demands and rules that can't be broken, but your punk ass has been playing games this whole time. You know how badly I was hurt in my last relationship and you promised me you wouldn't betray me. Fuck you, Brian. I'm out of here, and I'm done with you!" she replied, lumbering past him with Carmen in tow.

Brian kicked the chair where Nadia previously sat and stormed off in the same direction.

It was like watching a movie except without the popcorn, and speaking of which; boy was I hungry!

20

Brian

I didn't know why Gabby had suddenly flipped her wig on me, but she was gonna hear about it as soon as I handled my business in the kitchen. Nadia and her bitchy friend were walking so fast in front of me that I didn't even bother to try and catch up. It was clear that nothing I was going to say at this moment was going to cool Nadia's heels and frankly, I needed time to figure out what I really wanted to say.

I expected Trent to be on my heels, but either he wasn't as concerned about my possible fling with Gabby as it appeared, or he was biding his time. I stopped one of the waitresses in the corridor on my way back. "Tell Veronica to make sure a waiter or waitress gets to table 8 in party room 1 now! And I also want whoever was supposed to be assigned to it fired tonight!"

The skittish bleached blonde vixen scurried away to do my dirty work as though her job was on the line; and given my mood, it probably was.

"Okay, what the fuck is the problem?" I yelled to the five or six staff members present as I busted through the double doors leading to the kitchen.

"Somebody knocked an entire batch of crab meat on the floor and it was a significant amount of what we had prepared for service tonight. I didn't know what we should do. I know there was a full delivery yesterday but..." my assistant chef Ray rattled off frantically. "I didn't want to go to it without your approval."

He was 5' 10", brown-skinned and looked like Luther Vandross when he was fat, but he was a hell of a cook whose professional resume was impressive. I'd never admit it, but he might even cook better than I could, given his experience.

"Who the hell is somebody?" I yelled. "Because somebody is going to cover the loss out of their own paycheck!"

Their faces tensed; one or two of them cleared their throats, but the majority eyeballed the 5' 3" light-skinned girl wringing her hands, wearing her hair in a loose ponytail and with a stream of tears running down her face. Her name escaped me, but I knew she was new.

"I... I'm sorry I...I was moving too fast to get the sauce from the stove and I accidentally bumped the tray they were being prepared on," she explained meekly.

"Ray, go down to the reserve refrigerator in the cellar. There's additional crab meat down there that was meant to cover us for tomorrow and next week's service through Friday. Take only enough to replace the amount she knocked over, and I'll place a new order Monday morning," I ordered, while leering at the girl. "What's your name?"

"Danielle," she squeaked.

"Danielle, you'd better step up your game from here on out. I'm serious about deducting the cost from your check, too."

"Yes. I'm sorry," she replied with sad, puppy eyes.

"Umm...excuse me, sir, but I've got some orders to get out to the main room," a scrawny Ray-J-looking waiter said, holding three plates on a tray.

I glared at him and stepped out of his path. "Get back to work, everybody!"

I exited the kitchen and headed towards Gabby's office to get in that bitch's ass, but I heard her and Trent talking in his office at the front of the hallway.

"Yeah, but you got me looking like a clown in here, meanwhile while I'm partnering with the man who's banging my wife. Yeah, we have an open marriage, but you know this is not at all how we do things, Gabby!" Oh yeah, he was angry.

"I know, baby, and I'm sorry. I just didn't know how to say it to you after he was pretending like he didn't already know me that day in your office. I was caught off guard, and plus he hated me then. Believe me, he was not nice to me when you weren't around. But one day we actually talked about it, and he started flirting with me. I don't think you want to hear the details, but there was still a little bit of attraction there that we needed to get out. Allow me this one indiscretion and let's just move on, Trent. I got over you fucking your ex-girlfriend in our house, which was a clear violation; so I think I deserve a pass for this one."

Well, well, well. So the sneaky bitch was gonna put it all on me. She was the one who pretended not to know me first; and she was the one pushing up on me!

"A pass? What the hell are you talking about, a pass, woman? We made an agreement to tell or ask each other when we were planning to fuck someone we used to date. What happened to that? Funny how you conveniently should get a pass after we added that rule; but you're constantly bringing up how I violated it before it was a rule!"

"Lower your voice. I know what we agreed, but this was more complicated than that. I didn't even expect him to be one of my choices. It's not like we got all emotionally involved just because we used to be together. In fact, there were probably less emotions than with other lays under the circumstances."

"Uh huh, then why would you want to tell his girlfriend?"

"I didn't tell her. She's just a smart cookie who figured it out by my body language."

"Like I said, what was the goddamn purpose of you having an exchange that made it clear to her that you slept with him? Especially if your body language showed you were fucking him, because your body sure as hell doesn't talk like that when I'm around. Why would you care if she knows? And what the hell were you thinking, pulling this shit at our restaurant while we've got two big parties going on?"

I heard a chair slide, and realized it must've been one of them moving closer to the other in the chairs lining the wall by his office door. I leaned my back up against the wall outside Trent's office and listened. I knew whatever she was going to say was probably gonna be a lie, but I wanted her to get it out before I went in there and blew up her spot.

"Tara called me balling her eyes out yesterday because Brian told Ike she was having an affair. First of all, that wasn't his place to tell anybody anything about their marriage. Secondly, who is he to expose her when he's running around behind his girlfriend's back too? He's hated me and crucified me for years because I cheated on him in college, Trent. In college! I mean, get the fuck over it already! But he holds grudges like they cost him money to let go. I just...I just wanted to throw him under the bus like he does everybody else for a change."

"At the expense of our business and our marriage, though?" Now he was sounding more like the weak-ass punk I suspected he was.

"No, baby. I might not have gone about things correctly, but I wasn't sacrificing our business or our marriage for anything. I own that I wasn't forthcoming about my history with him. I was wrong. But that's all I'm wrong about," she pled.

My phone was vibrating in my pocket and when I saw that it was Ike, I started walking away from Trent's office and towards the back entrance of the restaurant.

"Hey, you okay?" I asked, answering it and silently cursing myself for accidentally leaving my Bluetooth on the kitchen counter earlier that morning.

"It's over," he replied.

* * *

If ever I'd heard a defeated man, he was one. Ike had been ignoring my phone calls since I'd broken the news to him, but this was exactly the news I expected and hoped to hear when I did. He'd finally cut that bitch off!

"Bruh, I know you hurtin', man. Where you at?" I asked, exiting the door out by the trash bins as two disconcerted employees dashed out their cigarettes and rushed inside behind me.

"In the house." He sounded like a zombie. Maybe even a drunk zombie.

"Okay, look. I'm gonna come by there as soon as I get out of here tonight. Is the bitch still in the house?"

"Yeah."

"You can come crash at my spot if you don't wanna stay there, man. I mean, what did the bitch even have to say for herself?"

"She just kept lying. She just kept lying to me, man. She just kept-on-fucking-lying," he repeated as though in a trance.

My usual inclination to bombard him with cynical jabs was diminished by the true empathy I felt for the guy. My best friend; my best boy, was in a bad place.

"Well, where is she right now?"

"Lying on the floor."

I was puzzled. "Lying on the floor? For what?"

"That's where she fell when I beat her to death with the pool cue," he answered calmly.

I paused, and then laughed when I got the joke. "Ha-ha! I know you wish you could."

He was silent.

"Ike. You're not serious, are you?"

"I was so angry!" He began crying through clenched teeth. "She just kept-telling-me-lies. Lies! I knew she was lying! You told me she was lying! The PI told me she was lying! I saw pictures! Pictures of that bitch fucking him in the backseat of the car I-bought-her! She had no respect for me, Brian! None!"

Holy shit, he was serious!

"When did you do this, Ike? When did you hit her? Maybe she's not dead."

"Last night. I did it last night. She's dead. I don't think it's possible to be alive and have your brains stuck on the end of a pool stick at the same time. Guess she shouldn't have come back popping more shit to me while I was playing pool, huh?" He laughed eerily, then sniffled and cleared his throat. "Don't worry, though; I got him, too. I texted him from her phone and told him to come over because I wanted to fuck. You know, he actually made it hard for me. Can you believe it? The motherfucka said he didn't want to disrespect her husband by fucking in my house. Can you believe that shit, B? As though dicking down my wife whenever and wherever he felt like it wasn't disrespectful."

He sounded amused...in a psycho sort of way. In fact, he sounded a lot like Gwen did when she taunted me before shooting me. I couldn't believe what I was hearing and frankly, I didn't know what I should do. He'd said a number of times that he would kill her and whoever she was fucking if she ever cheated on him again. I'd always thought that was an empty threat directed at me as a warning not to revisit that situation. Now I learned that he'd meant every word.

"So, he came over and you killed him, too?" I asked in disbelief.

He laughed that crazy-ass laugh again, and I no longer heard the cracking in his voice that came from crying.

"You damn right I did. I told him the door was unlocked and that I'd be waiting upstairs in the bedroom for him. And you bet your ass I was! See, I had the love songs playlist I made for her going on my iPod through the stereo. I lit our bedside candles, cut the lights out in our room, and I was gonna make up the bed to look like she was lying in it, too, but he got to the house faster than I thought he would." He sniffled and fumbled with the phone a bit before continuing. "Yeah, so anyway, I was standing behind the bedroom door when he got up to the room calling for her. Slick bastard stood in the doorway for a long time before he came in though. Almost like he knew something wasn't right. But he must've kept thinking with his dick, because as soon as he walked far enough in... BAM! I shot his ass with my nine-millimeter. As soon as he went down, I started beating that fucker in the head and in his screaming mouth with the hammer I was holding in my other hand. I wanted him to suffer for all the pain he caused me. I had to stop when I switched to hitting him with the claw side and it got stuck in his skull. I got tired of trying to pull it out. Down goes Frazier! Down goes Frazier!" He hollered as his breathing sped up and got heavier.

He was definitely off the deep end now. What do you say to a crazy man who's just killed two people?

"Ike..." I didn't know.

* * *

"I got big balls after all, huh, Brian? I bet you never thought I would do it, did you? Now who's a pussy? I'm not a pussy. I've never been a pussy. I was just in love. I should've listened to you, B. I should've listened to everybody." His rough sobs came suddenly, and I looked at the cell phone as though it were a portal to an alien language. She'd driven my boy crazy.

I put the phone back to my ear and asked, "So you've been there all day with the dead bodies? Don't they smell?"

"Smell? No, not yet," he said, as though he was just now thinking about it.

"What have you been doing all this time? Are you just planning on staying locked up in the house until...until...?"

"Until the cops come get me?" He sounded somber now and sighed deeply.

He was silent for a few moments, and just as I was about to call out his name he said, "I've been sitting with her mostly. Talking to her; explaining myself. I know she can't really hear me but, I talk to her anyway. I mean, I've tried to give her everything she wanted, Brian. I let her spend money I didn't have on stuff she didn't need, and I put up with taking shit from everybody about her cheating on me, too. Believe me, that shit wasn't easy either, B. You think it was easy for me to pretend like my ego wasn't crushed all these years? And then to find out she was pregnant, too? Man, I was not gonna be on the Maury Show sitting next to Teddy trying to figure out which one of us was the father of my wife's baby."

My mouth dropped open.

"Pregnant?"

He sighed again. "I found a positive pregnancy test in the trash when I got home. I meant to take that little notice of humiliation to my grave...or at least not confirm that I knew about it while I'm alive."

"Aw, fuck, man. I'm just gonna leave and come over there now," I told him, as I went back through the door and headed towards my office to get my keys. "I'll come get you and bring you down to the precinct.

Or I can just wait there with you if you want. Do you want to call the police, or do you want me to do it on the way?"

He howled. "You do it on the way."

"Why are you laughing?" I asked, feeling a ball growing in the pit of my stomach.

"No reason. I guess there isn't anything for me to laugh about, but, you gotta admit that I'm the last person you ever thought would be in this situation, huh? I can see the look of shock on Chuck, Doe-boy, Fred, and the fellas' faces now. 'Ike? Our boy Ike? Nah!' they'll be saying."

I reached my office, grabbed my keys and wallet from the top drawer of my desk and headed back towards the front of the restaurant. To hell with what was going on in the restaurant tonight; the kitchen was gonna have to handle itself.

Trent was exiting his office as I passed it and grabbed my arm. "Brian, we need to talk."

"I can't right now," I answered, annoyed, pulling away from his grip, still with the phone to my ear. Didn't this fool see me on the phone? "I gotta go."

I didn't have time to spar about his trifling wife and their dysfunctional open arrangement. My boy was in crisis, and if he'd really done what he claimed to have done—which I was sure he had—this was going to be the last time I was going to see him without two layers of Plexiglas and a phone between us.

"Go?" Trent said with a panic-stricken look on his face. "Look, I just want to talk to you for a few minutes and clarify some things. You can't leave. We're at capacity tonight."

"Not now. I'll be back," I told him, as I made distance between the two of us and continued my stride towards the front of the restaurant. "Hello?" I said back into the phone.

"Hey, Brian, I just want to say that I really love you, dawg. I know we've been through a lot of shit together and had some fallouts, but I knew you were my boy, my brother. I know my family won't understand this, but you understand me. You make sure to tell the police my side of the story, too. I don't want people talking about me like I killed two innocents, because these motherfuckers were far from innocent. Shit, I'm the only innocent in this scenario, except the baby maybe." He paused. "I really wanted a baby with her too, B."

Truth be told, though, I did understand how he could have done what he did. If given enough time, I probably would have beaten Gabby into an early grave back in college myself.

"I know you did, bruh," was the only response I could manage as I approached my ride in the parking lot.

"Okay, well, you better call the cops now. I love you, bro," Ike said, before abruptly hanging up.

I couldn't explain it, but my entire body suddenly felt like a mass of Jell-O and tears bitterly made their way from my eyes as I slowly dialed 9-1-1.

21

Julian

I sat at the head of the long table while Tia straightened the crown on my head and ensured it wouldn't mess up my beautifully flattened hair. It was fake gold with purple rhinestones in it, my favorite color, and was also gaudy and just as fabulous as I liked it. Raul had done a wonderful job putting balloons all around the room and hanging purple streamers wherever he could. I had no idea anyone was going to decorate it for me but of course, my BFF Tia saw to it that I would be pleasantly surprised.

All of my really good friends came to celebrate with me. Two of my former neighbors when I lived with my mother, the only three people I remained friends with from high school, a handful of loyal clients and their guests, a couple of boy toys I remained close with, and various friends I'd made over the years. I was especially happy that my salon family came out to support me, because I probably interacted with them more than anyone else in my life. That fine-ass Sean brought his sexual chocolate-looking self with his brother, Donald. As it turned out, old boy looked a lot better in person than he had in that picture Sean showed us at the shop. He still wasn't my type, but he wasn't quite the dog I originally thought he was.

I wondered why he acted so strangely when we were introduced, but quickly found out the reason behind it. He knew my brother Brian. I guess we favored each other so much that it made him uneasy. I'm sure it didn't help things much when Brian actually came in to say hello and saw him sitting at the table looking like a church mouse in the midst of cats.

True to form, my brother acted like a complete clown, cracking insulting jokes and laughing at them himself, regardless of whether they were funny or not. Sean wasn't too keen on his brother being the butt of anyone's joke, and he warned Brian to knock it off after enduring a couple of minutes of it (I hadn't intended that pun but, it was one).

Brian didn't take too kindly to being checked, and assumed Sean was Donald's new man. When he found out Sean was Donald's brother, he backed down a bit, and limited his interactions solely to me. It was obvious that he was pretty busy anyway, so he didn't stay for long. But the fact that he even bothered to come in and acknowledge me brought me a little bit of joy. Maybe one day we'd be close the way I'd always hoped I would be with him. But...he wasn't the center of attention at that time. I was.

"Here's your gift from me and Jason," Raul said, handing me a small box while looking sheepishly towards his light-skinned boyfriend who, quite frankly, looked like he was checking out the ass on my ex-boyfriend Martin.

Raul's lime-green pant suit was the epitome of ugly, and it clashed with all of my fashion senses. That little weasel Jason should have told him it was atrocious, but then again, what would he know about fashion, since it seemed he was wearing the same beige pant suit for every occasion Raul ever brought him to. "Boooo!" Alarms were going off in my mind like gangbusters.

"Humph, thank you," I said, taking the gift and looking slickly towards Tia. "I sure hope it's not from the same place you got that hideous suit."

Raul gasped and clutched his pearls. "Hideous? Clearly you don't know anything about being unique. Kanye has this same exact suit in red, I'll have you know. Let's not act like a birthday bitch today, okay?"

Just as I was about to read his little Puerto Rican ass, my sister and her fiancé approached.

"Happy birthday," Brenda said, pulling a card from her purse and handing it to me as I stood and we embraced.

"Thank you, sugar. I'm so glad you came!" I exclaimed, genuinely happy to see her. I had to admit, I was equally as happy to see Lane's fine ass as well. Oooh, chil', he was scrumptious! "Lane," I said, shaking his hand.

"Happy birthday. Nice decorations," he replied, putting his left arm around Brenda's waist.

"Attention! Attention!" Tia called, now at the other end of the room, tapping a wine glass with a spoon.

The chattering minimized, and all attention was now on her as requested.

"On behalf of Julian and myself, I just wanted to say thank you to everyone for coming out and sharing my best friend's birthday with him tonight. We all know that this has been a rough year for him, and I'm just glad that he's gonna be here yet another year to continue to be my best friend and a great friend to all of you. He would rather that I don't speak his age, because of course we all know he looks way younger than he really is anyway," Tia smirked, and laughter scattered throughout the room as a waiter rolled in a huge purple and white sheet cake with my picture on it. She must've snatched it from my Facebook profile picture folder, but at least she'd chosen a good one. "Come on down here, birthday boy, and blow out these candles. I only put 10 on it so you should have enough wind, although I've been told your blow jobs are top rate." Again, the party erupted in laughter along with a few, "I know that's right!" cosigners in the crowd.

My sister blushed, and I sashayed down to the other end of the room as though I was on a catwalk, spinning a couple of times and flinging my hair from one side to the other. "Well, you'll get no argument there!" I declared.

* * *

I made the same silent wish I had made every year since my mother was committed to the asylum—that she would turn back into herself—and blew the candles out to a resounding round of cheers and whistles.

The waiter took the cake back to the kitchen to be cut, and I went back to my seat at the other end of the table. Serena, another one of my salon family members, was stacking the small group of gifts and cards on the table in front of my chair, and everyone else either took a seat or began to crowd around mine.

"Oh, am I opening them now?" I asked bashfully.

"I sure hope so, because I want to make sure I get my proper praise for my gift to you," Kendall chimed in, while brushing his Bieber hair from his face.

I perked up and said, "Well then, which one is that?"

He made his way from his seat to the gifts on the table and snatched out a small square box wrapped in shiny blue paper with a bow on top.

I read the note aloud, "To a great boss who has shown me that we only get better with time."

I grinned at the flattery and pulled off the shiny paper from the box carefully.

A Movado box! Wow, I was really impressed that Kendall had gone all out for me this year! However, that gratitude slowly faded when I opened the box to find a poor knock-off, gold and silver version of a true Movado watch. I owned enough Movados, Rolexes and Cartier watches to be able to spot a fake from twenty feet off.

Guests "Ooh'd" and "Aaah'd" when I opened the box, but I cut my eyes at him. "Kendall, where did you get this lovely watch from?"

He was beaming. "They had a great sale at Macy's and when I saw it, I knew it looked like your taste."

"Boy, bye! Go head somewhere with them Mount Everest-sized lies. No way in hell did you purchase this watch from Macy's. Child, I know a Fo-Vado when I see one. I mean, I appreciate the sentiment and everything, but I don't wear knockoffs. No, sir."

Kendall's face flushed, and the rising snickers didn't help. "Well...that can't be because...I mean, it was an outlet Macy's, but still."

I brushed his little gift to the side and opened one of the cards on the table. It was from Dianne, my ace-boon-coon since high school. We used to be more like best friends back in the day, but she met her Prince Charming a few years back and he convinced her to move to New Jersey. Now we only spoke sporadically on the phone once or twice a month.

'To my brother whom I miss dearly and always wish the best for, I hope you will finally be able to relax sometime soon, Love, Dianne and Rafik,' the card read. Inside of it was a gift certificate for a day of pampering at Mind Benders Salon & Body Works.

"Oh, yaaaas!" I whooped. "Girl, this is exactly what I need."

Dianne, who was a big and beautiful, brown-skinned woman with a short Anita Baker-style haircut, smiled and leaned into her husband. Rafik was a short, balding Haitian man who rarely spoke, at least not to me, and he nodded my way as well.

I saw Marco, my Dominican boy toy enter, holding a medium-sized gift-wrapped box. I hadn't seen him since the run-in we'd had with Nick at my place, but we chatted on a few occasions since, and I'd invited him to my party. I was pleasantly surprised to see that he not only found his way without the help of my transportation, but that he also brought a gift.

I grinned devilishly towards him as we made eye contact, and I drank in his all-black attire with the top two buttons of his Roberto Cavalli open. I was definitely going to have some of that for my birthday.

"Hey, sugar," I said, standing to hug him as he brushed past my friend Ryan, who was standing to my right.

"Happy birthday," he replied with bedroom eyes, setting the gift down in front of me.

I was showing so many teeth I probably could've held an all-white party in my mouth. I unwrapped the box to find a home wine making kit. I didn't even know they made such things, but this was right up my alley!

"Oh, shoot! Now this I could use. Tia, girl, get ready to stomp some grapes with your boy," I joked.

"No grape stomping needed," Marco said, smirking so that his deep dimples winked my way.

I chuckled and picked out the birthday card from Nick in the now diminishing pile of gifts and cards. I surveyed the room and beamed at the gathering of friends and family who came to celebrate me and noticed that Brenda and Lane, who were standing in my line of sight, looked unpleasantly distracted. Lane was preoccupied with a text message, and Brenda was reading it with him.

"Is everything okay?" I asked with a raised eyebrow. Whatever it was, they could have at least pretended to be interested in my gift opening and had the decency to read it afterwards.

"No, not really, but you go ahead and open your gifts and cards and stuff. We're gonna step out for a minute," Brenda advised, grabbing hold of Lane's arm.

"Well, what's wrong?"

"It's something with his cousin. You...you just go ahead and open your stuff and I'll tell you later. We'll be back," she continued in a hushed tone, as Lane's expression looked more afflicted than before and he started walking towards the doorway.

"Yeah, excuse me," he said, with Brenda in tow.

Now I was puzzled, and as nosy as I am, I was about to pause my gift exhibition and follow them, but I thought better and remembered to take baby steps. She and I still weren't close yet.

I opened the sealed envelope and pulled the card out. When I opened it, another smaller envelope fell onto the table.

"This one is from Nick, y'all," I said, mainly to the salon staff who knew our history. "At least he still gave me something!"

* * *

I began to read the short note aloud as I held the card in my left hand and picked up the smaller envelope with my right.

'To the man I've given my life and love to for many years. You know I've always been a creative gift giver and that hasn't changed, regardless of my status or yours, which hopefully will be the same very soon.' I paused and rolled my eyes at what I assumed was his weak attempt to divulge how much he still wanted us to be together. "Poor thing. Okay, let me continue. 'Enjoy your life in Atlanta, and I hope that you will think of me every day until the end of your days.' Well, that was quite an intro. This damned gift better be good!" I laughed, as I put the card down and began to open the second envelope.

It was plain and white, and its contents felt thin like paper as well. I imagined it was a gift certificate from Groupon or something like that, which had to be printed out online.

I pulled out the folded paper and opened it. I was confused momentarily.

It was a document addressed to Nicholas Maxwell Dempsey on the top left hand side, and it was from Piedmont Medical Family Practice. Below it was a bunch of Nick's personal information, medical jargon explaining what the testing was and below that, was a list of various tests that were performed. At the top of the list were the results for HIV-1 and under the results it read...POSITIVE.

There was a typewritten explanation of what the results meant, but it all instantly became blurry as I took in what I was viewing.

Nick was HIV-positive, and the motherfucker had intentionally tried to give it to me!

"Well, what is it?" Tia asked jovially.

"Yeah, he hyped it up enough. What is it? A trip?" Kendall inquired snidely.

I was speechless, and quickly folded the paper up before shoving it back into the envelope. I turned slightly as I got up and noticed the impaired expression on Marco's face. He was definitely standing close enough to be able to see it clearly. I wasn't sure, but he surely looked like he just swallowed a raw egg.

I, on the other hand, wanted to be anywhere but in the midst of a room full of people at that moment.

"Excuse me," I said, abruptly pushing past anyone in my way and rushing out of the room. I heard Tia and a few others calling out my name, but I ignored them and headed towards the bathroom with the envelope held tightly in my grip. When I saw one of my guests standing near the men's room talking to someone, I second-thought that option and detoured towards the front of the restaurant.

I needed some fresh air!

"Have a good evening, sir, and thank you for coming," the hostess said as I blew past her and a small waiting area of people waiting to be seated.

"I'm not leaving. Just getting air," I blurted out.

Once outside, I ran my hand over my face and sucked in oxygen like a crack head on a pipe.

My head was pounding, and I paced the side of the building by the parking lot with no purpose. God how I wished I had a blunt in that moment! I couldn't believe Nick had done this to me! So, he slept with me with the intention of infecting me? But if he was infected, who had he gotten it from? I went for doctor office visits every couple of months, and Nick was the only one I slept with unprotected.

All the while that fucker was crying and hounding me, had he been fucking someone else behind my back? Now I understood all of his little comments about giving me what I deserved. I was going to see to it that the son of a bitch got what he deserved if it was the last thing I ever did! I'd have him thrown in jail, sue him, or kill himself; whichever was the most convenient.

Dear God, no! Please don't let me have it too!

"Julian, what's wrong? Why are you out here?" Brenda asked, leaning out the window of the car parked directly in front of me.

I hadn't even noticed that anyone was in the car, let alone my sister.

"Oh...umm... I... nothing," I stuttered.

"What do you mean, nothing? Why are you out here instead of in there celebrating?" she continued, getting out of the car and approaching me. Lane was in the driver's seat talking to someone on the phone intensely.

"Forget about me. Why are you and Lane out here?" I questioned, happy that I hadn't yet shed tears as I was about to before she signaled me.

She was hesitant as she glanced from me to Lane, then back again.

"I'm not sure. His cousin, Ike, you know, Brian's best friend, sent Lane some cryptic text messages, but he wouldn't answer his phone. And then out of nowhere, the text messages stopped. The hostess said Brian left and he's not answering his phone either, so, Lane's worried about what Ike is up to."

"Cryptic messages like what?"

"Talking about how he never should've trusted Tara like everybody said, and not to worry about him because everything has been made right, and only God will judge, or some mess like that. I don't know. He's talking to their friend Chuck now since he only lives five minutes from Ike and he's going to go over there. Anyway, back to why you're out here," she pried.

The cell phone she was holding in her hand rang and she held up her index finger before answering it.

"Hey, Brian, are you with Ike? Because..." she stopped speaking and listened until her face turned pale.

She turned away from me and towards the car, peering at Lane through the windshield.

"Oh my God. Dead?" I heard her voice cracking, and saw her shut her eyes sedately.

Lane opened his car door and stood outside of it.

"Who's dead?"

22

Epilogue

I stared out the bedroom window as I rocked back and forth in the chair and hummed softly until the bundle of joy I was holding silently cooed and made light sucking noises as he faded into slumber. I never loved anyone as much as I loved my newborn son, and Lane was the happiest I'd ever seen him when he watched the miracle of his birth.

At 9 pounds 2 ounces, Blake Isaac Hamilton was a big baby and Lane boasted, "All the men in my family were born over 9 pounds. He's gonna be a big boy, just like his daddy."

The birth was one of the few shreds of sunshine in our lives since the night of Julian's birthday nearly six months prior. So much had happened, and most of it, not good.

Lane hadn't been quite the same since we found out that Ike committed suicide by gun before the cops arrived at his house and found the murdered and mutilated bodies of Tara and Teddy. Some days Lane would sit in his home office for hours doing nothing, and over thinking what he could have done to prevent it. Other days, he was angry that Ike would go to such extremes and cause such heartache for his family and friends. Whichever mood he was in, though, I was glad he talked to me about his feelings and hadn't shut me out. If anything, we were even closer now than we were previously.

Unfortunately, my brother arrived at Ike's house just minutes before the police and heard the fatal shot through the door. Luckily, he didn't have to add the sight of his best friend with his head blown off to his repertoire of already traumatizing memories. I heard that Ike had done some unspeakable things to Tara and Teddy's genitals, and that Teddy's body was horribly defiled. I wept as much for Teddy as I had for Ike because, despite the hurt feelings of the past, I still loved him. He didn't deserve the ending he met, even if he had somewhat brought it upon himself.

Despite the bad press, there were a lot of people at Ike's funeral. Brian, Lane, Chuck, and the rest of their friend group were pall bearers at the funeral, and the repast was held at Eat Your Art Out. I didn't attend Tara or Teddy's funeral, but I heard through the grapevine that Tara's was sparse. I was horrified to hear of her demise, but not particularly upset. She wasn't that great of a person in life, and I expected those people she'd burned hadn't bothered to show up to see her buried after death, either.

Brian was definitely affected by the events that transpired that day. He seemed to be operating in zombie mode for a number of weeks after Ike's death, and his typically cocky personality was a little less self-assured.

Eat Your Art Out was doing extremely well, and Brian was there more than anywhere else. But when he wasn't, he was usually trying to get up under Nadia for the better part of any day. He had a couple of long conversations with Trent, and even Trent with Gabby, to determine the future of their business partnership. It was decided that Gabby would only come to the restaurant by necessity and even then, she didn't need to interact with Brian without cause. The way Brian explained it, the reason was more to thwart any concerns Nadia might have in the future if she ever gave him another shot, than to actually prevent any naked sharing between them.

Still, with all of his efforts, Nadia was unreceptive to his attempts, and the last I heard, she was contemplating taking a job in L.A. For once in his life, Brian might not get what he wants.

Lane and I decided to go to the Justice of the Peace and tie the knot last month. Neither one of us wanted any more attention than what was already being placed on us after they discovered my mother's body at the bottom of Lake Lanier three months after she was supposed to have gone to Germany with Avis.

She hadn't called me before she left like she said she would, or since, but that didn't raise any red flags for me. My mother was notorious for forgetting to do what she said she would, and with everything else going on, it never crossed my mind that something might be wrong.

There was a lot of media attention about who the Jane Doe was once they found her, but they weren't able to identify her body until weeks later when they tracked down her dental records. Imagine my surprise when I got the call, and then a visit from the detectives on the case. Her death was ruled a homicide due to the crushed skull, which indicated that she was hit with a blunt object, and the fact that neither Avis nor Jenny reported her death, and many other factors.

Someone cleaned out my mother's bank account, was using her credit cards, and was impersonating her using her passport while traveling with Avis. It was obvious that Olivia underestimated the loyalty of her best friend Jenny; because Jenny not only looked like her, but now she was living her life as her.

Thus far, the two of them were still on the lam, but the police claimed to be optimistic about eventually catching them once they ran out of money. I was immediately ill when I got the news. No, my mother and I were not close, but she was still my mother, and I loved her regardless. Even Brian broke down when I told him over the phone before I began to feel sharp pains in my stomach and discovered I was going into labor.

Twelve hours later, my now nearly six-week-old son was born. The sensationalism of it all, considering my and Brian's close calls with death the prior year, brought a lot of unwanted television media to our doorsteps. In fact, the attention had just begun to die down in the last week.

Ikey, which Lane had already begun calling him, stirred a bit, and I continued to rock him, fingering his little toes. I knew I was supposed to be getting him ready for his godmommies, Rhonda and Athena, who were coming for a visit, but I had been up most of the morning comforting him through a slight ear infection, and I was enjoying watching him sleep peacefully.

Rhonda was lucky to only have served 15 days in jail and get twelve months' probation for throwing the brick that injured Nick. The fact that the victim didn't show up to court to testify on his own behalf helped her case a lot, though. Nick had been MIA since he'd dropped those HIV test results on Julian. Nick's mother claimed not to know where he was, and Julian was getting very little help through other resources to find him.

Anyway, Julian was going regularly for HIV testing, but hadn't tested positive in any of his visits so far. Ironically, Marco, although he was aware that Julian may still be in danger of contracting the disease, stuck around, and the two of them seemed to be building a pretty solid relationship.

I heard the doorbell chiming wildly, which could only be due to one or both of his godmommies pressing the button like impatient maniacs. I expected Ikey to wake up as irritated by their foolishness as I was, but instead he slowly awakened and looked inquisitively at me.

"Hey, my little dumpling," I said, smiling and tugging one of his precious little fingers. My heart fluttered with love as he gazed at me with those dark opal-colored eyes. I wondered if he'd grow up to look more like me or like his father. God rest his soul.

Enjoyed this book?

Please leave a review on Amazon or Goodreads to share!
Other releases by K.F. Johnson:
BEHIND CLOSED DOORS: LOVE HURTS
WHEN I'M BAD I'M BETTER
WHEN I'M BAD I'M BETTER 2
WHAT I'D DO FOR LOVE
WHAT I'D DO FOR LOVE 2
LOVE HURTS: SERIES COMPILATION
WHEN I'M BAD I'M BETTER FOREVER: SERIES COMPILATION
STABBED THIS CHRISTMAS: A NOVELLA

Join my mailing list!
http://www.kfjohnsonbooks.com

About the Author

"The Empress of romantic, murder, suspense", **K.F. Johnson** is a Queens, New York native residing in Atlanta, Georgia. As a child, habitually failing to make curfew before the streetlights lit, earned her numerous occasions on restriction where reading & writing became her main form of escape. Later, K.F continued to develop her talent while obtaining a B.A. in Psychology at Spelman College & acquiring an MBA. In 2012, she published her 1st book for her social media friends & family to see. To her delight, it went viral, repeatedly reaching #1 on Amazon's top 100 for its genre. Since then, K.F. has published multiple books, started One Ironwoman Publishing, been featured in magazines & nominated for numerous awards, both for her books & as an author. With her fan base cheering for more, this mother & wife has blossomed into a witty & cunning author, penning spicy, realistic & deadly tales of African American life to remember.

www.ingramcontent.com/pod-product-compliance
Lightning Source LLC
Chambersburg PA
CBHW071300190726
48292CB00007B/2627